Lost in Thought

First Book of the Sententia

Cara Bertrand

Copyright © 2014 Cara Bertrand
All rights reserved.

This book or any portion thereof may not be reproduced or used in any manner whatsoever without the express written permission of the publisher except for the use of brief quotations in a book review.

This book is a work of fiction. The names, characters, places and incidents are products of the author's imagination or have been used fictitiously. Any resemblance to persons, living or dead, actual events, locales, or organizations is entirely coincidental.

www.carabertrand.com

Hardcover ISBN: 978-1-935462-93-4
Paperback ISBN: 978-1-935462-94-1

Front Cover Design by BookBaby
Images courtesy PhotoXpress.com
Back Cover Design by Kristine Farrell

LUMINIS BOOKS

Meaningful Books That Entertain

This one is for Tim, for helping me rewrite my definition of possible every day. I love you.

Advance Praise for *Lost in Thought*
Amazon/Penguin Breakthrough Novel Award Finalist

"Compelling and solid, this paranormal thriller has it all: love, murder, intrigue, mind games, and a bit of mystery." – *Publishers Weekly*

"...my pick for the winner, a fantastic novel trying to break free...The boarding school setting is a lot of fun, and the chemistry with Carter snaps...Lainey and Carter begin exploring the provenance of Lainey's Legacy, the true extent of her powers, and just how those powers might be manipulated, the book starts to pick up momentum, leading to an action-packed ending with a twist that will leave readers clamoring for the next installment." – Gayle Forman, *New York Times* Bestselling Author of *If I Stay*

"...the novel is full of characters teen readers will enjoy spending time with, especially Lainey's vivacious roommate, Amy, and Carter, the mysterious and swoon-worthy love interest...a nice dose of romance, mystery, and supernatural thrills keeps the pages turning." – Jennifer Besser, Vice President and Publisher of G.P. Putnam's Sons Books for Young Readers

"X-Men meets teen romance...Fans of paranormal romance will find a lot to like in *Lost in Thought*; this vividly written tale sets the stage for an exciting series to come." – Jill Baguchinsky, author of *Spookygirl*

"The tale of Lainey Young's journey from being a seemingly normal girl with a secret to an extraordinary girl with many secrets will draw readers in and leave them wanting more! Cara Bertrand's sharp writing makes the unbelievable utterly believable, and the well-drawn characters likeable and equally despicable and, in Carter's case, irresistible. Tinged with mystery from page one, *Lost in Thought* keeps readers guessing from beginning to end, and will appeal to paranormal romance fans of all ages." – Amy Ackley, author of *Sign Language*

Lost in Thought

First Book of the Sententia

Cara Bertrand

Prologue

I t started innocently, but isn't that always how things start? My Aunt Tessa and I were shopping at a local antique store, pretty much my favorite way to spend free time. I picked up a heavy candlestick that looked classic, expensive, and at least a hundred years old. As I turned it over to check, I felt dizzy. I set it down, so I wouldn't drop it, and sat on an antique bench I probably shouldn't have. The dizziness passed, as quickly as it came, and I reached for the candlestick again.

This time I did drop it. When my fingers touched the tarnished silver, I had the oddest vision. In my mind, I saw a crying woman in an old-fashioned dress, complete with petticoats and a corset, looking down at a man in a similarly old-fashioned suit lying on the floor.

And bleeding from his temple.

I knew instantly that the man was dead and the woman, with the help of this candlestick, had killed him. I blinked and found myself right where I'd been, on the bench I shouldn't have sat on, with the murdering candlestick dented on the floor. We bought the candlestick, and its match, and I told my aunt that I got dizzy and needed to have some lunch. By the time I'd finished my sandwich, I believed it too. But that wasn't the truth.

The truth was far stranger.

Chapter One

T his really isn't creepy at all!" I said. "It's actually...beautiful. And only kind of in the middle of nowhere."

I'd seen the pictures in the brochure, of course, but didn't believe it could be as nice as the glossy images made it appear. The brochures were *supposed* to make us want to come here, right? But I'd been mistaken; the reality of this place was way better in person.

It didn't mean I'd like it, but at least it was nice to look at.

Aunt Tessa laughed. "Not all boarding schools are misty, remote places with dreary hallways and dark secrets, Lainey. You're right though; it *is* beautiful. And right in the center of town too. There's even a coffee shop across the street..." She trailed off as we slowed and turned through the heavy wrought iron gates of Northbrook Academy, my new home.

The campus was enormous, full of rolling green lawns dotted by clusters of trees and crisscrossed by several roads and smaller walking paths. A mixture of buildings, varied in age and size but all beautiful, interspersed the equally beautiful grounds. There were two ponds at the front of the property, to the left of the giant set of gates we'd just passed through. The main drive sloped gently up to where I could see athletic fields in the distance, tennis courts far to the side, and dense woods lining the many hilly acres between.

We pulled into guest parking outside the Admissions building, a small but handsome carriage-style house painted a cheerful yellow. In fact, I thought it was possible the building had *been* the carriage house in the early days of the Academy. I opened my door and was greeted with fresh, early autumn air tinged with pine and wood smoke. I stretched and turned in a circle, taking in the scenery and relaxing the tiniest fraction more. Only the most sullen teenager could fail to appreciate this place, and I was not sullen. It was a Tuesday, already several weeks into the fall semester. From the way the friendly woman at the reception desk fluttered about us, I got the impression my arrival was the most exciting thing that would happen all week.

Aunt Tessa and I were ushered into a waiting office. The receptionist offered us tea, which we both accepted gratefully. She returned nearly instantly with a tray bearing a tea pot, two elegant porcelain mugs, silver spoons, lemon wedges, a pot of honey, and actual cubes of sugar. Wow. There was even a buttery-looking cookie on my saucer. I stirred a drizzle of honey into my steaming mug and sipped. It was delicious and strong, just how I liked it.

Maybe I can get used to this place, I thought. I looked around the room while we waited. It was a first floor parlor-turned-office, with wide windows, bottle-green velvet drapes, and liberally dotted with antiques of a fine quality, at least to my somewhat experienced eye. I was speculating on the age of the well-worn but polished desk—it had to be even older than the school, which opened in the 1870s—when I became aware of the discreet sniffling coming from my left.

"Oh, Auntie," I sighed, but it was a loving sigh. My aunt, the pretty, overly-sensitive artist. This was the third time she'd cried since we left Maryland nearly ten hours ago. I wouldn't tell her this, because I was always the solid one, but I understood. I'd shed my tears in the shower that morning so she wouldn't notice.

"It's just, I'm going to miss you Lainey, and…" She sniffled a little harder for a moment. "I'm sorry, but I can't help but be worried about you too."

"Not to worry, Ms. Espinosa, we intend to take very good care of your niece," replied a new voice from behind us. A rounded, jovial-looking man with thinning hair and glasses strode into the room. I was pretty sure he would make an excellent Santa Claus at Christmas time. "George Callahan, pleased to meet you." He extended his hand first to Aunt Tessa and then to me, along with a momentary glance of be-musement he couldn't quite hide. "I'll be Miss Young's advisor for her two years here at Northbrook, and am advisor to all of the Legacy stu-dents."

He settled behind his desk, pulling a thick folder off the top of a neat pile. "Miss Young, we're extremely pleased that you've chosen to join us and especially thrilled to have another Legacy student. I will say, confidentially of course, that even though anonymous, your Lega-cy is one of our most generous. We'd wondered for the longest time if it would ever be claimed, and here you are. Now, I'm sure you'd like to get settled into your room, so we'll get through the admissions process quickly."

Dr. Callahan opened the folder and shuffled the paper-clipped bundles, handing a stack each to my aunt and me. "Here's the schedule we discussed on the phone, for you to review, Miss Young. Ms. Espi-nosa, if you'll help me through the rest of the paperwork…"

I tuned out at that point, while Aunt Tessa completed the stack of forms that would officially enroll me in the Academy and add me to the "prestigious ranks" of Legacy students, and thought about how I went from a traveling gypsy-scholar to a remote New England board-ing school student in only three days' time. See, my aunt was an artist, kind of a famous one, if you're into installation art and sculpture. She was also not really my aunt and the only mother I could remember. She was actually my godmother.

She couldn't have known what she was getting into when she signed up for that particular honor, and I loved her infinitely for never making me feel like anything less than her own daughter. We were used to the confused glances like the one even the good Dr. Callahan couldn't contain when we first met people, since we looked absolutely nothing alike. I was tall and pale, with a slender build and big hazel eyes, where she was petite and tan-skinned, with dark, mysterious eyes and lush Latin curves. There was little chance we'd ever be mistaken for directly related. The only feature we had in common was a similar shade of dark brown hair, though mine was pin straight and hers beautifully wavy.

Aunt Tessa had been my mother's best friend, like her sister really, since my mother wasn't close to the few distant aunts, uncles, and cousins that remained of her family. My father had no family at all. When I was little, Aunt Tessa would tell me the romantic story about how they were destined to be together, two virtually family-less kids who made one together. And I guess we were a happy family, Mom, Dad, me, and Aunt Tessa, until my parents were killed, along with ten other people, in a horrific highway accident when I was five years old.

I was already at Aunt Tessa's when it happened, and I never left.

Both of our lives changed forever that day. Aunt Tessa went instantly from a happy but poor graduate student to a single mother of a five year old with a huge trust fund to support her. My father was, for his relatively young age especially, shockingly wealthy. Millions and millions wealthy. My aunt always told me he was just a stockbroker, and I guessed he was an incredible one. After my parents' accident, I inherited almost everything, but for the million dollars they left personally to Aunt Tessa along with me. That brief period after my parents died while she finished her degree was the only time we lived in one place for longer than nine months.

Then her career started. And she was *amazing*. Soon, we were traveling all over the country, sometimes the world, while Aunt Tessa did her installations and sculptures. Most of the time we stayed for several months, but sometimes only weeks. Enrolling me in schools was pretty pointless, since we moved so frequently. I had a long string of nannies and private tutors except for an entire semester of my freshman year, when my Aunt served as a visiting professor at a big university in Boston. The university also ran a small private high school, so for the first time ever, I was in regular school classes. I had liked it, though, and I thought my short time there had prepared me pretty well to attend Northbrook.

But I'd never lived without Aunt Tessa before, and when we were living in Boston I had only just started to go crazy.

THE OFFICIAL STORY—the one that everyone but me believed—was that I had severe migraines, precipitated by dizziness and, frequently, fainting. I'd been to six specialists, plus two psychologists, in the last two years. At first, they thought it was an allergy, because the first four episodes occurred while I was in places notoriously full of allergens: antique shops.

I loved antiques. It was weird, I knew. Not something your typical teenager was into. But hey, it wasn't like I'd had much chance to be a typical teenager. I'd never spent much time of my own thinking about *why* I loved them, but one of my psychologists concluded it was the "lack of permanence in my childhood that led me to an unusual preoccupation with objects that seemed to have longevity." I concluded that guy was mostly an idiot with no appreciation for fine things, but he might have been on to something with the permanence.

When I thought about whatever antique I was admiring, I imagined its past, where it had been, what it had been through in its long life.

That kind of thing. I was fascinated by the idea that these items had years and years of history, that they had stories to tell and a sense of place about them that I guess my psychologist would've said I subconsciously yearned for myself. Turned out I was right about the stories the objects would tell, but at the time I thought they were the ones I made up in my head.

The first specialist determined that I was allergic to nothing. Nada. Not even dust. It was a great theory, I gave them that much, and I *wanted* it to be that simple, which is why I let them poke me repeatedly, rub things on my arms, and all around make me miserable for two months straight. In the end though, they couldn't explain my dizzy/fainting/migraine spells, and the allergist sent me to the nutritionist.

Because I was fairly tall—nearly five foot, ten inches—and slender, their next thought was that my problem was my diet. I needed to eat more, or better, or probably both. I could have told them this wasn't true, that my parents were both tall and slim, and that I ate plenty and exercised a lot, but I wanted this theory to be right too. Unfortunately, the nutritionist decided the problem wasn't my diet but caffeine specifically.

Coffee was, of course, my favorite thing, after antiques anyway. I was forced to abandon it for the next month, which would have been the most miserable of my existence if I hadn't just gone through the allergy testing. But instead of better, I was worse, having more episodes during my coffee-free hell. The nutritionist sent me to the first neurologist.

I went through two of them, followed by the first psychologist, two more neuros and, finally, the last psychologist. I was scanned, I was monitored, I was all sorts of tested however you can imagine. I was asked questions, I was listened to, I was talked *at*, and then finally I was simply watched. There was no solid explanation, nor any solid pattern, for what was causing my migraines.

Every one of my doctors tried hard to solve my problem, and in the end I felt bad for them. I wanted to stop the testing after the first two neurologists, but Aunt Tessa absolutely refused to let it go. The problem was not my undoubtedly excellent specialists. The problem was me. I wasn't honest with them, at least not entirely, because I had hoped they could find a medical reason for my headaches without my having to admit the full truth.

The problem was that I saw dead people.

Chapter Two

Or more specifically, I saw visions of how they died. Most lasted only a few seconds, a handful were gruesome, and I swore some of them were visions of how people were *going* to die. They would come with no warning except dizziness, usually right after I'd touched something or someone, and were followed by a severe headache. If I was lucky, I even fainted too, in between the vision and the migraine.

If someone were telling me this story, I'd probably have laughed at them. In fact, I knew I would, which is why I absolutely couldn't bring myself to tell the doctors and especially not the psychologists. Maybe the psychologists wouldn't have laughed—they were professionals, after all—but they would have written down immediately what I already knew: that I was crazy, or at least getting there on an express train. Of course, they would never have used the word "crazy," at least not when talking to me, and they would have tried to blame my condition on something, like my parents' deaths, or my untraditional lifestyle, and I couldn't bear that. Ironically, that's exactly what happened.

Aunt Tessa and I had been in Baltimore for several weeks, where she was teaching a class at her and my parents' alma mater. It was the first time we'd been back since the year after their deaths. We were walking through campus one afternoon when a dizzy spell struck. I swayed and put my hand out on the car next to us, a blue Cadillac Coupe Deville that some lucky student had obviously inherited from his parents or grandparents. It was a tank, showing its age in some rust and dents, but still solid and looked like it would run for years to come. I would never forget it.

It was the car that killed my parents.

It was over in a few seconds, the vision and the simple chain of events: an SUV in the right lane came up on a slower-moving bus and changed lanes too quickly, without looking. The man in the Cadillac honked and swerved, causing him to clip my parents' car instead. Their car spun radically to the right, where the SUV slammed into it and pushed it into the bus, which then rolled over three times before coming to rest on its side across the highway.

I saw this all clearly, as if I were right there, my mother desperately turning the wheel, my father shocked and disoriented from being asleep in the passenger seat, just before the SUV crashed into his door and took them out of my life forever. My parents died, the driver of the SUV died, and nine people on the bus died too. The Cadillac skidded into the grass median and suffered nothing more than a dented bumper.

I took my hand from the car, looked at my aunt, and crumpled to the ground unconscious.

WHEN I AWOKE in the hospital, I had a wicked headache and an appointment with my psychologist. Apparently I'd screamed, too, when I collapsed, and had been muttering about my parents, the car, the vision, as I drifted in and out of consciousness for three hours. The psychologist arrived and asked me gently what happened. I told him a slightly edited version of the truth: I got dizzy, put my hand on the car, and then passed out, remembering nothing after that. I did not mention what I'd seen.

The details of my parents' accident weren't a mystery, so it wasn't like I'd been babbling about something I shouldn't or couldn't have known. My aunt and the doctors were skeptical, especially about the importance of the car, but I stuck to my story of not knowing what had happened. And in a way, I didn't. I only knew that I was crazy and that the whole crazy incident had made me exhausted.

My psychologist determined that, big surprise, I was exhausted. He went further though, blaming the exhaustion on the psychological stress caused by my constant life on the move and, of course, my return to the city where my parents died. He prescribed three remedies: that I take an antidepressant, I get out of Baltimore, and, lastly and most importantly, once I got wherever I was going, I *stay* there. He did not want me to move again for my last two years of high school.

Whoa. My first thought was I wasn't prepared for that. I *liked* my life, thank you very much. I was mentally ready to slow down once I went to college, but I thought I'd have two more years to enjoy this wanderlust lifestyle with my aunt. Instead, I kind of felt like I'd been in a car wreck myself, going from moving fast to stopped dead in the blink of an eye.

Aunt Tessa instantly blamed herself when she heard the psychologist's proclamation—for bringing me here, for not thinking more about how such a lack of stability would affect me, and on and on—and would not be deterred from the plan despite all my protests. She was on the phone immediately with Uncle Martin to discuss our options when he announced the most surprising thing of the day. Given the day we'd had, that was really saying something.

Apparently I had a guaranteed place at a prestigious boarding school—Northbrook Academy, in Northwestern Massachusetts—

already waiting for me, whenever I decided to show up. My aunt and I took this as a bit of shocking news since neither of us had ever heard of the place.

Uncle Martin's voice resonated from the speakerphone in front of us. "You see, Tess, Lainey's trust fund has some unusual clauses, as you know. One of those is for a Legacy placement at Northbrook…"

"But why didn't we know about this?!" Aunt Tessa interrupted, a little angry. "Could Lainey have been attending that school this whole time? Legacy implies family history there, right? Whose Legacy is she? From Allen's or Julie's family?" Allen and Julie were my parents. "Neither of them went there, I'd remember."

"I'm sorry this is a surprise, Tessa. To you too, Lainey; I'm sure you're there listening. It's not that I didn't want to tell you. I wasn't allowed."

"Huh?" was my brilliant contribution to the conversation. I was sure this Academy would be hugely impressed.

"I don't pretend to understand all of Allen's wishes, but most of them have turned out to be quite wise," Uncle Martin continued. "And regardless, it's not my place to question them, merely execute them. His stipulation was this: Lainey was only to be proposed the opportunity to attend Northbrook if she *needed it*. And before you ask, I don't think Allen planned to send Lainey to the school either. He was very explicit that if and only if a situation in Lainey's life made her attendance at Northbrook the most desirable course of action was I to present this opportunity. As to what would necessitate her attendance, he left that to my discretion."

He sighed. "Uncle" Martin was not technically my uncle either, but I loved him nearly as much as Aunt Tessa. He was my trust fund manager and one of my father's oldest friends.

"Believe me, Lainey," he continued, "when your headaches began to be a serious concern, I spent considerable hours contemplating if it was time to make the offer. But you've never seemed unhappy to me, certainly not *depressed*"—he said it as if it were a dirty word, something the psychologist had defiled me with by the mere suggestion, and I smiled for the first time that afternoon—"even with the headaches, and I've always thought that with your aunt is exactly where you wanted to be. And you're right, Tessa. Legacy status at Northbrook is usually established by a family member. Lainey's, however, is anonymous. The trust says nothing more than it exists, how to claim it, and that her acceptance will be immediate and fully funded, provided she meets academic admissions criteria which, I assure you, she does admirably."

We all stopped to digest everything Uncle Martin had put out there. It was a lot to take in, not to mention that he always talked like the big time financial manager he was. In my whole life, he'd never treated me like a kid and never apologized for it, which was one of the many reasons I loved him. I also trusted his advice.

"Well…what do you think, Uncle Martin?" I hoped his opinion would confirm the surprising one rapidly forming in my mind.

"I think it's something you should seriously consider," he said. "Naturally, I familiarized myself with the school as soon as I accepted the position as executor for your trust. It's a fine institution, one of the finest in the country, with many distinguished alumni and a robust academic curriculum. I wouldn't hesitate to send my own daughter there, and since you're the closest thing I have to one, Lainey, I wouldn't hesitate to send you either."

"This is all happening so fast, Martin," Aunt Tessa said. "Why don't we get the literature, and…"

"Okay," I interrupted.

"Okay what?" My aunt turned to me, confused.

"Okay, I'll do it," I said. "As long as I like how it looks once I can check it out. But if it looks okay, I'll accept. I'll go there."

Aunt Tessa was kind of frantic. "Lainey, there's no hurry here, no pressure. You don't have to decide this minute, or even today. Why don't we take a week to consider your options and really look into the school…"

"No," I interrupted again. I was determined. "If my father made it an option for me, even a bizarre secret one, he must have thought it would be a good place for me. Uncle Martin agrees. It's already October. If I'm supposed to find a school and stay there, I'd like to start sooner than later. If it's not creepy, I'll go there. How soon can we set it up, Uncle Martin?"

Turned out "soon" was by the end of that day. I had all of one day to pack for my new, stationary life. Aunt Tessa, when she wasn't crying, protested the entire time. I didn't have to go so soon, I should take time to rest and recover, I shouldn't feel like I *had* to go to this school, even if it was already paid for, and so on. I kept telling her I *wanted* to, and I kind of did. Uncle Martin personally couriered over all of his literature on the school, and after an hour looking at it and everything I could find online, I honestly thought it looked great.

What I didn't tell my aunt was that, more than anything, I did *not* want any time to "rest and recover" because I knew all I would do was spend it going crazier. I already had a hard enough time keeping the images of my parents' spinning car out of my head. Aunt Tessa also tried to insist that she go with me, not only to drop me off, but to stay. I absolutely refused, which I think made her cry more than anything, and it was all I could do to prove my unwavering love for her company.

I finally convinced her with mostly the truth: I would feel guilty if she gave up her planned projects, and it would not help me recover. I didn't think I was going to recover anyway, but I *would* feel guilty about Aunt Tessa being stuck in the middle of nowhere with me. In the end, and after a few more tears, she gave in, as I knew she would.

We left for Northbrook before sunrise on Tuesday and I tried very hard to look forward to it every mile of the way.

I DIDN'T REALIZE I'd fallen asleep until my aunt was whispering my name and gently shaking me awake. As if falling asleep in my first meeting at my new school wasn't embarrassing enough, I was also pretty sure I snorted, and maybe drooled on myself. Just a little.

Dr. Callahan looked sympathetic though and offered a kindly, "I'm sure you're tired from your long drive, Miss Young. We're all set, if you'd like to go to your room and start getting settled?"

Still embarrassed, I nodded, offered a sheepish "thank you," and was so ready to get out of there.

Chapter Three

My room was in a grand building called Marquise House that overlooked the two ponds at the front of campus. It was certainly impressive, more Gothic than Victorian, with three stories of dark siding, a deep, shaded front porch, and decorative spires at all the many peaks. *So maybe this is where they're hiding the creep factor,* I thought as I knocked on the door, but when we were greeted moments later by my dorm attendant, Ms. Kim, we entered into a surprisingly bright—and completely cobweb free—foyer with gleaming woodwork and a large central staircase.

Ms. Kim was a slight, pretty woman with sleek dark hair, equally dark eyes, and creamy skin I could only describe as the color of antique lace. I was at least seven inches taller than she was. But she was friendly and direct, wasting no time getting down to business. "You must be Miss Young. Lainey, correct? Glad to have you. Follow me up to your new room. You'll be on the third floor. Stairs only, sorry," she added with a smile. We followed.

As we headed up, she told me I'd be rooming with Amy Moretti, also a junior, and "one of Northbrook's most promising and popular students." So no pressure there or anything. I would probably hate her. "Miss Moretti," she continued, "volunteered to share her room with you, since there were no other openings in any of the junior and senior dorms." Okay, maybe I wouldn't totally hate her.

Ms. Kim stopped at the end of the third floor hallway and handed over a set of keys. I opened the door into a surprisingly large room, especially considering only one girl had been living in it before my arrival. And though I expected something hastily rearranged with all the best spots already claimed, it was immaculate, divided perfectly equally, and painted a soothing, pale blue color. A large bay window dominated the back wall, with a cozy looking padded sill underneath and two cushy chairs arranged on either side. A blue and cream patterned rug rested in the middle of the room, dotted with plush pillows for lounging, and each side of the room boasted a single bed, a small desk with a built in bookshelf, and a tall dresser. One side, obviously meant for me, was bare, save for a neat stack of text and notebooks already delivered and waiting on my desk.

Amy's bed was covered in a beautiful pale floral comforter that looked about a foot thick, with at least four pillows and a stuffed bear at the head. Her desk was filled with precisely arranged books and papers, a sleeping laptop sitting in the center. A few framed art prints decorated the walls on her side of the room, along with—and this worried me a little—a large, old, and expensive-looking chart of the Periodic Table of Elements. I almost thought it was an antique; it seemed like there were some elements missing from the ends, as far as my very fuzzy memory of it could recall. A door at one end of the room led into a small but sufficient private bathroom with what I assumed was an original claw foot tub with a shower, a pretty pedestal sink, and a classic black and white hexagon tile floor. Like everything else at the school so far, my room was beautiful.

Move-in went pretty quickly, since I hadn't had time to pack much, and then it was time for Aunt Tessa to leave. But not before she had one more cry, this time as she folded the last of my sweaters into their drawer. I hugged her and, to my surprise, I cried a little too.

"I promise I'll miss you every day, Aunt T," I told her truthfully.

She pushed my long hair out of my face while her tears dried up, repeating all of the things she'd said before: how she'd miss me, that I had to call her often and let her know I was okay, how I could come home at any time—*any time*—if I didn't like it here. I nodded, hugged her some more, and then she was gone. Just like that, I was alone.

I looked aimlessly around my room, not exactly sure what to do with myself. I picked the student handbook and campus directory out of the stack on my desk and settled on my bed to familiarize myself with my new life. I promptly fell asleep.

I WAS AWAKENED from an unexpected sleep for the second time that day—I couldn't deny I was a little exhausted—but this one was not so gentle. The door banged shut, followed by a little scream, and then a softly muttered, "Oops! Oh, shit." I bolted upright, silently praying I hadn't snorted and wasn't drooling again.

"Sorry! Hi! I'm Amy. You're obviously Lainey, at least I sure hope so, otherwise I don't know how you got in here, and you're in the wrong room. I totally wasn't expecting you until tomorrow, but I guess when they said 'first day' they meant your first day for classes. Anyway, yeah, wow, you're gorgeous. I told them if I was taking a roommate, I wanted a hot one, and they delivered! A total heartbreaker, I'm sure. What have you done so far? Are you all unpacked? Need help?" She ended with a happy and hopeful smile. I was amazed she wasn't out of breath.

"Hi!" I squeaked, cleared my throat, and tried again. "Uh, hi, yeah, I'm Lainey. It's nice to meet you. And thanks for volunteering to share your room with me. You didn't have to do that, and I appreciate it. I didn't want to room by myself, and I'm glad to be with someone in my grade…"

While my mouth babbled and then ran out of steam, I observed her. She was adorable, probably five and a half feet tall, and a little overweight, but in a way that really didn't matter. She was soft curves and all the right proportions. That painter Botticelli would have loved Amy Moretti. Her face was round and clear, with gorgeous olive skin, deep brown eyes, astonishingly perfect eyebrows, pillowy pink lips, and a shoulder-length rush of well-tamed curly brown hair. Effervescent, like soda or champagne, was the best word I could think of to describe her. She practically bubbled with good cheer. I felt pale and subdued in comparison.

"Yeah, me either!" she replied. "I had this great big room to myself and after about three days I was like, 'well, this is freaking boring,' and I was planning to change for a roommate in spring semester, but when we heard you were coming and they didn't know where to put you, I was at Stewart's office the next day asking them to shove you in here."

I'd hardly had to be shoved in, considering we almost could have fit a third person in this place, I thought, before I realized my brain was wandering and I was still sitting on my bed, clutching my student handbook, while Amy was still standing and smiling at me. I recovered my senses and stood up.

"Oh, damn!" she said. "Guess I won't be borrowing your pants after all." She held out her hand and I shook it. "Amy Moretti. Nice to meet you. I'm just your average student, no special Legacy status. My dad only contributes in the multiple thousands every year, and I hear it takes at least a multiple of ten of that to get Legacy, so somebody must *really* like you." She laughed, and I actually laughed too. Her personality was instantly infectious, and I understood what the administrator had meant about Amy being one of the most popular students at Northbrook.

"Lainey Young," I replied. "And honestly, my Legacy is a tiny bit of a mystery. It's anonymous. I'm not sure if my dad established it or not."

"Huh. Well, I love a good mystery! Are you hungry? I'm hungry, and it's almost dinner hour. Let's go on that tour I'm supposed to give you—bring your schedule, okay?—and then get something to eat. You can tell me all about you, and I'll dish all of Northbrook's secrets and lies while we're on the way."

I WASN'T SURE what her plans were for the future, but Amy would've made a great tour guide if she wanted to go that route. The more time I spent with her, I began to think she might be great at whatever she decided to do. She took me around most of campus, pointing out the dorms and who lived there, the class buildings, the common areas— library, dining hall, study lounges and recreation rooms, chapel, fitness center (otherwise known as the gym)—and the administrative buildings, including an infirmary and our very own post office. This place really was a miniature town.

She circled all of my classroom locations in pink marker, drawing arrows between them to indicate my best route each day. We circled back around and she glossed over the faculty housing at the eastern edge of campus. The assortment of houses and cottages abutted the largest stretch of woods surrounding campus, which Amy also noted was full of trails.

"Believe me, it's no accident you have to pass the faculty-guards to get to them," Amy explained. "The school goes to *extraooooordinary*"— she drew out the word for emphasis—"measures to protect our virtue and try to keep us from each other...but of course, we're all pretty smart here, and adults have been failing at protecting kids' virtues since the beginning of time, so it's not so hard to get around their extraordinary measures, if you find someone worth sneaking for anyway, and there is a pretty healthy selection of candidates, I'll admit," she added with a giggle. I smiled back at her.

I wasn't a girl who'd had a lot of steady boyfriends, seeing as I almost never went to school and never stuck around for more than a few months, but I'd been very practiced at stealing kisses from the sons of my aunt's customers after all those dinner parties I'd been forced to attend. In the last two years, I'd spent a fair amount of time on college campuses getting chatted up by the freshman and sophomore boys—I'd always looked older than I was anyway—and taken on a lot of dates. My aunt didn't expect me to be a nun, and she trusted me enough to respect myself and her curfews, both of which I did. The prospect of being somewhere long enough to have an honest-to-goodness relationship both frightened and thrilled me.

As we finally made it to dinner, right before the main dining hours ended, I filled her in on my personal history, spilling out the entire story of the accident and my bizarre but amazing upbringing. I told her about the headaches and occasional fainting too, but obviously not about the crazy. Still, she was sympathetic.

"Oh, that totally sucks. And I'm sorry about your parents, but your aunt sounds amazing. I only wish I'd been half the places you've been, though Cleveland isn't that exciting, I bet. My dad's just a doctor in Boston, and my mom's chief occupation is me, though since I've been here since seventh grade, I'm not entirely sure what she does with herself all day anymore…"

We filled our plates and plunked down at a table while she continued in her fast, but enchanting, way of talking. "Seriously though, I hope you're not bored out of your pretty skull here, after your life on the road. I like it though…the classes aren't boring and some of the kids are spoiled babies, but most of them are pretty cool. The town's not big, but it's nice, and we're kept pretty busy anyway." Amy, I was beginning to realize, could carry a conversation by herself better than anyone I'd ever met. I was quickly in danger of liking her immensely.

Amy waved hello to a few people as we sat down, but no one joined us. "I told everyone to leave me alone when you finally got here," she confided, "so I could have at least a few hours to get to know my new roommate myself. Pretty much all the rest of us have been here since at least freshman year, or earlier, and I wanted to keep them from pouncing on the fresh blood before you've even been here twenty-four hours."

I learned as we ate that her "just a doctor" father was actually Chief of Surgery at a big hospital in Boston. She thought she might follow in his footsteps, or maybe become a researcher or biomedical engineer; she was still deciding. I told her about my weird hobby and how I dreamed of owning my own antique store. In comparison, that suddenly seemed not very impressive or ambitious, but she seemed to think it was a great idea.

"That sounds *fabulous!*" she gushed. "Way more glamorous than me in a lab coat all day." I thought that curing cancer was probably more glamorous in the long run, even if the clothes weren't as good, but I appreciated her enthusiasm. "You'd be like...a historian of the everyday! I can picture you wearing the sexiest vintage dresses and sweaters, passing on little bits of history to your customers. I'm totally jealous. Maybe I can be your assistant! I'd look great in glasses and vintage boots, carrying a clipboard and taking your notes."

We continued to chat on the way back to Marquise House, but I was fading quickly. On top of the dramatic last few days, I'd been up very early for our drive that morning and had a busy day ahead of me. It wasn't late, but I got ready for bed as soon as we got back to our room. Amy went to her desk to work on some homework, and promised to be quiet and let me get a good sleep.

As I drifted off, I mused about her calling me an "historian." I'd never quite thought of it that way and I liked it. Maybe being the keeper of small, seemingly inconsequential bits of history was not such a bad life to lead, and maybe it was a more important job than I thought.

Chapter Four

My first day was an absolute blur of students and teachers, of remembering my way from building to building with only fifteen minutes between classes, even with Amy's helpful map, and of introducing myself over and over at the beginning of each class. I was exhausted by the time it was my lunch hour, but I had yet to meet with Headmaster Stewart. A note handed to me at the beginning of my second period Statistics class told me that was when she expected me.

I made my way to the Administration building, one of the prettiest on campus. Tall and Victorian, with a round front tower and loads of gingerbread trim, it was situated almost exactly in the center of campus so that you passed it on your way to nearly everything. It was also painted an unusual but surprisingly attractive pale lavender color. At least it was easy to find.

I climbed the porch steps and opened the screen door into an old-fashioned entryway. I had no idea where to go, up the stairs or to the bustling parlors on the left and right, and was a little bit nervous, so I just stood there like an idiot, admiring the beautiful antique mirror and console table. A boy who looked to be in maybe the eighth grade and also about to wet his pants came tripping down the stairs and almost crashed into me. He skidded to a stop, rapidly spilling apologies, and I asked him for Dr. Stewart's office. He pointed up the stairs and fled out the door. His look of abject terror did nothing to help my nervousness, but I made my way up the stairs anyway. Slowly.

The pleasant woman at the desk ushered me straight into Headmaster Stewart's huge office suite, sitting me down in the anteroom with a cheerful, "Welcome to Northbrook! Dr. Stewart will be right with you." I didn't have to worry about my growling stomach because she waved me over to a delicious looking lunch spread that was laid out on an antique sideboard. This was my kind of place. While filling my plate, I wondered if the furniture was all original, and mentally complimented the original owners on their excellent taste. I was just putting a slice of apple with cheddar in my mouth when the interior door opened and Headmaster Stewart beckoned me inside her office.

She was tall, a few inches taller than me even, and so thin that I wanted to hand her my sandwich, out of pity or suddenly feeling incredibly fat, I wasn't sure which. Her face was narrow and calculating but not openly unfriendly. I knew at once that she could be imposing when she needed to be and downright terrifying if she wanted to be. The poor kid running down the stairs was proof of that. She wore a somewhat unfashionable ensemble of long dark skirt, heavy-heeled pumps, and button down shirt, topped by a scholarly plaid jacket. She was saved from total frumpiness by the fact that it all fit her thin frame well, making her look blade sharp, and adding to my feeling that she could cut me down with one look if I didn't impress her. I swallowed and smiled tentatively.

"Hello Headmaster Stewart, it's nice to meet you. Thank you for lunch."

She laughed, and my tension eased by a tiny bit. "It's you I should thank for lunch, Lainey—it's Lainey you prefer, isn't that right?—

because it is Legacy students, like you, who help keep our Academy running at the level our current students and alumni have come to expect."

Unsure how to respond to that, since I knew so little about this school and its expectations or my apparently special Legacy status, I went with what I thought was a safe, "I'm very happy to be here."

"And we're delighted to have you," Dr. Stewart replied. "I know your transition here has been rather unexpected, but I hope you'll adjust quickly and come to enjoy your few years here."

I thought that "unexpected" was a pretty big understatement, since I went from never having heard of this place to being a full-time boarding student with a fully funded scholarship in about seventy-two hours, so I decided she was being tactful. In fact, from the way she was eyeing me as she talked, I got the impression Headmaster Stewart was as curious about me as I was about this entire situation.

She was a professional though, and as I worked through my lunch, she gave me a brief history of the school, most of which I'd heard in the Admissions building the first day, but I listened politely anyway. She moved on to how glad they were to have me—actually, she mentioned that one several times—emphasized her high expectations for me, and commented on how impressed she was with my worldliness, as she called it. I wasn't entirely sure if she meant it as a compliment. She touched very briefly on my "medical concerns" and assured me that the school would do everything it could to help me. Then she threw a curve ball.

"There's a long-standing tradition of student cooperation here at Northbrook," she intoned. This seemed both obvious to me and also ominous. I wasn't sure what she was getting at. "Each student performs four hours of service at the school per week—your assignments will be determined next week—and a team activity is compulsory each semester. Do you have any preferences, or any areas of sports expertise?"

For a moment, I was excited. I liked the idea of service to the school and I hoped to get back to my regular martial arts practices, one of the things I would miss most about my change in lifestyle. "I've taken martial arts since I was a kid, actually!" I told her. "I'm a brown belt in kickboxing and a blue belt in karate."

My excitement deflated with her frown. "That's wonderful," she said, though her tone implied exactly the opposite of wonderful. "However, we focus more on cooperative sports…You're rather tall, so I thought perhaps basketball?" she added hopefully.

I panicked a little, not wanting to be a disappointment at my very first meeting with the headmaster, but team sports and I were practically complete strangers.

"I've never had much chance to play basketball, but I'm willing to try?" I ended my sentence like a question but I couldn't help myself. I wanted to please this woman, so she wouldn't make me run from the room like that poor eighth grader on the stairs. And, I admitted to myself, so she wouldn't tell me my Legacy was an accident and send me packing three days after I arrived. As nervous as I was about this whole staying-in-one-place thing, now that I had it, I was surprised that I wanted it more than anything.

But my panic was not necessary, this time anyway. We determined that my "unique upbringing might not have been conducive to traditional team activities" and I learned the compulsory team requirements were not quite as cruel as I thought. There were all kinds of "teams," including musical ensembles, ballet troupes, creative writing groups, debate clubs, and even a media production team. In the end, I was enlisted for the team sport that had the most individual performances: the swim team. A quick call to the athletic office had me scheduled for my first practice the next morning.

After a few more assurances that the school was "so delighted to have me" and that they were "certain I was going to be a valuable member of the student body," my meeting with the headmaster was over. As I hitched my bag over my shoulder and was about to leave, Dr. Stewart said two things that, at the time, I assumed were separate thoughts, and I didn't take either for very important. Not until much later I would realize I'd been wrong on both counts.

"I know your class books were delivered for you, but I'm sure you'd love to visit the bookstore yourself," she suggested. "We're lucky to have it as a benefit to Northbrook." I nodded and turned to go, but as I opened the door she added in a light tone incongruous with the serious look on her face, "This is a special school, Lainey. We can't wait to see what special part you'll be."

WHEN CLASSES ENDED for the afternoon, I decided to do as the headmaster suggested and check out the bookstore. I had plenty of homework, sure, but about the only thing I liked more than shopping for books was shopping for vintage books. Turned out I was in luck.

The bookstore was across the street from the main campus, easily the largest business on the block. The stone façade was three stories high, with wide, book-filled windows on the first and second floors. A discreet wooden sign on a decorative iron bar proclaimed it, simply, "Penrose Books." I pushed open the weathered brass door and walked into my new little slice of heaven.

Penrose's was everything I ever dreamed a bookstore would be. It had warm yellow light streaming through the windows onto row after row of shelves that stretched almost to the high ceilings. Where the sun couldn't reach, what looked like old-fashioned gas lights lit the space in a soft, inviting glow. On one end of the floor was a long wooden counter with an antique register that must have weighed a hundred pounds resting at the corner. On the other side was a reading lounge with many stuffed couches and chairs, a few small tables, and a giant fireplace that was clearly still used on the colder days. A handful of students were already there talking, reading, or doing homework. The entire place smelled like leather and paper. It was fantastic.

I didn't see anyone who appeared to be working there, but I wasn't looking for anything specific. After a quick glance around, I followed an intriguing sign that read: FIRST EDITIONS AND RARITIES, 2ND FLOOR to where it pointed up a wide staircase with polished brass railings.

It was quiet and cozy upstairs, with even more rows of books than downstairs, and the same soft light making the entire place relaxing and incredibly inviting. I thought I was the only customer up there. At the far end of the floor, I found FIRST EDITIONS. There was a second, smaller staircase, one that must have been hidden behind the register area on the first floor, blocked with a chain and a small sign reading EMPLOYEES ONLY in a fancy script. If I thought the downstairs smelled great, this area was even more amazing. Now it smelled like *old* leather and paper, a wonderful combination of pipe tobacco, cotton, and time. I wanted to move my bed over and sleep in this section every night.

I was gently thumbing through a pristine leather-bound edition of "Modern" Poetry, circa the early 1900s, daydreaming about who might have owned it in the past, when I was suddenly jolted back to the present day.

"That's one of our best editions; you must have a great eye," came a soft—and highly unexpected—voice from behind me. I gave the most embarrassing, girly little shriek and spun around, nearly dropping one of the best editions in the store unceremoniously onto the floor.

He was handsome, tall, several inches above six feet, and lean but obviously muscular, all long legs and graceful limbs. His hair brushed over his forehead, curling at the ends. It was the unnamable color between brown and blond with brighter gold in some places, as if he spent lots of time outdoors. Or was just really lucky. Beautiful liquid blue eyes with darker edges topped a strong nose, narrow and straight, and lips that were perhaps a little too thin but complemented the rest of his features. He wore a simple t-shirt with jeans that fit perfectly, not too tight, not too loose.

He was the kind of guy I'd admire approvingly, if I saw him on the street or in the dining hall, but he was not the stuff of dreams, or so I thought. And then he smiled at me. Suddenly he became not just handsome but *really* handsome, entrancing even. I couldn't look away. Didn't want to either. I realized that I'd been wrong. He *was* the stuff of dreams, because he was *real*. He was a boy you didn't fantasize about but actually knew and dated and were envied by other girls for it.

Of course, in the few seconds between when I turned around and he smiled, I couldn't have made such a detailed inventory of his physical charms. Initially I had only a fleeting impression of cute boy, tall, unexpectedly talking to—and smiling at—me, but it would come to seem as if I always knew him exactly as he was, that I couldn't remember him as anything less than everything. Eventually I would know his face better than my own, than anyone's. But I didn't know that then. I didn't even know his name.

He coughed and gave me a look that was charmingly abashed. "Hi. Sorry. Didn't mean to startle you." Another smile. "I'm Carter. I work here."

Wow. He worked in the bookstore. Could he tip the perfection scale any further? Before I could respond, I heard a woman's voice, somewhat muffled as if on the first floor, call, "Cartwright? Are you upstairs?" I looked at him questioningly.

"Uh, yeah. Short for Cartwright. It's an old family name, kind of a tradition. Thankfully nicknames are a tradition too, so Carter it is."

I laughed. "Well, I'm Lainey. And I understand old family names, because that's short for Elaine."

"It sounds like we have something in common then, Lainey. I'm sure that's the first of many."

That's about when I blushed, a particularly bad habit of mine. But I hoped it was a pretty blush that made me look fetching, instead of shy and awkward, which I so suddenly was. Not knowing what else to do, I looked down at the book in my hands.

Thankfully Carter appeared to be neither shy nor awkward. "I haven't seen you here before," he said, looking at me as if he was trying to remember something. "Are you at the Academy? I thought I knew all the students."

"I just started, actually. Apparently I'm a Legacy, but I didn't know that until three days ago."

Something slight changed in him when I mentioned being a Legacy, or so I imagined. I couldn't pinpoint what it was, but I felt it, as if the air tightened around us. "A Legacy? Really? Who's your Sponsor?"

"That's the thing. I don't know."

Now he looked at me questioningly. "You're on Legacy, but you don't know your Sponsor?"

I shook my head. "No, I really don't." How did I explain without telling this boy my whole, tragic life story? "I...it's anonymous, and I don't know if my father established it or if it's from someone else. I haven't had the most traditional upbringing, I guess you could say, and I don't know much about my family. My parents died when I was young," I finished lamely.

"Well Lainey, I think you just became the most interesting girl at Northbrook."

Okay, I blushed again. How did he keep doing that to me? I started to say something, a thank you, maybe, but I was interrupted by the same woman's voice, nearer and a little more irritated.

"Cartwright! I hear you upstairs! I need your help sorting the new collection of..."

But I never heard what the new collection was, because a heavy crash sounded from not far below, followed by a breathy, "Oh damn," and a much louder, "CARTER!"

"Sorry," the boy in question offered. "I'd better go help my aunt. I'll see you soon, Lainey," he called over his shoulder as he loped quickly down the stairs, but not before I'd seen something that confirmed I was going crazy. I could have sworn that just as the whatever it was crashed downstairs, his eyes made a strange flash, becoming entirely dark in the center, surrounded by a pale, watery blue line.

AMY WAS ON her bed, flipping through a magazine, when I got back to our room but she tossed it aside when I came through the door.

"Hi!" she bubbled. "How was your first day?"

I sat down across from her and told her about my classes, my meeting with Headmaster Stewart, signing up for swim team. "And I went to the bookstore," I added, frowning as I picked up my backpack and moved over to my desk.

She noticed the frown and frowned herself. "You didn't like it? I *love* going there."

"No, no, it's a great bookstore. I only saw a little bit of the place, but they seemed to have everything. I can't wait to go back and really poke around, sit by that fireplace maybe." She laughed, and I looked back at her, confused. "What?"

"It's a great bookstore, I'll give you that, but that's not why we all love going there. Did you meet Carter?"

I gave a small, strained smile. "Yeah, I met Carter."

"And *that's* your whole reaction? 'Yeah, I met Carter?'" She mockingly imitated my voice, pretty well I might add.

Now I laughed, a real one. "He...seems like a good employee," I offered. She threw the magazine at me, but I ducked and it landed harmlessly on my desk, a little ruffled, but perfectly readable. I tucked it in my bag for later.

"I was right. You *must* be a heartbreaker if you can be this casual about Carter Penrose."

I was pretty sure that, between the two of us, she was the true heartbreaker, but I simply smiled and said, "Okay, let's put it this way…I wouldn't mind doing some of our studying over there whenever you suggest it."

"That's more like it! I'll tell you though, the sitting area is always full of our classmates. The younger ones and the new ones get dressed up before they go, and make excuses to ask him for help with something, *anything,* especially if it involves a trip to the upstairs, where they can really turn the flirt on. But after a while you realize you just go to enjoy the scenery. It doesn't help that he remembers *everyone* and is so freaking nice all the time. I think a spark of hope lingers in all of us, but I've never seen him hang out with anyone from the Academy outside the store, except for some of the guys on the track team. And Jill. She swears they're not dating, but we hate her anyway."

I didn't know who Jill was but decided to hate her a little too, just on principle. "Does he go here? Or to the town school?"

"Not anymore. He graduated last year. Or I should say 'graduated,'"—she made little air quotes around the word—"since I swear he only played sports and used the library. He's ridiculous smart and did most of his classwork at home with his aunt as a tutor. She's super nice too, if you didn't meet her. They live on the third floor, above the bookstore. Anyway, I think the school just wanted to let him run on the track team and bring up their average SAT scores, not that they're not stupidly high anyway, but that's how good he is. I mean, I'm a genius and he gives *me* a complex. What I can't figure out is why he's still here—not that I mind—and not in college, getting his PhD in astrophysics or something. But he's been working at the bookstore as long as I've been here, and I've asked, but he doesn't seem to be going anywhere."

"Wow. Well…maybe that's his flaw," I said. Amy raised one of her pretty eyebrows. "He's got to have one, right? I was thinking at the bookstore that he was a little too perfect. Maybe he's got no ambition."

"I guess," she replied skeptically. "If that's it though, it wouldn't make me kick him out of bed, unless it was to go do my homework for me and then come back."

I rolled my eyes, but laughed anyway, because, my weird feeling aside, I thought maybe I didn't disagree.

Chapter Five

I saw him the next morning. I was surprised, though I'm not sure why. After lying in bed pretending to sleep got old, I decided to get up and clear my head before swim practice by learning the campus a little better. It was cool out, bordering on cold, but crisp and refreshing. The sky was the pearly gray of early morning but sure to be clear and bright later. New England autumn at its best. I tugged down my sleeves against the chill and headed off toward the ponds.

Main Street was still and empty beyond the gates. I skirted the big pond and followed the path past the Admissions building. Penrose's stood dark and silent across the street. I was supposed to be clearing my head of the weirdness, so I purposefully turned up a branch that led toward the middle of campus, putting the bookstore at my back and pushing thoughts of the cute, disconcerting boy to the back of my mind. Of course, then I saw him.

I was coming out between, according to my directory, one of the science buildings and the Infirmary when Carter ran past me. I was close enough to call to him, but I kept quiet and watched him instead. He was jogging quickly, his stride sure and even, sweat making his shirt cling to his back and outline his broad shoulders. Watching him for only a minute, I could understand what Amy had said about the school wanting him to run on their track team.

He didn't seem to be doing anything suspicious though. I don't know what I expected, shifty glancing around maybe, a secret meeting at the woods' edge. But he was just running. Fast. I came out from beside the building and took the same turn he had on the road that bordered the woods. When I crested the small hill, he was already disappearing into the trails behind the faculty quarters.

I shook my head and mentally slapped myself for my foolishness. Just because I was going crazy didn't mean that everyone around me was in on it. This was all on me. I hadn't had a dizzy spell and nothing truly strange had happened since I arrived. The longer I thought about it, the less I believed I'd seen anything at all yesterday. I was nervous about being here, nervous about my growing craziness, and trying to make myself feel better by making everyone I met seem as weird as me. I took a trick from all of Aunt Tessa's yoga classes and concentrated only on my breathing until my mind was sufficiently relaxed and I could enjoy my early morning walk.

I got to the gym a little early for swim practice. "Gym" wasn't really the right word for it. Athletic complex was closer to the mark, but even that barely did it justice. It was enormous, modern, and as nice as any of the student centers at the biggest universities where my aunt had taught. The pool—or the natatorium, as my admissions counselor had called it—was in the back.

I found the girls' locker room and Coach Anderson's surprisingly cheery little office with ease. She directed me to the equipment room, where I was told to help myself to whatever I wanted, and assigned me a locker. I changed quickly and headed out, grabbing a towel from the generous stack by the door. Really, I could get used to this prep school thing. Coach Anderson didn't waste any time and sent me straight into the pool for an evaluation. I was no swimming star in the making, but

I was strong, and she thought I'd be a good distance swimmer by the end of the season.

The other students had started to trickle in during my test, some of them stretching, a few in the Jacuzzi to limber up, but most of them covertly—or openly—staring at me. Talk about awkward. Nothing like meeting a bunch of your new classmates for the first time while in your swimsuit, dripping wet and breathing a little hard. Before I had time to meet more than a handful of others, Coach blew her whistle and gave us our workouts.

The time flew by. Or glided, really. Going back and forth, the sounds of the pool and the other swimmers, concentrating on what my arms and legs were doing, all of that lulled my overactive brain into a sense of calm and normalcy. When the final whistle blew, I realized I'd enjoyed myself, though I was sure I'd be sore tomorrow. I met most of the girls back in the locker room, promptly forgetting all of their names, before I quickly showered and hung my new suit in my locker to dry.

As I was packing everything else in my bag, listening to two of my teammates chatter, I noticed one of the girls watching me. She was small, a little over five feet maybe, and slim, with shoulder-length pale blonde hair and average features that were made completely irrelevant by the largest, widest blue eyes I had ever seen. It was all you could do to look away from them, and it reminded me of Carter when he'd smiled at me. *I* reminded my stupid brain to give the Carter thing a rest, and tried giving the girl a tentative smile. She looked away without returning it. I'd never caught her name, and it seemed as though she kept to herself, not talking with any of the other girls on the team. I knew that she'd been watching me though, had felt the weight of her gaze like the heavy, wet hair down my back.

I LOOKED AROUND for Amy when I arrived at the dining hall for lunch. I was starting, a little guiltily, to think of her as my Northbrook life raft, but I honestly liked her too. I would have chosen to hang with Amy even if she hadn't been my roommate, and when I spotted her at a crowded table, I knew I was far from alone in that. Thankfully, she seemed to like me too, or at least pity the new girl. She jumped up and waved me over.

"Lainey, ohmigosh, it's all I've heard all day," she gushed, and then adopted a husky, lower voice, "'Ame, are you rooming with the new girl?' and 'Ammmmmy, dude, can you introduce me to your roomie?' and 'Hey Ame, can I come study with you later at your room?'" She snorted. "I swear, I need a freaking whip and chair to keep the animals at bay, not to mention an allergy pill for all the over-excited testosterone I've been exposed to in the last twenty-four hours. Move over, idiot," she finished, pushing the guy next to her—I thought he was Caleb, from swim practice this morning—over, and dragging a chair for me from the table behind her, right out from underneath what looked like an unsuspecting freshman.

Had I mentioned I really liked Amy?

I sat and gave I-thought-he-was-Caleb a sorry-she's-crazy-but-thanks-for-moving smile, which, to my relief, he returned with a my-pleasure-and-we're-used-to-it smile of his own. I was introduced to the few others around the table I hadn't met in classes and settled into mostly listening to a lively conversation that touched on designer shoes, matter vs. energy, a recent action movie, and Shakespeare. I contributed a little on the two ends, was completely lost in the middle, and mainly thought to myself, *so this is what rich, smart prep school students talk about?* Really? I was musing about that when Amy completely side-swiped me.

"And Lainey and I are going to the bookstore after final hour, so bitches stay home," she announced, rather loudly. "You too, Caleb," she added.

I swore everyone there gave me a knowing look, but it wasn't only my table giving me the eye. From two tables over, a girl I hadn't seen on campus before, but could only describe as the future Miss America, was glaring at me while leaning down to talk to the almost-but-not-quite as pretty girl next to her. She stood, picking up her tray and making her way to the double front doors, and I amended my original assessment. Maybe Miss Universe. She was so perfect, I almost had to shield my eyes.

Oddly though, we didn't look entirely dissimilar. From the back, we might have been sisters. She had long brown hair, almost the color of mine, but it was layered with the most subtle amount of waviness, an effect most girls spent hours at the salon to achieve but I imagined came to this girl naturally. She was about my height and equally slender, with perhaps more natural curviness than I possessed and a sway to her walk that told me she knew how—and wasn't afraid—to use every inch of those curves. Her face was patrician and perfectly proportional with deep brown eyes that were sultry and memorable. This girl's beauty was epic, and I figured I knew who she was.

Everyone was already staring at her—I didn't seem to be the only one who noticed the glare she'd given me, and I figured everyone always stared at her anyway—so I ventured, "Uh, so I guess that's Jill?"

Amy looked confused for a second. "Huh? Oh! No, that's Alexis Morrow. She's as big a bitch as she looks—hey, if I looked like her, I'd probably be a bitch too, unlike you, Ms. Young and Gorgeous—but most of the guys don't care. Right, Caleb?"

Caleb had the good grace to glance over and grin—a very cute grin, I didn't fail to notice, and I was pretty sure Amy ate it right up—but his attention was clearly elsewhere for the moment. Honestly, I was amazed he even heard her. I completely ignored her seeming comparison of me to Miss Universe and tried to get to the bottom of this mystery. "So, that's not…uh, the guy from the bookstore's girlfriend?"

I tried for casual but didn't fool anyone. Hell, I'd already tipped them off by asking about the mysterious Jill in the first place.

Amy looked at me with exaggerated sympathy. "No darling," she said, patting my arm, "that's not 'the guy from the bookstore's' girl-friend,"—after two days, she could imitate me perfectly, which would have been irritating if I hadn't liked her so much—"though believe me, Alex has campaigned harder than anyone for the title. But Jillian's over there." And she gestured to a lone girl at a table near the edge of the room.

It was the blue-eyed girl from swim practice.

TRUE TO HER word, Amy collected me from our room after our last classes, practically pushing me out the door after throwing first a hair brush then lip gloss at me and refusing to relinquish my over-sized hoodie from where she'd snatched it off my chair and stuffed it under her pillow.

"Oh no. No shapeless sweatshirts for you today. I mean, Caleb and Jason were practically drooling on my desk by the time I sat down in first hour, after they'd seen you and your assets at swim practice. We're taking them on display over to Penrose's and seeing if we can't turn some heads. Half the guys at the Academy hang out there…and there's always some local talent to consider," she added with such an adorable wink I completely forgot I was supposed to be annoyed with her.

"Only two days here, and you're already a real pain in my assets," I fired back. Then I added, in complete honesty, "And I'm pretty sure Caleb wasn't drooling over me." His eyes might have strayed to Alexis during her grand exit, but they'd lingered on Amy repeatedly through-out our lunch.

She giggled and grabbed my hand before dragging me out the door. "C'mon, Heartbreaker."

We stopped at the coffee shop on the other end of the block before making our way into the bookstore. Mochas steaming, we snagged a couch near the fireplace I was surprised was empty, whether out of some unspoken rule or the younger kids' awe of Amy, I'd never be sure. But I didn't care either, since it had stayed cool enough outside that the fire was lit and I'd been forced to freeze without my sweatshirt. I couldn't get close enough.

We spread our books on the table in front of us and got to work. Amy pulled out some ridiculous-looking physics problems, which she actually seemed to enjoy. She even hummed a little while her pencil flew over the pages. It occurred to me then that when she'd joked about being a genius it hadn't been a joke.

Studying at the bookstore turned out to be a lot of fun, like social hour with a few books thrown in. None of Amy's friends from lunch, including Caleb, showed up, but Miss Universe was dominating a small, talkative group behind us. I could physically feel the dirty looks burning the back of my head.

I leaned over to Amy and spoke softly. "Uh, what's that Alexis girl's deal?"

Amy glanced over her shoulder and smiled broadly at her. I almost wanted to duck to avoid the killing look she threw at us next. "Like I said earlier, Alex is a bitch, a really pretty one. That's about her whole story. She's a super-rich only child who has been spoiled every minute of her life. She doesn't like anyone to be the center of attention unless it's her, and believe me, Lainey, that title has gone to you the last few days. It also doesn't help that I overheard her complaining to one of her bitchy friends that *she* overheard someone say Carter asked Jill about you. Nothing's secret at Northbrook, by the way, at least not for very long. Since Alex considers Alex the most beautiful girl on the planet, and Carter the only boy around here worthy of her attention, something she's made *abundantly* obvious, she can't understand why she doesn't have him. Seriously, for a girl who's such a good actress, she's not very subtle. Oh, and also, she hates me," Amy added, her sweet smile never diminishing.

What I thought was, *Carter asked about me?* but what I said was, "Why does she hate you?"

"Eh, because people like me, I think, even though I'm not tall and skinny"—she gave me a meaningful look, to which I stuck out my tongue—"and I do better in all our classes than she does. She might be pretty, and a bitch, but she's not stupid. In fact, she's smart. Very smart, even, not that it matters, since her future clearly does not lie in academics. But Alex hates to lose at anything, which is precisely the reason we're sitting here."

I was instantly suspicious. "What's *that* mean?"

"Well Lainey, I happen to like you." She punctuated her words with a grin I could only describe as devious. "I also happen to like Carter Penrose, as a person I mean, not just as the piece of fine man that he is. And I absolutely *love* to goad Alexis. So, genius that I am, my plan is to, in one brilliant move, catch you a hottie, hook Carter up with my lovely roomie, and absolutely ruin Alex's probably whole year, all while enjoying every minute of it."

"Wow. You're a real mastermind." If she heard my heavy sarcasm, she ignored it.

"Don't forget it," she replied cheerfully. "Oh, and no need to thank me, either. I don't do my good work for the glory." I threw my napkin at her and went back to my book, but I was secretly pleased. I hated myself.

I didn't have long with my poetry homework before her plan went into motion. Carter himself strolled into the lounge a few minutes later with an armload of wood for the fire. I'm not sure how he managed to carry it along with the weight of all the longing gazes he drew, but he made his way toward the fireplace with ease, saying hi or a few words to almost everyone he passed.

He paused a little longer at Alexis's group, and I heard some flirting so blatant and uncreative—"I see how you keep so fit, Carter, carrying such big wood around all day"—I nearly groaned aloud. After a few more exchanges, he finally brought his haul over to our dwindling fire.

"It's about time, Penrose; we're catching a chill over here," Amy launched at him as soon as he got close.

"I wouldn't want you to freeze your tiny brain, Moretti, so I brought a few extra pieces to stoke the fire," he offered back, along with one of those mesmerizing smiles. Clearly Amy and Carter were better friends than she'd let on. I caught myself smiling back at him, like an absolute idiot, and immediately returned my attention to my book.

Not fast enough though. "Welcome back, Lainey," Carter said, ducking down to catch my eye. I thought I blushed. *Again.* I *really* hated myself. "I was sorry to see you leave so quickly yesterday. Looks like you've had the bad luck to land yourself with Moretti here. Let me know if you need my help getting her to leave you alone."

"Very funny, Penrose," Amy retaliated. "Ms. Young happens to have the good fortune of being my roommate, and I am here to protect her from the likes of pretty boys like you."

I came to my senses and started acting like the normal Lainey Young. "It's true," I broke in. "She's got my best interests firmly in hand. I'm not allowed to date until I'm at least twenty-two."

"Well that's a shame," Carter replied. "Moretti, why don't you tell her about your dating history, hmm? I'm sure that will scare her off from it for at least five years."

"Build my fire, Penrose, I'm busy doing Physics," she said, and this time *she* threw my napkin, which he dodged, and we all watched it sail into the fire. It combusted instantly.

Carter stoked the fire then sat on the arm of the couch next to me, leaning over toward Amy's notebook. "What are you working on?" he asked with obvious interest. "Need help?"

He smelled good, like fresh-cut wood and boy soap. Suddenly *I* was in danger of combusting. This was getting a little ridiculous. It wasn't like Carter was the first hot guy I'd ever seen. I mentally chastised myself, but it didn't really work since he was so close to me. He hadn't *had* to sit on my side of the couch. He could have sat next to Amy, but no, he purposely sat next to me, and leaned over in a way I'd usually interpret as flirtatious. Huh. This day kept getting more interesting.

Amy snorted. "Not today, and not from you, buddy. I've got it well under control," she said. "But, just to amuse you, it's kinematics. I know you love that. And since I'm perfectly capable of managing this without you, why don't you help Lainey with poetry. That's way more confusing than mechanics any day." She pulled a horrified face and Carter laughed.

"I *do* love mechanics," he said, then turned to me, "but I'm not so bad at poetry either. What have you got?"

"Well, I'm pretty sure I've got it under control too, but I don't mind sharing. It's Ezra Pound." I held up my book for him to see.

"A good one," he said. And then he recited the whole poem. Without looking at it.

I was struck stupid, and stared at him for a moment, probably with my mouth hanging open. Amy, however, was grinning and muttered, *"Showoff!"* under her breath.

I recovered. Sort of. "Wow. Guess you like this one, huh?"

Now he grinned. "You could say that." He looked ready to say more, but the service bell at the register gave its little ring. Carter rose and waved toward the counter at the far end. "Sorry to run off, but duty calls. More poetry some other time?" he asked me, not even sar-castically, but in a way that seemed genuinely hopeful.

Amy, naturally, answered for us. "You'll see us here again, Penrose, don't worry. Now go help your customers before they steal some-thing." He headed off to the register and she turned to me, absolutely radiating pleased-with-herself-ness. "Well, *that* went even better than expected."

Chapter Six

The next several weeks sped by in a predictable pattern. I got up and swam, went to classes, hung out with Amy, studied at the bookstore, made friends, completed my weekly hours of service at the library, and tried not to get in trouble while looking for it over the weekends. In a word, I became normal.

And it wasn't boring. In fact, I kind of liked it. More than kind of. I thought it was great. Maybe it was novel to me, after so many years of constantly changing scenery, but there was something nice about waking up each morning and knowing where you had to go, what you had to do, and, especially, that you'd do the same the next day and the day after that. Amy swore I'd be bored out of my mind by Christmas, but I didn't believe her. I was surprised most of all that being stationary was almost as liberating as moving all the time, just in a different way.

By the end of about my first week and a half, I completely abandoned the antidepressants I'd been prescribed. I knew they were important for some people and it wasn't that I was embarrassed to take them, but besides not believing they'd cure my problem, the last thing I felt at Northbrook was depressed. I'd easily found my place with Amy and her group of friends as well as fallen into the comfortable rhythm of classes and studying. I was quite possibly as happy as I'd ever been.

I missed my Aunt Tessa, of course, some days pretty badly, but she sent me a small care package—fresh cookies, a little antique trinket, a new book she thought I might like—or a letter every single week. At first she was calling almost daily, but I put a stop to it quickly. I needed to learn how to live independently, I told her. I think she cried a little at this, but she understood. We made a standing date to talk on Sunday evenings. I looked forward to each call, which I'm sure she could tell and not-so-secretly pleased her. But she could also tell that I was happy at Northbrook, and that pleased her more than anything.

"I'm proud of you, Lainey," she said one night, kind of abruptly, since we'd been talking about a project I'd barely started working on and had produced nothing to be proud of yet.

"Thanks, Auntie. That means a lot to me. But why?"

"You've really taken to your new environment, sweetheart, in a way that impresses me and Uncle Martin too," she explained. "It's not that I didn't know you were adaptable; God knows if I've made you anything besides a little crazy, it was that." She gave a small laugh. "But you haven't just adapted. You're flourishing. And it was *you* who chose to take this step in your life. I didn't want you to. But I see I was wrong, and I'm so glad to have been." After a pause, she added, "I love you, Lainey. No parent ever wants to see her baby grow up, but I couldn't be prouder of how you're doing it."

I admit I got a bit teary after that little speech, but it was the good kind. Mostly. I couldn't help but be unnerved by her "a little crazy" comment. Even though it was in jest on her part, I knew it to be true. Or at least I had been sure it was true before I started at Northbrook. I'd been mercifully headache-free since my arrival. They'd come at least once a month since I was thirteen, and I was going on six weeks with no dizziness, no visions, and no headaches. I was beginning to believe, just a little bit, that maybe the doctors had been right and all I really needed was stability and structure.

The best part of that whole stretch of first weeks was Halloween. I'd trick-or-treated as a kid, but nothing compared to the production Northbrook put on for the town. It was *incredible*. For the entire week beforehand, all of the students dropped their assigned service work and transformed the campus into a giant haunted Halloween spectacular.

We prepared spooky stations and funny stations, hayrides and bonfires, ghost stories and face painting. We filled bowls with every candy imaginable, plus healthier options like apples and little bags of popcorn. A sophomore girl named Brooke, who was part of Queen Alexis's court and therefore usually shunned me, got to run a gypsy-style fortune telling booth. The gold and green striped tent was lit only by battery powered candles and filled with brightly patterned pillows and rugs along with a low wooden table topped by a crystal ball, giving the whole thing a very authentic, very exciting feel. Plus Brooke was really, really good. I almost swore she was telling real fortunes.

She "practiced" on the Academy students—even some of the faculty—and as we saw our friends come out wide-eyed and convinced, of course we all wanted a turn. I dutifully waited in line with everyone else. Amy went in before me and was nearly bursting with pleasure when she came out a few minutes later.

I gave her a speculative smile. "How's your future looking?"

"Brilliant, and chock full of yummy treats for Halloween, but that's all I'm telling you," she said before practically floating back to her task.

My turn, I poked my head in tentatively and exclaimed, "Oh wow, Brooke, this is fantastic! You look awesome." She was in her gypsy costume, complete with long skirt, layers of wispy scarves, and heaps of undoubtedly expensive gold jewelry, plus heavy dark eyeliner and mascara that made her lashes look impressively thick and long. She might have shunned me because of Alexis, but I didn't get the impression she was as mean as the rest of that clique. She was in character too.

"Velcome, Elaine Young, to my fortune parlor," she said, with a convincing accent full of r's rolled in a way I could only describe as sensuous. Between that and her gorgeous face, I suddenly understood why there were so many guys in line outside. "You vould like to hear your future, yes?"

"Sure," I replied. "Lay it on me."

Her berry-stained lips curled up into a mischievous smile and she glanced down at her swirling crystal ball. As she did this, for only a second, I swore her usually gold-flecked brown eyes appeared to flash a radiant shade of amber and I gasped. She looked up at me quickly, a hint of surprise showing in what were her perfectly normal, mostly brown eyes, before she said in her normal voice, "Oh. Uh, you okay?"

"Yeah, sorry," I mumbled, and offered the first, and lamest, excuse that came to mind. "Thought I saw a spider."

She rallied. "Ve shall proceed." She briefly looked down again, and then focused on me with a smile. "More than anything, you vant to know what brought you here, yes, Elaine Young, and vhat causes your headaches? It is because you are special, Elaine Young, and you vill find that out soon, I am certain of it."

"Whoa," I breathed. I didn't really tell people about my headaches, though Amy had warned me there were no secrets here, but Brooke was right. That *was* the question in my mind I most wanted answered. There had been no more clues to my unusual Legacy and no crazy visions so far, but her calling me "special" brought to mind my first meeting with Headmaster Stewart. And the strange trick of the candles that had caused me to see Brooke's eyes as a different color also reminded me that I had seen—or thought I had—a similar strange effect in my first meeting with Carter Penrose. As I mulled over her weird prediction and the strange connections, she brought me back to reality, also as if she'd truly been reading my thoughts.

She dropped her excellent accent and leaned over, whispering conspiratorially, "And there's a certain local boy you hope will finally move past the flirting stage, yeah? I think you've got that one locked up too, but you didn't hear *me* say that." She giggled and switched back to her gypsy persona. "Your fortune is done now, Elaine Young. Be gone and send me the next vaiting truth-seeker."

I waved and smiled on my way out, but then dropped it immediately once I was by myself. She was *also* right about the local boy. The more time Amy and I spent at the bookstore, the more I too came to like Carter Penrose, as a friend, and yeah, maybe a little more than that. Not that I admitted it to anyone. I had always thought he was good-looking, sure, but I wasn't the kind of girl who was immediately interested in someone just because he was hot enough to make me blush or give my stomach little somersaults.

I was, however, very much interested in a guy who was incredibly smart, brilliantly sarcastic in a way that was both funny and sharp-witted, and who was genuinely polite and nice. To *everyone*. Frankly, I was the tiniest bit in love with the boy from the bookstore. Despite Amy's pronouncement that she was trying to hook us up, she never really pushed anything, and I didn't try to do more than be myself and flirt back when he flirted with me. But it was getting a little frustrating.

Even I could see that Carter hung out with Amy and me more than anyone else, and though I could tell he was naturally flirtatious—which is exactly what, according to Amy, caused hope to burn eternal in all the Academy girls—he definitely devoted extra attention to me. Don't get me wrong, I liked it. A lot. But I would have liked to get beyond that and, oh, have him ask me on a date or something.

I'd gotten a few other offers from guys at the Academy, one of which I accepted. I went with a senior named Garrett, a friend of

Caleb's who played with him on the baseball team. He was quietly funny and tall and a little bit shy, which was actually what I liked about him most. We'd gone to—where else?—the bookstore lounge for a coffee by the fireplace. I imagined about a million first dates had happened in the very seats where we sat, since the bookstore and the Academy were both over a century old. Of course, back then, first dates were chaperoned, and I almost felt like mine had one too.

In my peripheral vision, and in the periphery of my mind, I always knew where Carter was in the shop. And he spent more than a necessary amount of time in my direct line of sight. Stoking the fire. Repeatedly stopping to chat with the group across from me. Wiping non-existent dust off a few of the coffee tables. He didn't speak to me, except to say a friendly hello to both of us—he knew Garrett, of course, because he knew *everyone*. However, I did catch him, more than once, while he performed whatever task he'd devised to get into my vicinity, watching me. One time he scowled openly. I took a little smug satisfaction that Carter seemed bothered by my date, and maybe I played up my flirtation with Garrett the tiniest bit.

Garrett didn't seem to mind. In fact, I had a good enough time that I let him kiss me goodnight when we got back to campus. Turned out my shy boy was pretty good at it, and I think I let it go on a little longer than I should have, since before I realized, the curfew bell was ringing and I was rushing off with a little bit of a flush and a, "Thanks, I had a great time!" thrown over my shoulder.

I hung out with Garrett a few more times, but he didn't seem to be in a hurry to make me his official girlfriend, and I was not in a hurry to be in a relationship. With Garrett anyway, I finally admitted to myself and to Amy when she pressed. I enjoyed Garrett's company, and I *definitely* enjoyed the few times I kissed him, but when I thought of the term "boyfriend" in my head, he was not who I pictured.

I tried to tell myself I wasn't interested in being in *any* relationship, but I'd never been a particularly good liar, and especially not to myself. Things were unchanged between Carter and me, hovering at a stage of casual friendship and go-nowhere flirtation, so right before our Thanksgiving break, I decided to try something different.

THE HOUR RIGHT after classes ended was the quietest time at the bookstore, since most of the Academy students were at team practice or service hours. I took a moment when I stepped through the door to close my eyes and inhale the gloriousness that was Penrose Books. It never failed to smell amazing. I let out my deep breath slowly then opened my eyes. And literally felt them widen in surprise.

"Oh!" I gasped. Carter was standing mere inches from me, regarding me with a measured, thoughtful look I noticed from him on a regular basis. It meant he was deciding whether or not to say something.

"I do that too sometimes, when I come down first thing in the morning," he said softly. "One of my favorite moments every day." Then he switched back to his usual flirtatious self. "Except for when *you* come through the door. To what do we owe this pleasure? Since your first week, you haven't been here so early in the afternoon."

Shit. I hadn't come up with an excuse. "I...had someone ask to switch hours with me at the library, and I...couldn't study in my room because they're fixing our window. I thought it might be quiet over here this time of day. I remembered that it was practically empty the first time I came in." There, that didn't sound too bad.

But Carter smiled at me, and if his smiles were usually dangerous, this one should have been illegal. He looked at me for a moment with obvious, knowing delight, as if I were wearing a blouse as see-through as my excuse. "Well you're right about that; you have the place, and me, mostly to yourself. I recommend today the couch by the fireplace, always your favorite, I believe," he said and gestured grandly to the empty lounge area.

Or almost empty. At one of the small tables by the windows sat Jill, as inconspicuous and quiet as always. She had some books open in front of her, but at the moment she was studying Carter and me with the curious, weighty gaze I'd become used to. I gave her a small wave and took up my favorite couch by the fireplace, as suggested.

If I enjoyed studying at the bookstore when it was busy, I doubly enjoyed it when it was empty. I didn't know why I hadn't tried it sooner. The store was quiet, except for some crackling of the fire and the occasional jingle of the register when the one or two customers checked out. Jill made almost no noise whatsoever, so I could almost imagine that I *was* alone, with my books and my covert studying of Carter. He seemed to make everything he did look effortless and as if he enjoyed it, including mundane tasks like shelving the new magazine issues.

As he was hauling off the last stack of outdated magazines, I heard him say, "I'm going to take a break now, Aunt Mel," when he passed where she was perched at the counter, reading a newspaper.

She actually glanced at me, which necessitated a quick duck of my eyes into my book, laughed, which told me I hadn't been quick enough, and said affectionately, "No problem, Cartwright. I'll hold off the hordes of customers."

Melinda Revell bore a good amount of family resemblance to Carter. She had the same naturally wavy, not-quite-blonde-or-brown hair, a sort of caramel color, and similar blue eyes, plus a dusting of freckles that made her more cute than pretty and very approachable. She smiled often, and genuinely, her eyes crinkling at the corners in a way that made her even more likeable.

When Carter reentered the lounge area for his break, he headed straight for me, carrying a small load of firewood under one arm and a book under the other. "Penny for your thoughts," he said mildly, as he set his book, a thick tome of what looked like short stories by Russian authors, on the table and stacked the logs in the low-burning fireplace.

"Sorry, not available. My thoughts are far more valuable than a penny," I replied with a smile.

He turned from the fire and gave me that measured look again, for the second time in one visit, before saying, "I'm sure they are." He sat down on my sofa, perhaps a little closer to me than was absolutely necessary, I noted with internal delight.

I stuck my finger in my own book and rested it in my lap. "Who was the original Cartwright anyway?"

"A grandfather many greats removed," he replied. "He was famous, you know; invented the power loom. Quite a namesake to live up to, but I'm trying. Who was Elaine, Elaine?"

"My mother's great-grandmother, or so Aunt Tessa tells me. She wasn't famous though. My middle name is Rachel," I added, "but I don't know who she was, if anyone."

Surprising me exceedingly, he said, "In the Bible, Rachel was a thief. What have you stolen lately, Lainey Rachel Young?"

Surprising *myself* even more, I said, *"This,"* and leaned over and kissed him lightly on the cheek.

To my relief, he looked surprised but not horrified, and thoughtfully touched the spot where my lips had touched him. Once more I got *the* look. "No, that was given freely. But it won't stop me from asking you to return it someday, at a time of my choosing," he added playfully, along with one of his dangerous smiles for good measure.

Very quietly, from the area of the windows, I heard the most delicate of derisive coughs. I'd completely forgotten about Jill's presence, and that she was kind-of-maybe Carter's girlfriend. But Carter was sitting with *me*. Confused, I leaned over and in a low voice started to say, "Carter, can I ask…" when he chuckled.

"No," he said.

"I'm sorry. Forget it."

"No," he repeated, and continued softly, "that's not what I meant. I meant, 'No, Jillian's not my girlfriend,' despite what you might have heard. And I'm not gay, either," he added, "in case you heard that one too."

I blushed. "I…hadn't heard that second one. But Jill, yeah, there's, um, some healthy debate about your relationship, I guess you could say."

He laughed. "Well, *I've* heard some not so subtle speculation about the second one since I haven't accepted a few, ah, slightly more than friendly advances from some of your classmates. But it's not that I'm not flattered, by the advances, I mean, not that I care if anyone thinks I'm gay either. Well most anyone anyway. It's just that I try to resist dating Academy girls, since I kind of went there and I've always worked here. Most of the time I think they see me as a…trophy, or a contest prize, you know?"

I thought he underestimated his level of appeal, but instead of telling him *that*, I said, "So, c'mon, you expect me to believe you don't date anyone, even Jill?"

"Jill and I really are just friends," he said seriously. "Actually, she's like my cousin. We have…common interests. And she *definitely* encourages me to stay away from Academy girls. Some of your classmates are not very nice, you might have noticed."

I snorted. "You're not kidding." I spared a fleeting thought to wonder how *Jill* felt about being considered like a cousin, and then added, "And you're also not answering my question."

He laughed again. "You're really *not* shy, are you, Lainey? First time I met you, I was sure you were just going to be a pretty, quiet girl who loved books. But to answer your question: you forget—unlike all but a few of the Academy students, I grew up here. All my previous girlfriends have been from town. There isn't one right now though, a local girl, I mean. In case that was your next question."

I wasn't shy, that was true—if I had been, my transient life would've been pretty difficult—but hoped he didn't think I was like those other Academy girls, looking to toy with the local boy. I was trying to figure out how to say that without embarrassing myself completely, but Carter saved me from it.

"That's what I like about you, Lainey," he said. "You're not quite what I expected, and you're not like the typical Academy girls. You're not like anyone," he added quietly, almost as if he didn't realize he'd said it out loud.

I opened my mouth to respond but didn't get the chance. The front door jingled and a loud group of my classmates laughed their way inside, heading for the lounge that had filled in around us. I'd been so absorbed, I hadn't realized. Carter stood, grabbing his entirely untouched book off the table.

"As much as I'd rather not be," he said, "I am still at work and need to get back to it." As he turned toward the register, he added, "You know, you should go say hi to Jillian while you wait for your roommate's trail of clues to lead her here. She's a little quiet sometimes, I know, but I think she'd like you."

"Uh, sure," I said, hoping I didn't sound too hesitant. Jill *was* quiet, and hadn't really taken to my attempts to befriend her yet. But I'd follow his suggestion and give talking to her one more shot. I left my book and my bag on the couch to save my spot and headed over toward her table.

I didn't make it.

I was about four steps from Jill when it hit, a familiar wave of dizziness. I reached out to steady myself, my fingers brushing the hair of the student sitting in the chair nearest to me. She was a pretty freshman girl with light brown hair and a friendly smile. I didn't know her name, but in that moment I *did* know she was going skiing over Thanksgiving break and would not be coming back.

In a swift vision, I witnessed the girl catch the edge of her ski on some ice and frantically spiral her arms before tumbling over sideways and sliding head-first into a towering light pole.

She did not move again.

I blinked and, instead of the dead girl, saw Jill. Her pale blue eyes, already enormous, appeared a strange, deep shade of indigo as they widened even more in surprise. Blackness invaded my own eyes then and I dropped toward the floor.

Chapter Seven

When everything came back into focus, I found myself lying on an unfamiliar bed in a dark room. The door was open a sliver; a slice of light sneaking in from the hallway offered the only source of illumination. I remembered the freshman girl, and the vision, and Jill's surprisingly strong hand around my wrist right before I collapsed. What I didn't remember was how I got wherever I was. What I could see gave me no clues to my whereabouts except that I was in a small, generic bedroom. I was contemplating letting myself go back to sleep when I heard soft voices outside the door. It was a jumble of frantic whispering, from which I caught only snatches.

"…do with her?…"

"…can't carry her over to the infirmary, Cartwright…"

"…think she doesn't know…"

"…definitely no idea…"

"…Legacy, she had to be…"

"…Brooke Barros said…"

"…Jill and I…watching…hadn't seen her do it before…"

Tired of being discussed just out of earshot, I cleared my throat and called out, "Hello?" The conversation abruptly ceased, and after a second, Melinda pushed open the door. I could see Carter lurking behind her along with his Uncle Jeff, Melinda's husband. No Jill, at least not within my line of sight. The cast of characters in the hallway answered where I was anyway. I must have been brought up to the Revells' and Carter's apartment above the bookstore.

"Oh, Lainey! Sorry honey, we didn't mean to wake you," Melinda gushed from the doorway. "Are you okay? Do you need anything? Water? Do you want me to shut the door? You rest here as long as you need, don't worry."

"No, no, it's okay," I said, sitting up a little. "I…" didn't know how to finish that. What was I? Confused, definitely. Curious about their whispered conversation, absolutely. I decided to start small though. I switched on the lamp next to me so I could see them better and asked, "How long was I out?"

They tentatively made their way into the room, Melinda coming to sit on the edge of the bed.

"Not long," she answered. "Just a few minutes, really. I had Carter bring you up here to get you away from the bedlam. Your classmates are a little hysterical, I'm sure you can imagine."

Great. Now they all knew my problem, in the most sensational way possible. At least I would make a good story. I was pretty sure by the time I got back to campus, half the students would believe me dead, and the other half would think I'd accosted Jill and she knocked me down. "Great," I said out loud this time. "Who's watching the store?"

"Jillian's taking care of it for us. She helps out all the time." Melinda was apparently the designated talker here. "Not that I think she has to do much more than babysit right now," she added with a frown.

"It's okay," I told her. "This isn't the first time this has happened, though it's the first time since I got here, and definitely the first time I've had the chance to become an object of gossip for an entire school, but I'll recover. Sorry about the disruption to your evening though."

I looked around at them. Melinda was frowning again. Carter was watching me with a blend of concern, surprise, and for some strange reason, smug satisfaction. Jeff was completely unreadable. "So," I said. "What is it that I don't know?"

That caught them off guard. Sort of. Carter blinked, Jeff was, well, still completely unreadable, and Melinda froze before stepping up again. "I don't know what you mean, honey," she said. "You fainted. Jillian said it looked like you got dizzy first. I thought Carter told me you had a history…"

"Oh, come on," I interrupted. I hated being rude to her, but I couldn't let them pretend there wasn't something going on here. And they *knew*. I knew they did. "I know this isn't just some migraine thing I've got. I've always known, just been too afraid to tell anyone. But I know you guys know what's causing them. I heard you. So tell me. *What don't I know?*"

My question came out more forcefully than I'd meant it to, but I couldn't help it. I sensed that finally, *finally*, I would get some answers to this sickness that had been plaguing me for three years. And I knew, suddenly, that this was why I'd come to Northbrook. If it hadn't been for the visions, I never would have ended up here. I felt sure that, somehow, my father had known this would happen.

After a minute of no answer I demanded, "Well?!"

Carter coughed but only looked at his aunt. My champion came from an unexpected source.

"Just tell her, Melly," Jeff Revell said softly before he turned and slipped out into the hall.

Melinda sighed and started, hesitantly, "It's…complicated, Lainey."

"I'm not surprised it is," I replied. "If it weren't complicated, all of my many doctors would've figured it out by now. What I don't understand is why you all seem to know exactly what's wrong when years of testing couldn't tell me."

"It's because they really couldn't, Lainey," came from Carter. He was still hovering a few feet from the bed. "What's wrong with you...well, it's not *wrong*, it just is, but not even the best doctors would be able to explain it, unless you find the very right one. We know you didn't see any who could because they'd have told us."

Okay. This conversation was getting stranger by the second. I thought I might throw up, but I wasn't sure if it was because of my rapidly developing migraine or the battle between *freaked out* and *angry* raging in my stomach. "Okay, what the hell is going on?" I looked back and forth between Carter and Melinda. "One of you better explain, fast, before I get up and run out of here, headache or not. You're scaring me."

Carter slipped from behind his aunt and knelt down on the floor next to me. He put his hand out toward me, but I flinched away and he let it drop to his knees. "You don't need to be scared, Lainey, not of us, not ever. I'm sorry."

"I don't want to be," I said, and realized, as my voice cracked, that tears had started to slip down my cheeks. "But you're not making that very easy right now. Please. What's going on here?"

"Lainey," Melinda started gently. She leaned over to place her hand on my arm and I let her. "You are different. Special. Along with many of the Academy students, and Carter, and me. You're not ordinary, but *extra*ordinary. The simplest way to put it is that you, like us, have ESP."

I stared at her stupidly for a minute. Had I really just heard that? I found my voice again, and found that my tears had been mopped dry by skepticism. "ESP. Extrasensory Perception. Come on!" I said. "That's not even funny."

Except they weren't laughing.

"ESP," I tried again. "So you're trying to tell me that what, I can predict the future? And you can too?" And then as my brain caught up to my words, I gasped and clapped my hands over my mouth. *"Brooke,"* I whispered between my fingers. "I…I swore she was really telling fortunes. I heard you mention her in the hallway. Jesus. You're not kidding."

"No, honey, we're not," Melinda said. Carter still knelt beside me, in what had to be an uncomfortable position, but he showed no evidence of it. He was watching me so intently I could almost feel him willing me to believe them.

"Oh God! I knew it!" I shouted. "I really *am* crazy!" And then I started to cry in earnest.

I CRIED FOR a long time. Melinda hugged me, making soothing noises but not really saying anything. When the sobs finally slowed, and I felt like I could breathe enough to speak again, I said, barely audibly, "Please tell me this isn't real."

At least Melinda was tender in her denial. "I can't do that, honey. It *is* real. Very real. But you're *not* crazy, and you don't have to be scared of it, I promise."

Carter spoke for the first time since my breakdown. "It's not like you see on TV or read in books, and especially not like the trash they print in those tabloids," he said earnestly. "'ESP' isn't even what we call it, not at all, but it's the easiest way to explain it to the uninitiated. We knew you had no idea, and honestly, we weren't entirely sure either, but since you were a Legacy, we thought you must at least have the genes. So we've been waiting for you to manifest…which you finally did this afternoon."

"I'm so confused," was all I could come up with. "The...visions"—I'd never mentioned them out loud before— "are...they're *real?*"

"They are," Melinda replied. "Or they could be, if it's a future vision you see," she added thoughtfully. "Can you tell us...?"

But she was interrupted by a loud knocking and then Amy's voice, a little frantic, coming from somewhere nearby. "Carter?! Melinda? What's going on? Is Lainey up here?"

I opened my mouth to call out to her, but before I could speak, Carter leaned over, gripping my arm, and whispered emphatically, "She doesn't know, Lainey. She's not part of this." He let go and stood up before calling out, "We're back here, Amy. Everything's okay."

She burst into the room moments later. "Jesus, shit, Lainey, I thought you were *dead.* Oops, sorry, Melinda. But what the hell happened?! Kids are freaking out all over campus, saying you'd, well, *died* at the bookstore, or...but Jill didn't *look* like you'd punched her, and Jeff said you were up here and everything was fine..."

As I'd predicted, according to rumor I was either dead or had gotten in a fight with Jill. I actually smiled. "I am fine, Ame," I told her, a huge, enormous lie. "I was over here studying, and then unfortunately had one of my dizzy spells. Jill actually caught me, and I'm guessing kept me from cracking my head open when I passed out." I turned to Carter for confirmation.

"Definitely. I'd be downstairs mopping up your blood if Jill hadn't saved you from landing skull-first on the coffee table," he joked, lightening the mood in the room. I imagined the tension had been thick enough to touch before Amy arrived. Then my skittish brain started to wonder if I *could* touch tension, if I tried—I had no idea what this ESP thing really meant—and I think I started to pass out again, because I heard Carter say, "Whoa!" and grasp my arm.

I looked around the room at all the concerned faces then smiled over at Carter. "Oops. Sorry. Guess I'm a little wiped out."

"It's okay, honey," Melinda said. "But if you feel up to it, it's probably time to get you over to the infirmary."

I *didn't* feel up to it. I absolutely didn't want to go anywhere until they finished explaining this crazy revelation to me, until my questions were answered and I felt like I understood what was going on with my own head. But unfortunately, that wasn't possible. The whole campus already knew about my episode, so keeping it to myself wasn't an option. I knew I'd have to go to the infirmary, and call my aunt, and have people fuss over me for probably the next few days, before Thanksgiving break started.

This would also probably cause my first trip off campus—Aunt Tessa and I had planned to spend the holiday in Boston—to be canceled and ruin my entire break. I sighed, and started to get up. I noticed that Carter continued holding my arm, even though that wasn't strictly necessary anymore. He didn't let go until I was standing steadily.

"Yeah," I said dully. "I'm ready. Let's get this over with."

I WAS FORCED to spend the night in the infirmary. Carter and Amy followed me as I followed the nurse all the way back to the room that had already been reserved for me. In addition to the standard slippery, squeaky beds with paper sheets used during the regular daily visits for head and stomachaches, our infirmary had four private rooms in the back. The nurse left us with a slightly disapproving glance at Carter and a promise to be right back.

I plopped morosely onto the bed and looked at them pleadingly. "Please don't abandon me here."

"Absolutely not!" Amy cried. "I'll fake cramps or something if they try to make me leave. Nobody argues with you when you say you have female problems."

Carter laughed and set my bag down on the floor next to my bed. "Well, I think they'd probably argue if I tried to fake cramps, and I'm sure I'm not supposed to be back here anyway, but"—and he looked at me meaningfully when he said this—"I'll come back tomorrow, if you're still here, or you can come see me at the store after they let you out."

"Okay…and thanks. For, uh, everything," I finished feebly.

"My infinite pleasure," he said. And with that, he slipped out the door.

Amy waited about four seconds before she pounced. "Are you all right? Shit, Lainey, I was so worried! What happened? You weren't fighting with Jill, were you? I didn't believe it, but she's so weird, I couldn't be sure. I really thought you might be dead though, the way some of the kids were carrying on. Some freshman girl said you practically collapsed on top of her. And is it true? Carter swooped in and carried you up the stairs? Maybe you should faint more often if that's the case."

I laughed. It felt good to laugh, and some of my tension eased out of me just by being around Amy. "I'm fine. Really. This is no different from the episodes I've had for years, except that it had to happen in the middle of the crowded study lounge. And *no*, of *course* I wasn't fighting with Jill! Jeez. I was going to say hi to her because Carter suggested it. He insists they're just friends, by the way, since I know that will be your next question. And I guess it's true that he carried me up the stairs, but I was unconscious, so it wasn't as thrilling as you might imagine. I'll have to mock-faint if I really want to experience it."

"Right. That sucks. I guess I'll have to stick with imagining it for now. And I *knew* you weren't fighting with her," she muttered. "But, hey! What were you doing over there anyway? You usually work at the library this afternoon!"

Busted. "I, uh, switched my hours this week and…thought it would be quiet over there, so I could get some studying done before break," I offered, praying she'd buy my excuse but knowing she wouldn't.

And she didn't. Not even a little bit. "You little minx!" she shouted, half outraged, half amused. "You were hoping to flirt with Carter without any witnesses! So did you? And don't beg off that you have a headache. You're fine enough, I can tell by the bright pink color you just blushed. Gawd, you're even pretty when you're embarrassed. I hate you. Now *spill.*" So I recounted our conversation, and how I had kissed him. Even though it was only a little peck on the cheek, she practically applauded. "Nice. Spontaneous and bold. I couldn't have planned it better myself! Maybe that will get him off his ass and onto asking you out."

"I doubt it." I tried and failed not to sound dejected. I told her about the rest of our conversation, his swearing off Academy girls, and the bit about Jill too.

"Cousin, huh?" she said dubiously. "Wonder how Jill feels about that. But, anyway, bah. He likes you. He treats you differently than any other Academy girl I've seen him talk to the last four years. He'll come around. I know it. I might have to kick him in the shins, but he will."

I giggled. "Don't do that; he won't be able to run, and I like seeing him jog around campus!" I played off her comments with lightheartedness, because I couldn't tell her the truth, that Carter had been so attentive to me because he'd been waiting for me to "manifest," as he put it. I felt suddenly like a lab experiment, like I'd been a research subject without my knowledge or consent. I didn't like that feeling. At all. My early anger returned with surprising intensity.

"Hey," Amy said gently. "What is it? You're crying. Is your headache coming back? I'm sorry. I shouldn't be bothering you."

"No, no! It's not that at all. I'm just frustrated"—the truth—"I thought maybe the dizzy spells and migraines were going away"—sort of the truth—"and I…really want to be normal, is all"—the total, absolute 100% truth, especially now that I knew beyond a shadow of a doubt that *normal* was the exact opposite of what I was. I gritted my teeth and wiped the tears away forcefully. I was *not* a crier, damn it.

"Oh, hon, I'm sorry," Amy sympathized. "But normal is overrated. I've never been normal, and I'm perfectly awesome. So are you. We'll figure this headache thing out some day, I promise." The nurse opened the door then, wheeling a cart full of standard nurse objects, and ushered Amy out of the room. "I'll go get some of your stuff and bring my homework back to study here for the night. And I'll stop and let Caleb know you're okay; he was worried too," she said and headed out the door.

As Brooke had predicted, Amy and Caleb had—*finally*—hooked up during the Halloween festival and become an official couple almost instantly. Amy asked Brooke one day how she'd known it was going to happen, and she just laughed and said, "Anyone with eyes knew *that* was going to happen." I'd agreed with her about that—it *had* been plainly obvious—but now I suspected that Brooke had *known* a little more than she let on. Still, I liked Caleb. He was sweet, and smart enough to keep Amy interested, a rare feat. It was also clear he adored her.

I was surprised they hadn't gotten together long before, since they'd been here together since eighth grade and were so clearly smitten with each other. Caleb was not too tall for a guy, about my height, with sandy hair, deep brown eyes, and open, even features in a still boyish face that I was sure would grow into an incredibly handsome man's as he got older. He was a standout on our otherwise mediocre swim team as well as, I was told, the baseball team's starting second baseman.

Amy bustled back into my infirmary room, looking a little flushed and very pleased, not too long after the nurse left me. The nurse had asked about a million questions and gave me all the standard tests—temperature, bright lights in my eyes, poky thing in my ears, and blood pressure, which turned out to be running high. I was hardly surprised, given my supreme level of agitation. I eyed Amy's happy glow and said, "Caleb's well, I take it."

She grinned a wide, satisfied grin. *"Fantastic,* actually, and says hi and hopes you're feeling better. He walked me back over here and, well, it's early still but gave me a *proper* good night. Damn proper. You know how much I must love you, Lainey darling, since I'm in here, and not out there. Those swimmer's shoulders, I tell you. I absolutely melt."

"Spare me," I pleaded and gagged a little for good measure. She pouted, adorably, and I laughed. "Usually, I'm all ready for the vicarious details, but I'd rather not talk about your fabulous love life tonight. Let's talk about anything else, except for my fainting and your awesome boyfriend, deal?"

"You don't want to hear all the different rumors about your bookstore commotion going around campus? You can't imagine the crazy things I've heard," she said with a laugh.

"Okay," I agreed. "But only if they're funny. And I'm sure half the student body will be surprised to see me walking around alive tomorrow…"

It turned out to be therapeutic, hearing all the outlandish stories about my collapse and my alleged fight with Jill. Poor Jill. I hoped she wasn't being overwhelmed with questions too, like Amy, but I decided she probably wasn't. Jill was so self-contained and rarely seemed to socialize. She was more likely to be gossiped about than talked to.

Amy and I spent the brief time left before curfew chatting and, most importantly, laughing. I took a few minutes to clean up and change into something for bed. When the first bell rang, Amy started packing up her things.

"That's my cue, darling," she said. "I'll miss your snoring tonight. I've gotten so used to it, I'm not sure I'll be able to sleep in the quiet."

I threw my pillow at her but she dodged it neatly. "I don't snore!" I squeaked. "Do I?!"

"No, Lainey, you don't snore. I'd have told you already if you did, and probably asked to switch rooms. Some of us need our beauty sleep, you know? Okay, I've got to get back. Good night, roomie. Try not to scare me like this again, okay?" And with that she bent and kissed me swiftly on the cheek before heading back to our dorm.

I retrieved my pillow from the floor and was asleep almost before I got it back onto my borrowed bed.

Chapter Eight

I slept late the next morning and no one roused me for classes. I appreciated the chance to rest and think for a while after I woke up. Except I didn't *know* what to think—beyond that I needed to talk to Carter and Melinda as soon as possible—so I tried not to. I sat on my bed and did my aunt's deep yoga breathing instead. The nurse came in after not too long, towing her same loaded cart, and repeated yesterday's ritual. Despite the yoga breathing, my blood pressure was still high and I was not allowed to leave until it came back down to normal. Fabulous.

Amy stopped by briefly between two of her morning classes, but my biggest surprise came when a knock at the door was followed by Headmaster Stewart opening it and peeking inside. I was sitting cross-legged on my bed pretending to read a book but actually just moping. My aunt had indeed cancelled our Boston visit in favor of Thanksgiving at the Academy. Fun. I looked forward to seeing Aunt Tessa, sure, but I really didn't want to sit around at school all week. *Dejected* barely began to describe my mood. Until my bizarre visit with the headmaster anyway.

"Ah, Lainey, you're awake. Very good. How are you feeling?" she said, taking the one chair in the room and pulling it a little closer to where I sat.

"Fine, thank you, Headmaster," I replied. "I wasn't expecting a visit from you! It wasn't a big deal, not a bad episode at all, honestly. I don't even have much of a headache anymore. I guess my blood pressure is still a little high, so that's why they're keeping me here."

To my utter shock and confusion, she said, "Yes, well, your blood pressure is fine, Miss Young, within a completely normal range. I told the nurses that your doctors suggested a day of forced rest after episodes, and that was the medical excuse they were to give you."

"I...oh." Something in the way she'd said it led me to believe my doctors had given no such orders. "Is that true?"

"Is it true I told the nurses that? Of course. But no, your doctors had nothing to do with it. In the event of 'an episode,' as you call them, I merely wanted the nurses to keep you here until I told them to release you."

This conversation was becoming nearly as weird as yesterday's. I wouldn't have thought that was possible, but there I was. "I...don't understand, Headmaster Stewart. Did *you* think it was a good idea for me to have a day of rest?"

"Of course not, Lainey. Don't be foolish. You don't need rest at all," she replied, with a bit of a withering glance that made me want to cower. I caught myself and tried to sit up straighter. "You're perfectly healthy. I merely wanted the ability to talk to you in a secluded environment once we uncovered your talents. It took longer than I thought it would for you to manifest, but after speaking to Miss Christensen, I understand the delay. This environment, it seems, has been good for you, being full of young and healthy individuals and away from all those antiques you seem to love, burdened as they are with their long histories."

"Miss Christensen? You mean Jill?" was the response that came from my mouth, though I hadn't planned to say it. I hadn't planned to say anything at all. My brain seemed to be stuttering, like a car motor that would catch but not turn over. I felt like I needed a jump-start.

"Yes, Jillian Christensen. In addition to being a bright and discreet girl, she has a remarkably useful ability. She can recognize Sententia gifts, but only when they've been recently manifest. Your proximity to her yesterday afternoon was utterly convenient. The fact that she was able to touch you made it even clearer."

Unfortunately, none of this was remotely clear to me. "I'm sorry, Dr. Stewart, I…this is all a little new to me, and, well, I don't understand it much yet. I barely believe it, honestly. What is it that Jill does? For whom?"

"I was under the impression that Melinda Penrose"—she said Melinda's name as if she didn't *exactly* approve of her—"had explained. Did she not?"

"She…well, we didn't have much time. She told me I had ESP? Extrasensory Perception? And so did she. And Carter?" I added. I was doing it again, ending my sentences as if they were questions. Something about Dr. Stewart scared me into it.

She actually snorted. "The layman's explanation, of course. 'ESP' is what pseudoscientists and mentally unstable fringe members of society call it. We are *Sententia*, those gifted with perceptive abilities beyond the norm. Your gift is a fairly rare one, but perhaps not exceptionally powerful."

Okay then. *Sententia*, not ESP. Check. But that still didn't explain anything. "I…Headmaster Stewart, what is my 'gift'?"

She sighed, then muttered something about "Penroses" that didn't sound like a compliment, before saying, "Elaine, you are a Diviner. A Grim Diviner, to be specific. You perceive death. However, *you* will have to tell *me* whether it is past, future, or both you can see."

"A...Grim Diviner?" I tried it out, listening to how the strange phrase sounded coming from my own mouth, if it was as crazy a notion in my own voice as it had been in Headmaster Stewart's. And it *was* crazy, there was no doubt about that, but also...right? I couldn't quite wrap my head around it.

Was she *right?* All this time, had I been having real, *true* visions of how people were going to or had died, because of ESP or because I was this "Sententia"? If being able to perceive death was a gift, I wanted to return it. Immediately, and for what I hoped was a very large refund. Somehow though, I didn't think that was possible, so I went back to trying to accept it as real.

"Grim Diviner," I repeated. "A Sententia. And you say this is because of, what? A fluke in my brain?"

"Not a *fluke*, Miss Young, a *gift*. Being born Sententia is a *gift*. You are special and should be grateful for it. It is a rare but natural gift passed on through the genes. Yours, unfortunately, are a disturbing mystery, but I'm sure we'll get to the bottom of it. In the meantime, I will inform the Perceptum that your gift is manifest and we have uncovered its nature."

She seemed about to go on, when a delicate buzzing sounded from the pocket of her jacket. I'd come to learn that although the Academy had no dress code, Dr. Stewart had her own personal uniform, and appeared every day in a variation of the expertly fitted yet somewhat dowdy combination of long skirt, staid heels, and blazer I had seen her in at our first meeting. She extracted a slim cell phone, glanced at it quickly, and sighed again.

"Miss Young, you are free to leave the infirmary now. You will not return to classes until after break, and you will at all times maintain the excuse of your headaches to the general student population, *including* Miss Moretti. Let me be clear: under no circumstances are you to relate to her the nature of your gift or our conversation. As brilliant as she may be, she is not Sententia. Do you understand?"

I nodded soberly.

"Good. If you break this entreaty, I will know it, so do not be tempted. I'd already assigned Mr. Penrose to establish your Sententia heritage and have instructed him to continue your introduction into our ranks. He knows where you may speak discreetly, of course. Miss Christensen will be available to you as well and you may trust her implicitly. I dare say she'd be a more appropriate mentor than Cartwright, would that I could assign her." She rose then and headed for the door. "Welcome to the Sententia, Miss Young. I hope we'll be proud to call you one of us."

Though my mind was absolutely reeling with everything it had been forced to consider, there was still something important I had to know. "Headmaster Stewart," I called as her hand was on the door handle. "I…it's both. I see both, past and future…deaths," I struggled a little getting that word out. "And I saw, well, I don't know her name, but the freshman girl, at the bookstore. I saw her…die. Is…will it happen? Is it true? Can't I help her?!" I asked, a little frantically.

A very, very small look of sympathy crossed Dr. Stewart's face. "Is it true? Quite possibly. But unfortunately, no, you cannot help young Miss Thayer—Miss Christensen informed me she was the student whose proximity triggered your gift. She is not Sententia, and even if we could convince her that her death was imminent, we should not."

She sighed then and an unexpected bit of warmth, or maybe it was understanding, came into her eyes. "Sometimes our gifts carry a burden of knowledge, Lainey," she said. "Even if we don't want it, we must bear it. And though we may be special, we are neither gods nor superheroes, and must resist, at all times, playing at being either. I will be sorry for Miss Thayer's loss, if it comes to pass. In the end, what will happen will happen. I don't believe in fate, Miss Young, but I've been alive long enough to see that some courses are unalterable."

SENTENTIA. SEN—TEN—SHI—A. For a long while, I sat in my infirmary room, unwilling to get up and leave, repeating the term over and over in my head. I was Sententia. I had some form of ESP—*but that's not really what we called it*—that let me predict deaths or what was it called when you perceived the past? I didn't know.

It was that question that finally got me moving, over to my bag to pull out a pen and notebook. I'd spent long enough thinking in undirected circles, which was getting me exactly nowhere. I decided to tackle this unexpected new turn in my life just like the last one, the one that had brought me here: I would accept it as my current reality and start living it. This was no crazier than when I thought I was simply crazy; the only difference was now I knew the visions I saw were real. Or possibly real.

So I started a list. I wrote down everything I could remember about what Headmaster Stewart had told me and then, when I exhausted what I knew, I started in on what I *needed to know*. I tried to go with basics first:

How does this "gift" work?

How did I get it? (Something about genes?)

And then I moved on to the harder things:

How many Sententia are there?

What can Sententia do?

Why does it seem like there are so many of us here at this school?

After staring at my list for a while, I added one more, remembering a word Headmaster Stewart had mentioned briefly but struck me as ominous:

What is the Perceptum?

Satisfied, I gathered my things, thanked the nurses for their excellent care, and made my way out onto campus.

BACK AT MY room, I treated myself to the longest, hottest shower I'd taken since my arrival. I stood under the spray until it started to run cool, organizing my thoughts while I let the hot water carry away some of my tension, pretending I could feel it flowing down the drain. It helped, more than I expected, and I spared only a fleeting moment of guilt for whoever in Marquise House wanted to shower next.

I was absently brushing out my hair when a soft knock sounded at my door, followed by an equally soft, "Lainey?" Ms. Kim, come to check on me. I called for her to come in, expecting her to ask how my head was feeling, so I was utterly surprised when instead she said, "So how are you doing with the revelation?" as she closed the door behind her.

Whoa. *What the hell is going on in this place?* I thought. It seemed like *everybody* knew what I was but me. "I, uh…so, you know?" was the brilliant response I managed to offer.

She smiled her kindly smile. "Yes, Lainey, I know. Headmaster Stewart informed me and the rest of the faculty of your manifestation. I'm Sententia too, of course. My gift is mild, but a pretty helpful one for a teacher: when I ask questions, people want to answer them. It only creates a little bit of encouragement though, no impetus."

"Well… I guess that explains why I always want to stop and talk to you when you ask how my day has been," I said. "I'm not sure what you mean by impetus though."

"Some more powerful gifts manifest with a measure of force behind them, an impetus. If my gift were that strong, people wouldn't just desire to answer my questions, they'd be compelled to. But impetus of any kind is rare, and a very powerful gift indeed, so its rarity is probably a blessing."

"I…don't think my gift has any impetus either," I ventured.

"No," she replied. "It doesn't appear that way. It's often difficult to be a Diviner of any kind, and I'd imagine a Grim Diviner is most difficult of all. We're lucky your Legacy brought you here, no matter how strange the circumstances."

Boy did she have that right. "I do feel lucky to be here, Ms. Kim," I told her. "As…strange as this all is, I can't deny that I've liked it here. *Like* it here, I mean. I don't think that will change, at least I hope not. Is…well, is something expected of me? Now that I've manifested, I mean, and everyone knows?"

"No. No, Lainey. Nothing about your time as a student here should change. It's your *awareness* that has changed. Now you know, and you can begin to explore your gift or, more importantly, learn how to control it. You have a little to learn about being Sententia too, and that's actually why I'm here."

"Oh!" I said, surprised. "Are you going to help teach me?"

She laughed. "No, unfortunately that's not my job; I'm only an English teacher. I came to tell you that Carter Penrose is waiting for you downstairs. Being your mentor is his job."

"Oh!" I said, surprised again, in a different way. "Okay. I…guess I'll go see him." I grabbed my bag, my list of questions inside it, and my sweatshirt from my bed. Ms. Kim waited for me at the door and I was ready to follow her down the stairs when I thought of something. "Ms. Kim? I wanted to ask, um, who else knows about…my gift? About my being a Sententia?"

Thankfully she understood what I was getting at. "The other Sententia students haven't been told anything, Lainey. We are…fairly strict about students discussing their gifts *openly*"—the way she said it led me to believe they discussed them all the time in private—"because of the number of non-Sententia students here. Jill Christensen is the only other student who knows. Given the nature of her ability, she tends to know the gifts of most Sententia she encounters. But she learned how to keep her secrets at a young age and has never proven to be anything but trustworthy. Now, maybe we shouldn't keep Mr. Penrose waiting any longer? I'm sure you have a lot of questions for him too."

Did I ever.

Chapter Nine

He was waiting on the porch steps, elbows propped on his knees. When I opened the door, he stood abruptly, already wearing his familiar measured look along with something new, a touch of wariness I'd never seen him exhibit before. He looked almost exactly the same as the first time I'd seen him—black t-shirt, comfortable jeans, handsome face—but it seemed as if I was looking at someone entirely new, and a little foreign.

"I'm your *assignment*, huh?" I said. It came out not at all like I had intended. I'd meant it to be light and teasing, but my real emotions betrayed me. Instead of a joke, my question was a bitter, angry accusation.

He blanched. "Lainey, I...I wanted to tell you, but I wasn't allowed. I had to wait until we were sure. I'm sorry."

"Don't be," I spat at him. "I don't need your sorry. Let's get to work. I have a lot of questions, and it's apparently your *job* to answer them. Where to, Mr. Penrose?"

"Lainey, please." A tiny bit of pleading had crept into his usually confident voice. Like yesterday, he reached out his hand as if he would touch me, but seemed to think better of it and let it fall before I had the chance to smack it away. "Please don't be like that. I don't...you're not..."

"Save it, Carter. *Where to?* I really do have a lot of questions and nothing but time for the next two days to get them answered."

He sighed and stepped down off my porch. "Do you want some coffee first?"

"Yes," I replied. "Your treat."

I ACTUALLY WANTED coffee, a cheese croissant, and an apple Danish. Carter manfully paid for everything I chose, without complaint or comment about the caloric content of my lunch, and waited patiently while I painstakingly perfected my blend of cream and sugar. He bought nothing but black coffee for himself. As we walked from the coffee shop to Penrose Books in silence, I blew on my coffee and watched the steam rise slowly into the sky. I imagined my anger dissipating with it, being replaced by something heavier and slower-burning: embarrassment.

How humiliating, I thought to myself. Of all the things I'd learned in the last twenty-four hours, the hardest to stomach was that Carter had paid so much attention to me because he was instructed to. I was an idiot of the highest rank, a status I was not used to. Lainey Young had never been a girl who chased after a guy before, or got depressed when one didn't return her affections. But then, I'd always been the girl who'd be gone in days or weeks. Rejection, I suddenly realized, had a painful and lasting sting.

Thankfully, we reached the bookstore before my stupid brain could do any more moping, but instead of going through the front door, Carter walked right past it. I slowed my steps behind him and looked around in confusion. "Where are we going?"

"Upstairs," he replied. "There's a seventh grade class doing a project in the store, and I thought it would be better if we avoided them."

"Don't want to be seen with me anymore, now that the secret's been discovered?" This time I had been *planning* on bitter and angry, but what I came out with was dejected. I *really* had to get my mouth and my brain on the same page. Clearly my mouth was determined to give me away.

Carter stopped in his tracks and looked at me for a long moment. He swept his hand through his hair roughly, blue eyes glinting in anger. If I wasn't supposed to be so pissed at him, I'd say it was the sexiest he'd ever looked.

His voice was quiet but intense. "God, Lainey, is that what you think? That I don't want to be *seen* with you? That I don't obviously enjoy your company, or...or that I wouldn't be the envy of just about every guy at Northbrook within"—he glanced down at his watch—"approximately twenty-three minutes if I was witnessed by the seventh grade class escorting you through the bookstore and up to my apartment? I know you're hurt, and you have reason to be, but I've never thought you're stupid!" Quickly, he added, "I'm sorry. *I'm* the idiot here, and I'm not angry with you, but with myself. I..."

But it was too late. I knew it was coming, and I tried desperately to keep it in, but I couldn't help it. I was stressed beyond comprehension, angry, and confused. I burst into tears. Again.

Carter's eyes widened for a second before he cursed sharply under his breath. "I'm sorry," he repeated. "God, I'm *such* an idiot." Then he put his arms around me.

Supposed to be angry or not, I let him. And it felt good. He was warm and strong, and right then, I felt like neither. He said nothing more, but didn't move to let go until I'd stopped shaking and sniffling into his shoulder. I was vaguely aware of his hand making slow circles on my back. As my tears dried up, I realized we were still standing in the middle of the sidewalk, fairly awkwardly at that. I was in serious danger of crumpling my buttery, delicious lunch and spilling my coffee down the fronts of both of us.

"Ugh! I'm sorry," I said, running the back of my hand holding the pastry bag across my cheeks. "I don't usually do that. Really. My auntie is the crier."

Carter smiled, a perfect, genuine smile that did wonders to brighten my dark mood. "It's all right. I think you deserve at least one good cry. And I deserve to get sniffled on. C'mon. Let's go upstairs."

As WE TRAVELED up the less elegant back stairway that led to the apartment on the top floor, I was struck with a curious thought.

"Carter, who owns the bookstore?"

He glanced over at me. "Um, well, technically my aunt owns half and I own half. Why do you ask?"

"I was just wondering…if you…well, to be totally honest, I was wondering what you're still doing here. Most guys your age would be off living it up at college somewhere."

He laughed as we rounded the last flight of steps and he led me through the door into their cheerful eat-in kitchen. "I guess," he replied, "though I think I have a pretty great life here too. I mean, usually I spend all day with books, which is nice enough, and then there's today. How many college guys can say it's part of his job to sneak a beautiful co-ed up to his apartment?"

Har har, I thought. But I did appreciate the compliment, if not the reminder that I was part of his job. He kicked out a chair from the table for me and sat down on the opposite side after getting me a plate and napkin for my lunch. I put down my coffee and pulled out my notebook and pencil. I had already decided to treat this whole crazy situation as academically as possible, considering that most Sententia kids grew up understanding the world they lived in. I felt behind the curve.

Carter sipped his coffee expectantly while I organized my thoughts and polished off my croissant. Most guys would have been bored or tried to fill the silence, but not Carter. I quickly added patience to my rather lengthy mental list of his virtues, while reminding myself that I really was hurt and angry with him. His hug notwithstanding, I hadn't forgiven him for deceiving me.

I looked around the kitchen while I licked the last crumbs from my fingers. It wasn't large, but comfortable and well laid out, full of original woodwork and had a huge, definitely original cast iron sink with gleaming white enamel. Overall, the room had an artful balance of modern and historic that made it a pleasant place to be. Warm sunshine streamed in from the window over the sink. I tapped my pencil on my list and, feeling overwhelmed, decided to start at the top.

"Okay," I said. "I...know what I am. And I think I understand it. I mean, it just gives a legitimate reason for the visions that I've always thought meant I was crazy. I...perceive deaths. That sucks, by the way. It's a crappy gift if I ever got one. But it is mine, right, so I guess I just have to accept it."

"Yeah, we can't exactly choose our gifts," he said, half smiling. "Yours is pretty rare, in a way. And, uh, yeah, kind of sucky. For what it's worth, I'm sorry it's the one you've been dealt, but I have a feeling if anyone can handle it, it will be you. And with luck, I'll be able to help you learn to control it better."

"Thanks. That would be great. Honestly. Can I learn how to stop having the visions altogether?" I asked hopefully.

"Ah, no. Probably not completely. As a Diviner...the past and future tend to be a little insistent. But with practice, most Sententia have some level of control over when they use their gifts. For you it will mean first learning how to use yours at will, not just when a vision comes to you spontaneously."

"So...you're basically saying it will get worse before it gets better?"

"Pretty much, yeah. Sorry," he tacked on at the end.

I sighed. "No, I understand. It makes sense. But it's not something I'm looking forward to."

"You're right," he agreed. "If I'm going to get to spend time with you, examining people's deaths is not exactly how I'd like to do it."

I looked up at him from where I was scratching notes in my notebook. He had an impish grin on his face that suited him, like any kind of smile. It was contrasted by the sunshine streaming in from behind him, lighting up his golden-brown hair like a halo. Angelic and devilish, all at once. That wasn't a bad metaphor for Carter Penrose, I thought.

"Honestly Carter," I said peevishly, "it would be a lot easier to be pissed at you—which I still am, by the way—if you weren't so damn charming all the time."

That only made him grin more widely, which was infuriating, but all he said was, "What's your next question, Lainey, or do you want me to talk in general and let you stop me along the way?"

"No, I have a list." I waved it at him. "Like I said, I get what I am, but how did I get this way? How does it even work? It doesn't seem possible. I...never believed this kind of stuff was real before."

"Well, the first question is fairly simple. You got this way because one of your parents—in your case, definitely your father—was Sententia too. He's about as big a mystery as your gift—I can't find any helpful public records on his birth parents at all—but he must have been one of us. Anyway, our gifts are genetic. How it works? That's a little more complex."

He paused briefly, as if trying to decide exactly how to explain it. There was a buzzing energy about him, a strange mix of boyish excitement and intellectual interest that had me leaning forward in my seat. I was fascinated already. Whether it was more about our topic or my tutor, I couldn't be sure.

"It's...well, it's brain power," he continued. "A function of your brain. An *extraordinary* function of your brain. Average people can't do what we can do. Historically and, uh, pretty simply, we just call it Thought." Something in the way he said it made me think it was Thought, with a capital T. "As for the specifics, I can't explain to you the exact process because none of us knows exactly. We have theories, sure, but the mechanics are...scientifically vague. You've probably heard how 'humans only use 10% of their brain potential' or some similar statement, right?"

I nodded.

"Well, that's not precisely true; no one can accurately determine what percentage of the brain we use or don't, but it *is* true that the mind's capabilities are extensive and many of its functions are still basically mysteries. Honestly, most scientists will tell you what you said before: it's not possible; this stuff isn't real. Unfortunately they're wrong, because we're living proof to the contrary. Just because they can't explain it, or can't *believe* enough to accept it, doesn't mean it's not real."

"I suppose this explains why my zillion brain scans didn't show anything," I muttered. I took a few sips of my rapidly cooling coffee while I processed everything he'd said. "But...so how *is* it possible that I can touch something or someone and perceive its past or, especially, its *future?* You said scientists don't *believe* it, and that, well, that means whatever explanation you've got requires a 'leap of faith' or something, right?"

He cocked his head at me, hair still shining in the sun, that contemplative gaze strong on his face. "You really are amazing, you know that? Most unidentified Sententia *do* go crazy when—if—they ever learn the truth. You're not just not going crazy, you're adapting fluidly. It's incredible."

Sometimes I wondered if Carter really was more than eighteen years old. Most of the time he seemed like a normal, if highly intelligent, teenager. But then sometimes, when I listened to him discuss neurological theory, or when he said things like "adapting fluidly" as a compliment, I couldn't help but think that Cartwright Penrose was somehow more gifted than even your average Sententia.

"You're right about the 'leap of faith,'" he continued. "Nowadays, if scientists don't believe something they might call it pseudoscience, science fiction"—he coughed—"crazy bullshit. In the past, when it wasn't *science* that ruled as popular theology, what did they call it when normal humans could do things they *shouldn't* be able to do? Witchcraft, magic, *heresy*…or, rarely, *miracles*…" He watched me as he trailed off expectantly, waiting for me to come to my own conclusions.

Finally, I said, "You're talking about God."

I'd even managed to say it only slightly incredulously because, really, what other explanation could there be?

Chapter Ten

I'd never been particularly religious, because Aunt Tessa wasn't, but I liked to think I was faithful, in a way. I believed there was something greater than us out there, that being a good person—being polite and kind to others, being grateful for and sharing your good fortune, treating the Earth and all its creatures with respect—would somehow be rewarded, and that karma would revisit people who weren't. In my head, I called that higher power "God," and I mostly tried to stay on His good side. I did use His and His son's names blasphemously all the time, but I was pretty sure, in the long run, that wouldn't count too poorly against me. I did not, however, expect anyone would ever tell me I'd been particularly gifted by Him.

"God," I repeated. "You're telling me that we...have mental gifts from God." I couldn't help but think back to how Headmaster Stewart had said we Sententia were *not gods* and shouldn't play at it.

"God, Vishnu, Brahman, Allah, Mother Nature, *collective conscious-ness,* yes," he said seriously. "Whatever you prefer to call it. *Something* greater that connects us all, past, present, and future, and that science cannot—yet—explain or accept. Something connected you to Ashley Thayer. What do you see, by the way?" he added. "I only know what

Jill told me, what she could sense, that you're a Grim Diviner. She doesn't—I don't know how your gift manifests."

"Didn't Dr. Stewart tell you?"

He made a derisive noise. "Headmaster Stewart takes her pleasure in telling me as little as possible, absolutely nothing if she can get away with it. Before you got here, all she said was, 'Cartwright, there's a new student starting tomorrow.' I knew it was important because she was talking to me at all. So no, she didn't tell me about your gift, or any conversation you've ever had with her."

I would puzzle over that one later. Headmaster Stewart seemed not to like Carter and his aunt, and I couldn't imagine why. "I..." started to answer his question then hesitated. I'd never openly discussed my visions before, but I thought if there was anyone I'd want to tell, it would be Carter. Or Amy. But I *couldn't* tell her, so Carter it was.

"I get...dizzy. That's the only way I know it's going to happen, and then I have a vision. Of what happened, or is going to happen. It's very fast, only a few seconds, and I sometimes...*know* more than I can see. Yesterday, I saw Ashley. She's going skiing and will fall on some ice and...slide head first into a light pole. Do you think it will really happen?" I added, ever hopeful that he'd say no. He answered, instead, with a question.

"Have you had other visions that you *know* were true, that happened as you saw them?"

I thought of my parents, and the horrific, absolutely accurate vision that brought me here to Northbrook and face to face with my peculiar gift. "Yes," I whispered. "It was my parents."

He reached across the table and put his hand over mine. I'd long since stopped scribbling notes in my book, but I was surprised at the touch nonetheless. His hand was larger than mine and, exactly like I'd felt earlier about his arms around me, warm and strong.

"I'm sorry," he said, and I knew he meant it. "And I'm sorry to have to say that you're probably right about Ashley too, then. The future is never definite, but a specific vision from an accurate Diviner makes it...highly probable."

I spent a moment mourning the highly probable death of a girl I didn't know while enjoying the comfort of Carter's hand on mine. Reluctantly, I withdrew it and looked back at my list.

"What can you do?" I blurted out then thought better of it. "Or is it rude to ask that? I'm sorry, if it is." To my relief, my impertinence was rewarded with a laugh.

"To a stranger? Yeah. It's kind of like asking how much money someone makes, or a woman's age, or a man's...shoe size. But we're friends here, so it's okay." He winked at me, and I blushed because now I felt a little like an ass, and also because I couldn't stop myself from thinking about, well, you know—his shoe size. I decided to cover my embarrassment with boldness.

"Okay. So how big *are* your shoes?"

He laughed again, that delighted, dangerous smile playing over his face. "*Very*. But to answer your real question, technically I am a *Recordatio Perficio,* though my real function is Historian."

For a few seconds, all I could think about was my first day here, when Amy had suggested that in the future I'd be an "historian of the everyday," and here I was, face to face with an Historian of the Weird. I filed that thought away onto my ever-growing list for later and said, "You're going to have to help me with the lingo here. Is that first one Latin? Like 'Sententia' seems Latin."

"Exactly. My job is to catalogue historical evidence of Sententia and research new reports. I'm good at it partially because of that first one. In modern terms, we say I have a photographic memory."

I was sure my eyes widened. That would explain a lot about him. But I had to ask anyway. "For real?"

"For real."

"Prove it."

Without hesitation, he recited, word perfect, my notes from yesterday and list of questions. That I had only barely held in front of him for a few seconds.

"But that might not be exact," he added with a smile, "because your handwriting is atrocious."

"The scary thing is that it *was* exact, and my handwriting *is* atrocious. Wow. I mean, it's not a very long list, but I think I believe it could have filled the page and you'd still have gotten it."

"Probably," he replied, but his mild tone told me what he really meant was *undoubtedly.* "So, which one of those do you want me to answer next?"

"I guess the first one we haven't gotten to yet…how many Sententia are there?"

"Now? Some number of millions. Even point five percent of the world population numbers in the tens of millions…we estimate Sententia represent around a tenth of a percent, which is still over six million."

"Wow. I mean, I guess a tenth of a percent isn't really very much, but six million people is a lot of people."

"It is. But honestly, that number is just an educated guess. And it doesn't mean all of them are…active, so to speak. Probably half of them are dormant carriers of Sententia genes."

"Then why are there so many of us at Northbrook?" I asked. "That's *not* a coincidence, obviously. Is this some…Sententia training school or something?"

"Well, mostly you're here for a great education," he said, and I couldn't help but get the sense he was stalling. It worried me. "Northbrook is, first and foremost, an excellent college preparatory school."

"*But?*" I interrupted him. "There's a 'but' or something here and you're not getting to it. Why is that?" I studied him. He looked...wary again. That couldn't possibly be a good sign.

"We're all here because of...the last question on your list," he finally answered. "This school was established by the Perceptum as a place for generations of Sententia to meet one another, make connections, and, if necessary, learn how to manage their gifts and, most importantly, be discreet about them."

"Interesting," I said, because it *was* interesting. So Northbrook kind of was a Sententia training school, at least in part. "So what *is* the Perceptum? And why are you so hesitant to talk about it?"

"I..." Carter started then paused. "I'm not hesitant about the Perceptum," he said. I didn't fail to note the contradiction between his words and the hesitation as he spoke them, but I kept that to myself. "At all. It's just that this is the hardest part to introduce to unidentified Sententia. Sometimes it...scares them."

"Okay, well by saying that you've totally scared me, so spill it. Please. What is the Perceptum?"

"It's how the Sententia are organized, or networked. It also serves as a governing body." After a beat, he added, "And technically, I work for them."

I took a while to think about this, because on the surface, I didn't get why a Sententia organization scared some people. So I came to the conclusion that one of the things the Perceptum did *was* scare people. I just didn't know why and I wasn't sure I was ready to either.

Carter's voice interrupted my spinning thoughts. "I'd offer a penny for what you're thinking, but I already know that's not enough. I'm sure I can't afford the going rate, so I'll just have to wait until you're ready to share."

"That's right," I said lightly. "But...I think you'll need to wait a little longer. It's late. The bookstore is probably crowded with students, and it will be hard to get out of here without being noticed. And don't you have to work?"

He gave a gentle little laugh. "I *am* working, remember? Not," he added hastily, "that spending the day with you feels much like work. But to answer your question, Jill is covering my regular shifts at the bookstore today and tomorrow. I am entirely your devoted servant for these two days."

Well didn't that *sound good,* I thought to myself, and then kicked my left shin with my right foot, because I. Was. Still. Pissed. At. Carter. And irritated with my brain for not sticking with the program.

"You don't have to be angry with me, you know," he murmured.

I glanced up at him sharply. "I...uh, what?" was my eloquent response. Did he read minds too? Shit!

He was looking at me in that contemplative way he had, but there was something more than that, something that made my nerves tingle and my heart beat a little faster than it should have. "Sometimes you're not very good at hiding what you're thinking...it's like I can see the thought processes as they flow across your face. I'm pretty sure you were reminding yourself you're supposed to be mad at me. And that you literally kicked yourself to emphasize it. I...don't want you to kick yourself when you think of me. I *am* sorry, Lainey. For not being up front with you. For having to watch and wait to see what you might do. I didn't want to."

He paused then and, if possible, looked at me even more intensely than before. I thought I might have held my breath. "Well, no, that's not true. Honestly, having to watch you is the best assignment I've ever had, but I *couldn't* tell you. What if you really weren't Sententia? What if you didn't manifest? I had to wait and know for sure, not because I'd been instructed to, but because I would have hated to drag you out of your perfectly acceptable reality and into mine if I hadn't needed to. But I'm glad you are part of this world, because if you weren't, I don't know how long I could've pretended friendly indifference, how long before my *wanting* to tell you won out over my better judgment."

"I...understand," I said, and I realized that I did. Maybe he was right. Maybe I didn't have to be *angry* with him...but there was still too much that I didn't understand. I also wasn't sure I could trust what I *thought* he was saying. I was afraid it was wishful thinking, and a little more afraid that it wasn't.

So I decided just to ask. It was better to know than to wish, right? "And what do you mean, about...about..."

As I groped for the right question, he laughed softly, a despondent little laugh. "I mean, Lainey, that—despite being probably the worst idea I've ever had—I'd like nothing more at this moment than to kiss you, if you'd let me."

My breath caught, and I'm sure my cheeks flushed. "I...don't think that's a good idea," I said, though at least half of me thought it was a *great* idea.

He smiled, a woeful kind of smile that matched his laugh. "Neither do I, but I still want to."

I had no idea how to respond, nor how I wanted to, exactly. I was afraid though that if I opened my mouth I would say, or do, something I wasn't quite ready for.

"It's okay," he said. "You don't have to say anything. I just thought that's what you were asking and...that you ought to know. I was *never* faking wanting to be around you, Lainey. I meant what I said yesterday, that you're not like anyone I've ever met. You might be an Academy student, but you're so far from an Academy *girl*. I'm not entirely sure how to deal with that, but I'll figure something out. If I'm lucky, you'll be *my* girl. When you're ready."

So he *could* read my mind, whether or not he knew it. I smiled tentatively and echoed words he'd spoken to me only yesterday. "You're not shy either, are you, Carter?"

The dangerous grin returned. "Not at all."

AMY POUNCED AS soon as I opened the door to our room. "Where have you been?!"

"I…" was all I got out before she continued the attack.

"Did you know that you are, in fact, pregnant with Carter Penrose's baby, and that's why you passed out at the bookstore yesterday, after fighting with Jill?"

"WHAT?" I squeaked. Only six weeks here, and already I was *pregnant?!*

"That's what I said." She nodded somberly for emphasis.

"That's…ridiculous!"

"I *know!*" she replied. "I told them so. Because for sure if anyone I knew was sleeping with Carter Penrose, *especially* my roommate, I'd already have bragged about it to everyone *else* I knew, after getting all the details for myself first, of course." She narrowed her eyes at me. "So really, though, where have you been?"

"I…" was all I got out again.

"And why did some seventh grader see you outside the bookstore hugging Carter and crying before you went around to their back stairwell with him, hmmm?"

I walked over and dropped my bag on my desk while I waited this time to see if she was done. "I *was* over at Carter's," I admitted, because it was futile to deny it. I gave her the highly edited version of the story. "I didn't have classes today and…Carter was off too. He asked if I wanted to get some coffee and there was this class in the bookstore, so we went upstairs. Seriously, we sat at his kitchen table. You've seen it. No big deal."

She snorted inelegantly and derisively. "Riiiight. No big deal. Sure thing. But you're not sleeping with him yet, right? You'd tell me?"

I flushed what must have been an incredible and practically instant shade of bright crimson. "No! God. NO. Jeez. I've only known him for a few weeks." I was bumbling for words, and it came to me that I was protesting too much despite that it was totally true, so I thought I should just be frank about it. "I mean, we're not even dating. And, honestly, I've...never before. So. I wouldn't do that, even with him. Not so soon. Okay?"

Something about the look on my face must have given away my tenuous emotional state. Amy softened and stood up to hug me. "Okay, yeah, totally okay. I'm sorry. I didn't mean to embarrass you. And...I know you wouldn't have, not so quickly, even if you weren't, you know. *Pure.* I was just teasing. *But,*" she said, releasing me to arm's length, "it sounds like it *is* true that you were hugging Carter outside the bookstore and crying."

I sighed. "It's true. I was depressed. He helped. I don't know what else to say."

"Mm hmmm..." She nodded thoughtfully. "Well, if depressed is what it takes to get his arms around you, I guess it will do for now. And you *really* just sat at the breakfast table?"

"Well, yeah."

Now *she* sighed, dramatically and for emphasis. "Oh Lainey, my sweet, virginal roommate. It didn't cross your mind that he took you up to his apartment in the hopes that you might spend your time...elsewhere?"

I think my flush came back, strong and deep, but I decided to be honest with her. Mostly. "I...think he wouldn't have minded that," I murmured. Of course, then she squealed so loudly I almost had to cover my ears.

"HA! I knew it. *Fantastic!*" She was practically vibrating with glee, and was so delighted that I had to smile in response. "Uh, so why *did* you just sit at the kitchen table then?"

"It's...complicated," I hedged, not knowing quite how to explain the situation without *really* explaining the situation. I almost laughed when I recalled how Melinda Revell had said the exact same thing to me the day before.

Amy did laugh, a jolly, mischievous one. "Oh Lainey, it's really not. It's actually pretty simple, and even if you didn't know how, I bet Carter is a natural at it. Besides, I *know* you've been practicing on and off with Garrett. Hey, it's not because of Garrett, is it? You know his A Number One priority is sports, right? Plus, I think he's hopelessly in love with Alexis. I've...caught him mooning over her sometimes. It's surprising; I thought a nice guy like him would have more sense than that. But...there is something compelling about Alex, and not just her beauty. I can't put my finger on it."

Right then I realized that Alexis, along with probably *all* the Legacy students, was Sententia too.

"No, it's not Garrett," I said. "I had no expectations from him. He, uh, was nice for practice though." I smiled as I flopped on my bed.

Amy giggled approvingly. "That's my girl. So really, what's the problem? You want Carter; Carter wants you. This story sounds like the *opposite* of complicated to me. I'd say it was a little boring, and, honestly, *way* too easy for you. I've *seen* his girlfriends at the bookstore occasionally over all these years—he's had a healthy selection, not that that should surprise anyone—but you know, I'd really like to *know* at least one of them, especially if it's you."

"I'll see what I can do to satisfy your burning curiosity," I replied dryly. "I'm just...hesitant, I guess. And I think he is too. He's got his whole hang up on not dating Academy girls, and I...well, honestly, I've never been anywhere long enough to think about how I might like a guy after a year...or what might happen if it doesn't work out and then I'm not gone anyway. I guess I'm scared."

She looked at me for a while before saying, "Lainey, just this once, why don't you try living where you are *right now* instead of where you'll be six weeks or four months from now. You don't have to overthink it. If it doesn't work out between you, well, that *happens*. God knows I've had plenty of relationships that were over before they started, and loved almost every minute of them..." I coughed, an amused cough, to get her back on track. "Right. I'm saying you can't go into a relationship being afraid of what might or might not happen. If it doesn't work out, I promise you, the world won't end and there will be other boyfriends."

If only that would turn out to be true.

Chapter Eleven

I stayed in bed an extra-long time in the morning, luxuriating in the cozy comfort of my blankets, letting my mind review the last two days and every miraculous revelation they'd contained. Amy was long gone and the room, the whole of Marquise House, was quiet and peaceful. I watched dust motes drift lazily through the sunbeams lighting my room to a warm yellow glow as I tried to come to terms with this strange gift I'd been given.

I thought for a long time about Ashley Thayer, about how I could possibly save her, but ultimately I could come up with no real solution. I could warn her, but would that stop her from going on her ski holiday? I doubted it. How would I explain to her what I knew? And if I explained it, how could I make her believe it? I didn't think I could. Most likely, I'd be written off as crazy.

Finally I came to the conclusion that, however difficult it might be to accept, Headmaster Stewart had been correct. I was not a god, and I couldn't save everyone. I determined then that I would try to figure out how to do *some* good with my gift, but I also steeled my spine and prepared to bear the burden of knowing some people's deaths would be out of my hands, even if they were in my mind.

It was time to start my second day of Sententia orientation. I tried pretending this was like the first week of college would be, but unfortunately that didn't make it any less bizarre. After another guilt-inducingly long shower, and after blow-drying my hair, carefully selecting a sweater, jeans, and boots, and even applying a little bit of makeup, I was ready to call Carter. I was also an idiot, because despite repeatedly telling my brain that I was *not* getting ready for a date, for goodness sake, my fingers couldn't quite keep from smoothing my hair or adding a little more mascara.

He seemed to have been waiting for me.

"Lainey, about time."

I detected a sincere crankiness in his voice, something I'd never heard before. He perpetually seemed in a good mood. Seriously, it was almost annoying. "Uh, good morning to you too."

"Are you ready?" He practically interrupted me. "Meet me behind the store."

I had no idea what his problem was, nor what he was planning, but I wasn't doing it on an empty stomach. "But I haven't had breakfast yet!"

"Exactly," he said and hung up. Okay then. I grabbed my coat and headed across the street.

BEHIND THE STORE, in addition to the back entrance to the building, turned out to be where Carter parked his car, a small, older model, in decent condition and surprisingly clean inside. Having never had one of my own, even now that I could legally drive one, I was insanely jealous. When I came around the corner, he opened the passenger door for me like a gentleman and gave me an appreciative glance up and down which made me glad I'd spent a little extra time on my appearance that morning, but then got in and started the car without saying a word. I tried to play along with the mystery, but we were halfway to New Hampshire when I couldn't take it anymore. The border being all of five miles from the school, I obviously didn't hold out very long.

"Where are we going?" I finally asked. "And what's your problem?" Maybe there was some sincere crankiness in my voice too.

He glanced over at me, then ran his fingers through his hair and frowned. "I'm sorry," he said. "I'm just hungry." Apparently hungry Carter equaled grumpy Carter. Duly noted. "But I wanted to surprise you," he continued. "We're going to breakfast…it's my favorite place." The way he said it, I got the impression his taking me there was special, important even. I kept quiet for the rest of the drive.

He pulled up outside a dingy, tiny place called simply DAD'S, with a sign that advertised breakfast all day. I opened my door to crisp mountain air scented like a greasy griddle. It was heavenly. In fact, I had a feeling this was about to be the best non-date I'd ever been on.

The restaurant consisted of a small, warm room that smelled even more strongly of delicious breakfast, with a short countertop and a handful of worn booths and tables liberally dotted with diners. A friendly-looking waitress pouring coffee across the way saw us and waved like we were regulars. She gestured we should sit anywhere, and I chose a small table near a window. The walls were an aged tin, as if we were in an old train dining car, and gleamed dully in the small space.

"I love it here," I said earnestly as Carter sat across from me.

He laughed. "And you haven't even tasted the bacon yet."

"I can already tell it's going to be amazing." In fact, as my mouth watered and my stomach rumbled, I realized I hadn't eaten much in the last few days.

The waitress bustled over with two cups of coffee and a single menu, which she handed to me. *So Carter was a regular,* I thought, which was confirmed moments later when the waitress said, "Hi, gorgeous. We've missed you lately," in a sweet country voice. I'd been a various city girl most of my strange life, but I'd come to learn that country voices were similar whatever state you were in. They may all have had a slightly different twang, but twang they did. I felt instantly at home here, and it was obvious that Carter was a favorite guest.

He smiled at her fondly. "I've missed you too, Mercy. And this is Lainey," he said, "a new student at the Academy."

Mercy eyed me curiously. "An Academy girl, huh?" She glanced at Carter with a touch of surprise, maybe even disapproval, which I didn't think had anything to do with the fact that I probably should have been in classes at the moment. "A pretty one though for sure, and you look like a city girl, but if Cartwright likes you, I'm sure we will too. Pleased to meet you Lainey, and welcome to Dad's. He's in the back at the griddle. I'll be back in a minute for you to tell me what you want."

"Thank you," I replied as she bustled away. I stirred sugar and cream into my coffee, while Carter sipped his straight, and asked him, "I guess you come here often…but not with Academy girls, huh?"

He laughed. "Yes, to both. Not even Jillian has come here with me. Strictly locals. Until now."

Wow. So his bringing me here *was* special. I felt privileged. And pleased. I got the feeling Carter was trying to convince me that everything he'd said yesterday was true. I sipped my coffee and nearly dropped it in surprise.

"It's good!" In my experience, diner coffee was at best average and most often terrible, but cheap, and a viable method for ingesting caffeine. However, *this* coffee was fresh, strong, and, best of all, didn't taste like it had been made the day before and sat on the burner since.

Carter smiled, as if he'd known I would appreciate the distinction. "Best coffee in three states. But don't tell the Andersons I said that," he added. The Andersons owned the coffee shop down the block from the bookstore.

"It will be our secret," I said solemnly and crossed my heart with my finger. "So what else is good here?"

"Everything." His tone was so serious, I didn't think he was exaggerating. When Mercy returned, he simply asked for "the usual" and she patted his arm affectionately before she left to put in our orders.

"They seem to like you here," I said. "And that you come here often."

"As often as I can, which lately, hasn't been that regularly. It's nice to be back. And with you."

I think I blushed, just a little bit, but it might have been the warm coffee I was drinking too, I couldn't be sure. I outwardly ignored the last part of his comment and asked about the first. "Why not lately?"

"Work," he said and smiled pointedly at me.

"I, oh…you mean me? Watching me?" Jesus. I suddenly felt bad for not manifesting sooner.

"Trust me, I haven't minded." He lowered his voice. "But…this isn't discreet. We can talk about that later."

Discreet. There it was again. I'd heard the term at least three times in only twenty-four hours. I lowered my voice too and said, "Okay, but explain 'discreet' to me first. I mean, I know what it *means*. But why does everyone keep saying it like it's either a compliment or an order?"

He sipped coffee and glanced around briefly to ensure there was no one nearby. "Let's just say it's the Perceptum's unofficial motto. Doing anything discreetly is akin to doing it well."

"Okay, got it." I would think through that more on my own. I also realized that if we weren't talking about work here then he kind of wasn't working. "But then…shouldn't you be working right now? You won't get in trouble, will you?"

He chuckled. "No. Unless you want to report me as slacking off."

"Not today, so far anyway, but who would I tell if I get annoyed with you? Headmaster Stewart?"

"For your purposes, that would probably suffice. As it is, she doesn't need much encouragement to try to make my life difficult."

"Why is that?" I asked. "She…doesn't seem to like you very much. Or your aunt."

He sipped coffee and nodded. "Constance Stewart only likes people with money or who she thinks can help her advance her position, preferably both. For the most part, my aunt and I are neither. She thought I could be one of those people, and I probably could if I wanted to, but I've made it very clear I'm not interested in her games. And my aunt…my aunt has something she wanted very much at one time, and she's never forgiven her for taking it."

"What is it?"

Carter smiled wanly. "Jeffrey Revell."

I gasped in surprise and choked on the sip of coffee I'd just taken. Well, well, well. I'd *never* have guessed that. Jeff Revell was an attractive man, it was true. He was taller even than Carter and broader too, with a muscular build and fair hair worn short, like a policeman's. In fact, he'd always reminded me of someone in law enforcement or the armed services, with his straight posture and quiet, watchful gaze. He seemed to be the very definition of the strong, silent type. More than a few of my classmates, I was pretty sure, spent so much time at the bookstore because they secretly hoped Carter's *uncle* would be working that night.

But Headmaster Stewart was so stiff and proper and overly self-sufficient. I couldn't imagine her as anything but the woman she was today, but she must have had hopes and desires and a past, just like the rest of us. It had never crossed my mind that she was around the same age as Carter's aunt and uncle.

When I could breathe again I said, "Wow. Uh, wasn't expecting that answer."

"I don't think many people would, not unless they were at the Academy with the three of them when they were students," he said, and he told me the story.

It wasn't terribly sordid or anything, which was a tiny bit disappointing. In fact, it was pretty simple. Jeff and Dr. Stewart had actually dated briefly, before Jeff realized he couldn't think of her as more than a friend and before Melinda came along. Dr. Stewart was heartbroken, but, Carter said, also knew what his uncle told her was unequivocally true. Afterwards, instead of making friends, she began in earnest her quest to become a powerful member of Sententia society, throwing all of her effort into ignoring Melinda and solidifying as many Sententia connections as she could.

"I'm fairly sure, though," Carter finished, "that if my uncle went and confessed his undying love to the Headmaster, or, really, even his desire to have an illicit affair with her, she'd take him without a moment's hesitation."

Our breakfasts arrived then, steaming and buttery. Carter's "usual" was an enormous plate that contained, I was fairly certain, several eggs, at least two pancakes, home fries, more than two slices of toast, and some of every single breakfast meat on the menu. My eyes boggled just looking at it.

He noticed my stare and smiled, scooping up potatoes as he went. "Jealous?"

I glanced at my plate, which was smaller by half than Carter's yet full to the edges with eggs and toast, and said, "I thought my breakfast was huge; I don't think I could eat that much all day!"

He snickered and then shrugged. "I run at least six miles a day Lainey, and I told you, I'm hungry. But take a bite of yours, and you'll realize it's so good that you'll want my order too, next time we come."

I liked the sound of next time, and he was right: my greasy breakfast was exquisite and exactly what I wanted. We chewed in happy silence for a while, and I marveled at the amount of calories Carter was loading into his trim body. He certainly *looked* like he ran at least six miles a day, and moved a lot of boxes full of books too. His omnipresent plain t-shirt stretched over broad shoulders and exposed his muscular arms, obvious even doing something as simple as lifting his coffee cup. I realized I was staring and looked away hastily, though unfortunately not before Mercy arrived at the table to refill our coffee cups and caught me.

"He's a handsome one, isn't he, our Cartwright," she said to me, with a wink and a hint of a smirk. Carter glanced away in pretend humility while taking another sip of his coffee, but I could see his broad grin.

"I've seen worse," I admitted, praying I wasn't blushing too furiously. Mercy laughed and patted my hand, maybe a little bit affectionately too, before leaving us alone again. Needing to change the subject, and not able to talk about what we *really* needed to talk about, I turned to the other topic on my mind. "I'm so depressed about next week," I told Carter as I sopped up egg with my toast, explaining how my aunt had cancelled our visit to Boston for the holiday.

"Don't be," he told me, punctuated by a wicked grin. "We're going shopping."

"Sorry?" I mumbled, completely indelicately, around my mouthful of toast.

His grin widened, and I would swear to you the boy smiled way too often if it didn't look so damn good on him. "We're going shopping. Antique shopping, actually. I thought you might like that, and there are plenty of places to check out nearby."

"Well, I *would* like that. I haven't been shopping or, really, anything since I got to the Academy, unless you count the bookstore and the coffee shop. But…why? It doesn't strike me as something you'd do on break or, um, ever…" I trailed off, curious, but a little bit excited. Maybe the week wouldn't be so bad after all.

"I don't know if I'd go so far as *ever*, but we need to…find a few things"—he eyed me meaningfully when he said this—"for you to…practice with. Antiques are probably our best options. Plus you already love them."

It took me a minute to understand exactly what he was getting at, but then I heard Dr. Stewart's voice echo in the back of my head as she'd said…*away from all those antiques you seem to love, burdened as they are with their long histories.* "Oh," I finally said. "Oh, okay. Well, hopefully it will still be fun. And I don't pass out."

"I won't let that happen," he assured me. I believed him.

Chapter Twelve

When we got back to campus, Carter suggested a walk, and led us through the Academy gates. We kept walking past the faculty quarters and straight onto a wide trail that quickly disappeared between the trees. Students, I knew, were expressly forbidden on the trails unless they were with a chaperone. I stifled a giggle. I thought I might need all my fingers and toes to count the number of my classmates who'd love to have Carter "chaperone" them into the woods.

Apparently he was reading my thoughts again, because when I glanced over, he was grinning at me. "This isn't *exactly* allowed. For you anyway."

"Well, I won't turn you in for slacking this morning if you don't rat on me for going into the woods unchaperoned, with a boy of unclear intentions."

He stopped short, grabbing my hand, and pulled me so close to him I could feel the warmth of his body and smell his fresh, soapy scent. I'm pretty sure I stopped breathing. "I thought I made my intentions pretty clear yesterday, Lainey," he said seriously, bending his head close to mine. I *definitely* stopped breathing.

But I wasn't quite ready for that yet, and he didn't move any closer without an invitation from me. We stood still for almost a full minute, me waiting for my lungs to restart, Carter breathing deeply, waiting for my permission. Finally I broke the intimate space and restarted our walk. He fell in step wordlessly beside me.

We walked along for a while without speaking. It wasn't uncomfortable, not exactly, but was charged with tension of a different kind. My brain, not to mention the rest of my body, was swimming with thoughts of Carter, of possibilities and fears, of kissing him or *not* kissing him, and wondering which I wanted to do. That finally got me on track, because though most of me was leaning—really strongly—toward the former, I still had some questions I needed answered.

"At…" I started, and my voice came out as an embarrassing squeak. I cleared my throat and tried again, before Carter had the chance to make fun of me. "At breakfast, you said something that made me curious, about Dr. Stewart, how she *knew* your Uncle Jeff was telling her the truth. Does that have something to do with her gift?"

"Perceptive," he said. "I mean in the general sense; you're very perceptive. And yes, that *is* her gift. Ever wonder why the kids are so terrified of her, beyond the obvious? It's because they can't lie to Headmaster Stewart. She's *Vidi Veritas*, a lie detector. If she's being lied to, she might not be able to tell you what the truth actually is, but she knows that whatever she's hearing isn't it. Though I hate to admit it, her gift is one of the things that makes her a great headmaster. She runs the school tightly and mostly fairly."

Yikes. I was glad I'd never been anything but truthful with her. I was also suddenly jealous of her awesome ability compared to my crappy one. I'd have *loved* to know whether someone was telling the truth instead of whether they were going to die.

"Uh, wow," I blurted. "That's…useful information. Do the students know about her gift, the Sententia students I mean?"

He laughed as he guided us onto a smaller side trail. "Oh yeah, they know. If they haven't heard from relatives who've attended, they learn pretty quickly in their first meeting when she tests them. And then tells them if they passed or failed. The general students don't know, not exactly, but you've seen how quickly word gets around campus. It's not long before they've all heard not to lie to her, because somehow she *always* knows."

"But no impetus," I said. "She can't force you." He looked at me, a little surprised, and I shrugged. "Ms. Kim told me about it. She said it's rare. So…what kind of gift would have that?"

"You tell me. Take a guess."

We walked for a few paces while I thought about it. I really didn't know much about Sententia, but I'd heard of ESP and other fictional, so I'd thought, mind powers before. I started with that. "Okay…what about, well, like telekinesis? Is that real? That would be a physical force."

"It's real," he confirmed. "We call them Thought Movers, *Sententia Permoveo*. That's where our history starts, actually. They're the earliest recorded abilities we've found. The most feared, too," he added, almost as an afterthought. I didn't have time to think about the strange tone in his voice before he went on. "But it's *not* like you see in movies. None of this ever is. Our gifts work quickly, almost in the blink of an eye."

"But…if it's so quick, then why is it so dangerous?"

"Even in short bursts being able to move objects with only Thought is plenty dangerous, believe me," he said gravely. "And it's more than moving objects. Thought Movers can…affect the *intentions* of things. Make them go from moving to not moving. Change directions. Sometimes they can change *people's* intentions too. They literally have the ability to *move thoughts.* One moment you're thinking one thing, and the next, a Thought Mover has moved your thoughts...somewhere else."

I shivered. This *did* scare me. It was almost inconceivable that someone could have the ability to move an object with nothing but Thought. But to be able to, literally, change someone's *mind...that* was impossible. Or it should have been.

I shivered again and realized we'd stopped moving. We were standing in the middle of the trail as I stared off into space, my brain whirling with possibilities. A breeze ruffled the fallen leaves around us and made the mostly bare trees sway overhead. I tugged my coat tighter and noticed that Carter was watching me, a small, concerned frown marring his otherwise beautiful face. His hair was a little windblown, making him look more boyish than usual, and his cheeks had a slight flush from the cold. I resisted the urge to reach up and smooth my fingers through his tousled waves.

"Uh, sorry," I said sheepishly and resumed walking. Once more he fell in step with me wordlessly. "I guess I got a little overwhelmed there. This is a lot to take in. I'm...having trouble believing this is all real, and it just gets stranger as we go along." He didn't say anything, but reached out and put his hand into mine. I grasped it gratefully.

Whatever else I felt about him, every touch from Carter was warm and reassuring. Or electrifying, but I wasn't thinking about that right now. When he made to let go, I kept hold. Today, I needed not only a guide through this craziness but also an anchor. Carter would have to be both.

"It is overwhelming," he said. "I keep having to remind myself that before two days ago you knew nothing about *any* of this...you thought you were a normal girl, albeit one who was going crazy. You still must a little bit. But you're *not.* I swear to you, you're not. You're—incredible, actually. I think most people would have run screaming long before now. In fact, I've seen them do it, and they were grown men."

I giggled, lightening my mood and some of the tension I'd let build up inside me. "Silly Carter. You should know by now that women are tougher than men."

He laughed, and swiftly, so I had no time to protest or resist, brought our linked hands up to his mouth and kissed mine, saying, "You're definite proof of that."

He dropped our hands back down just as quickly but did not let go. I blushed, but I didn't let go either. His lips had been warm and the tip of his nose cold, but the whole sensation made me tingle just a little bit. Our side trail came to a fork and Carter led us to the left. I had the sense that we were coming around toward the back edge of campus, working our way in a big circle.

I also realized I was stalling. I had a million more questions about Sententia abilities that I wanted to ask, but partly that was to avoid talking about the Perceptum. Whenever I thought about it, I got a bad feeling. I hoped that was because of a lack of understanding. The unfamiliar was sometimes scary, right? I needed to get familiar.

"Okay," I said resolutely. "I'm ready to hear about the Perceptum now. Make me not scared of it, please."

"You have no reason to be frightened, believe me. Very few people do." I noted he said *very few* and not *no one*. I was suddenly sure that whatever he said, or however much good the Perceptum did, I would never be entirely comfortable with them.

"The Perceptum…" Carter continued. "It's difficult and simple to explain, all at the same time. Like I said yesterday, the Perceptum is, most basically, the Sententia network."

"What's it mean?" I interrupted him. "The word, I mean. Perceptum. How does it…translate?"

"Oh. It means *perception* or *one who perceives*. Latin rarely translates directly," he added smartly, sounding exactly like one of my teachers.

I resisted the urge to giggle and nodded instead, saying, "Okay, Perceptives Network, got it. But that's not all. Yesterday you said something about 'governing body' too. Explain."

So he did. We walked and I listened. Carter seemed to enjoy the history lesson on the Perceptum and, to be honest, I didn't mind hearing it. In fact, it was more than a little interesting. My brain was working too furiously for my body to be cold, and though I was hopelessly lost in the woods, I was beginning to feel a little bit better about the whole thing until he got to the part about what the Perceptum did today.

It started, apparently, with idealism, and a handful of men including Abraham Lincoln. Everyone knew what he did, but I guessed only a small portion of people knew how he had Sententia help. After Lincoln's assassination, the rest of the men continued their mission to use their gifts to positively influence the world, but the more people they enlisted, the more dissent they had between them.

"Not everyone," Carter said, "has the same ideas about what would be positive for the world, right? But they realized there was a problem they could address, something no other group could: they could recognize when other Sententia were using their gifts harmfully, or recklessly, or without even knowing what they were. From there, they established what they called the Perceptum Council, which still operates today."

Carter remained quiet while I pondered. Helping end slavery was a pretty great contribution to the world, but that's not what they did anymore. Now they what? Regulated the Sententia population, it sounded like. That wasn't so bad, in theory, but I thought back to what Carter had said about how *not everyone has the same ideas about what would be positive for the world*. I didn't think everyone would have the same ideas about what was harmful or reckless either. So I said as much.

"They don't," Carter replied. "It's why there's a council. When Historians recognize and report...new or potentially dangerous Sententia activity, they vote."

"Okay, so that's your job? Investigating Sententia sightings in the wild?"

He laughed. "That's pretty much it, yeah," he said. "My aunt too. I also research historical records, trying to trace Sententia genealogy. And, lucky guy that I am, occasionally I get to do things like this," he said, squeezing my hand. "Not too long after they formed the Council, one of its members established Northbrook, in case you were wondering. I've already told you why. There are a few other schools, here and on other continents."

I already knew Penrose Books had been established the same year as the Academy, obviously not a coincidence. Between selling books and scouting Sententia, Carter's plate seemed pretty full. "What happens when you and your aunt find something?"

"Uncle Jeff investigates and the Council votes on how to proceed, based on the situation."

That was ominous. "What are the options?" I asked carefully.

"The question is usually about how best to contact them," Carter replied. "And then sometimes the Council votes to contact local authorities instead. Discreetly, of course."

Of course. "What these people are doing isn't always nice, huh? I guess that shouldn't surprise me."

"No, it's not," he said softly. "Sometimes it's very much not."

Carter came to a stop and, since I was holding his hand, so did I. I looked around, confused. We didn't seem to be anywhere specific, just at another fork in the trails, but it was not as quiet where we stopped. I could hear sounds and voices that were probably coming from campus. I figured if I wanted to look at my watch, I'd see that classes were over and that meant I should get back to say goodbye to Amy. But I had so many more questions and, honestly, I felt…calm out here in the forest.

I wasn't ready to go back to campus, even if I knew I should. I poked Carter and said, "What, are you tired? Why'd we stop here?"

He was good, I'd give him that much. He smiled and said, "I'll never tire of your company. But it's late, so it's probably not…discreet for us to go out the way we came. This trail"—he gestured to the fork to the left—"comes out at the top of campus, not very far from here."

I got what he was saying. "And you want me to go out that way, right? Gotcha. Where are *you* going?"

He shrugged. "I'll go back some other way, closer to the road. Doesn't matter where. I—Do you want to come to dinner tonight?" He asked abruptly, instead of whatever he'd been about to say, and almost…shyly, as if he wanted me to say yes but was genuinely afraid I might say no. It was the only shy thing I'd ever seen him do.

I wondered if Carter had ever had a girl resist his romantic advances before. Though, seriously, it wasn't like I was resisting too heavily. A few days before I'd thought *I* was pursuing *him*. I was just a little hesitant in light of recent revelations. And then everything he did seemed to come so easily to him; maybe he'd never really had to work at anything. I made a silent vow that, no matter what happened with us, I would be his biggest challenge. I thought he might need it.

"Just to the apartment, nothing special," he continued quickly. "And not for this, for work. To have dinner, though we can talk about all this, if you want. My aunt will be there too, and my uncle is home. Anyway, I thought, well, Amy is leaving tonight and I thought you might like to join us."

Carter's babbling was…cute. It was so out of character for him, I couldn't help but laugh. I poked him again, playfully, in the ribs.

"Thank you. And I'd love to come to dinner at the apartment. I'm sure it will be way better than the dining hall…and the company's not so bad either," I added at the end. I was rewarded with one of Carter's better smiles, broad and pleased, but, remembering my vow of moments ago, I couldn't let him get away with too much self-satisfaction. "Your aunt, she's great, you know?" I said, and smiled at him even wider.

He laughed. "She definitely is. Okay, come over at seven? We close the store early on nights before break."

"See you then," I replied. More seriously, I added, "And Carter? Thanks. For today, I mean. For…understanding." And then, much to my surprise, since I hadn't planned to do it, I reached my arms around his waist and hugged him.

He looked down in surprise but quickly followed suit, wrapping his arms around me and pulling me closer. "Believe me," he said, rustling my hair a little with his warm breath, "it was my pleasure."

We stood like that for a moment and it was…nice. Comfortable. In fact, I wanted nothing less than to let go of him and head back to a busy campus full of students and parents and noise and secrets. But it was time to, so I stood on my tiptoes, kissed him quickly on the cheek for the second time, and then headed out the trail. After a moment, I heard him leave at a light jog, as if six miles this morning and however far we'd walked this afternoon weren't enough for him.

I glanced back over my shoulder but I knew he was already gone. I couldn't keep from smiling a little though, because I had been right: even with, or maybe because of, our unusual topic of conversation, that really had been the best non-date I'd ever had.

Chapter Thirteen

I said a quick goodbye to Amy and then passed the time tidying up my half of the room in honor of my aunt's visit. Amy's half was already pristine, as usual. I tried to emulate her orderliness, but eventually I'd look around and realize I had sweatshirts on chairs, books scattered about, and my bag thrown wherever I first stopped when I came in the door. Aunt Tessa flew in from Baltimore the next day and would be staying in campus guest housing, at Headmaster Stewart's invitation.

I wasn't entirely sure what we were going to do with ourselves for an entire week but I knew the time would pass quickly. I was, however, a little stressed about the giant secret I had to keep from her. It seemed like, as it had before I'd come here, my whole life had changed in the course of only a few days. I was so much in the thick of trying to understand it that I was worried about slipping up, about being able to be the same Lainey my aunt had known. I *wasn't* that same Lainey, not anymore. However this newfound ability affected my future, it had already irrevocably changed who I thought I was.

Learning that I *wasn't* going crazy should have made me feel better, and I guess it had, in a way, but now, I felt...lost. I'd never felt that way before. Aside from the crazy, I'd always been happy with who I was and the woman I thought I'd become. Now I feared myself, just a little bit, and what I could do. I was pretty sure that what I needed was time. To adjust, to process, to learn more. Unfortunately, I didn't have much of it before I had to be at least an approximation of the old Lainey. I was afraid that if I was distant, or distracted, or seemed as if I was unhappy, my aunt would think it had been a mistake for me to come here, which absolutely wasn't true. More than that, it had been a *necessity*.

And I *was* happy here. In fact, I loved it. I loved being in classes with other students, instead of alone with my tutor. I loved Amy and having a dedicated group of friends. I liked, well, gossiping, which meant that you knew a place and its people and how its daily life unfolded. I'd never had much chance to do it before, unless gossiping with my aunt about the art world counted. Not many people related to that. I missed my martial arts classes, but I enjoyed swimming, and had even helped the team win a few relays at our meets.

I liked *going* to sporting events and cheering for *my* teams and *my* friends. I liked…Carter. I had loved my old life too, but never knew what I was missing: what it meant to *belong* somewhere. Even in such a short time, I felt like I was *part* of Northbrook and I thought it was because I'd allowed myself to become part of it. I knew that, for better or for worse, this would be my home for two years, so I'd better make it for better.

All these things swirled through my head as I cleaned and straightened, but I kept coming back to that phrase: *for better or for worse*. Just like Northbrook was now my home, for better or worse, being Sententia was now my reality. It's who or what I'd be for the rest of my days, part of me. But it didn't need to define me, I decided. As far as I knew, once I left Northbrook, there was no reason I needed to be part of the Perceptum or any other section of Sententia society.

Yet as I had that thought, my stomach twisted uneasily. I knew why, even if I didn't want to admit it to myself. It came back around, of course, to a boy. Leaving Sententia behind would mean leaving Carter behind. A small part of me thought that, in the long run, that would probably be a relief, for the best. But most of me wanted to cry or throw up at the idea of it. And *that* finally forced me to accept what I wanted, maybe *needed*, to do. I decided to take Amy's advice from the other day and pair it with my own. I would start living for where I was now, and for better or for worse, or possibly for incredibly stupid, with Carter was where I wanted to be.

TO MY SURPRISE, it was Jeff Revell who greeted me when I arrived at their apartment. Melinda waved from where she stood at the stove behind him.

"Lainey, welcome, come in," Jeff said in his deep, quiet voice, extending his hand to me. I shook it, and it was as strong and masculine as I expected. "We've never met officially. Please call me Jeff."

"Thank you," I replied, "and thank you for having me. Home-cooked meals are a real treat for me, even before I got to Northbrook."

"Well, we're glad you could join us," Melinda said as she bustled over to give me a quick and surprising hug. We'd never hugged before, but I liked it. It felt reassuring, motherly. I knew Melinda and Jeff had never been able to have children, though Carter had essentially become theirs the same way I'd become Aunt Tessa's. "I hope you like pot roast!" She promptly opened the oven, releasing the most mouth-watering aroma I'd smelled, well, possibly ever. Our kitchens, wherever my aunt and I'd happened to be, usually smelled like coffee or takeout.

"I'm 100% sure I'll like it, if that's what smells so amazing," I said emphatically. "Can I help with anything?"

"No, honey, not at all. You're our guest tonight. You can probably find Carter setting the table in the dining room."

"It's through there," Jeff said, pointing helpfully at one of the doorways.

I could see Carter smiling at me from the end of a big table, where he was folding napkins crisply and precisely. I'd never been in most of the rest of the apartment, though I knew it was spacious since it took up the entire third floor of the building. The dining room was, like the kitchen, cheerful and inviting, with more of the gorgeous woodwork that also decorated much of the bookstore and a large, probably antique dining set complemented by fresh, modern paint and place settings. I imagined the rest of the place was equally beautiful and well balanced. I kind of wanted to live there.

"Hi," he said from his post at the table end. That was it. I thought he might be…nervous. It was charming, in a different way than usual.

"Hi," I repeated with a smile. "Want some help?"

"Sure." He handed over his stack of napkins. "You can put these out. But don't tell my aunt," he added hastily. "Guests aren't supposed to help with anything."

"I heard that, Cartwright!" came Melinda's voice from the kitchen.

Carter smiled, but didn't take back the napkins. I noticed that he'd started clearing *away* a place setting.

"Is someone not eating?" I wondered. There were still four settings left on the table.

"Jill. She was supposed to join us, but she called right before you got here and said she wasn't feeling well."

"Oh! Well, that's too bad. I hope she's not sick for break. I'm surprised she's still here. Most of the students are already gone."

"She's actually from Wyoming, so she flies out on Saturday morning. There aren't many flights to Sheridan."

"Wow. Long way from home. Why doesn't she go to the school in California? That would be a lot closer for her," I said, before realizing how silly that was. "Oh wait, she's Legacy. Duh."

"Right," he said. "Though I think she wanted to go to Webber." That was the West Coast Sententia school.

"Is she not happy here? She's…kind of a loner, except for hanging out with you, I guess, but I think that's mostly by her choice. I know she does well in classes, and Headmaster Stewart gushes about her. She's a good swimmer too, one of the best on the team, besides Caleb. Kicks my butt." I was moving slowly around the table, arranging the silverware on my napkins, while Carter followed with wine and water glasses for each of us.

He laughed. "I've noticed that. For someone so tall, I thought you'd be better."

Carter came to my swim meets? I thought frantically. Well if *that* wasn't embarrassing, I didn't know what was. "I, uh, didn't know you came to our meets," I squeaked. What surprised me most was that Amy didn't tell me he was there.

"Guilty," he said, though he didn't seem very guilty at all, based on the sly grin on his face. "I've always tried to slip in at least for a little while to watch Jillian. And now you too."

"But…why didn't you ever say so?! And why don't you sit with Amy? She never noticed you there either."

The sly grin transitioned to a sheepish one. "Uh, yeah, sorry. I try to stick to the shadows. Some of your classmates give me shit if I'm noticed at the swim meets and not their field hockey games."

I snorted. "I don't need three guesses to know who you're talking about. I'm kind of surprised, actually," I said.

"That I don't go to field hockey games?"

"That you never dated Alexis."

He laughed again, a deep, belly laugh of true amusement. "Why on earth would I want to do that?"

"Well, you do seem to get along with her, and she's certainly not shy about making her interest known. And she's so beautiful," I tacked on at the end, deciding to go ahead and say what I really meant.

Carter gave me what I could only describe as a withering look. "I might like Alexis just fine, but I'd never date her. She's not looking for a boyfriend...she's looking for someone to worship her like a goddess. That's not going to be me, despite how much she might like it to be. And besides, she's not as beautiful as you."

I might have appreciated the compliment, but I returned his withering look. "C'mon, Carter. She's more beautiful than anyone, me included."

"That's just it, she's not," he said, and tugged me down into the chair I'd been leaning on as he sat next to me. "I mean, I know she's gorgeous. I'm not blind. But...see, the difference is, it's not that I think you're a girl who doesn't know she's pretty. It's that you don't think it makes you *special*. Alex thinks her beauty makes her something important and with her gift, people usually agree with her. That...that makes her less beautiful. I like to flirt with Alex—what guy doesn't?— but otherwise, I keep my distance."

That made sense to me from what I'd always observed of him. Carter was as attractive as anyone, and he certainly knew it, but he never acted like a jerk because of it. "What's her gift got to do with it?" I asked. "And what *is* her gift? Besides an unfairly beautiful face and a bitchy attitude."

He barked a laugh. "Those gifts are naturally hers, for sure. Her *Sententia* gift...basically, people want to believe her. She's *convincing*. Like charisma on steroids. It's why she'll make a great actress someday. You've noticed her flair for the dramatic already, I'm sure. We call her group *Praeconor* or Heralds. Their gifts project onto others."

So that explained why, like Amy said, Alexis was so compelling. I started to ask something else but was interrupted by Melinda striding into the room carrying a salad and rolls, followed by Jeff carrying a huge platter of magnificent-looking pot roast. "Dinner is served," Melinda sang, setting down her bowls and taking the seat across from me. Jeff took the seat at the head of the table.

Thus commenced an enjoyable dinner, one that tasted every bit as divine as it smelled. I complimented Melinda nearly every time my mouth wasn't full of her amazing meal. We talked comfortably while we ate and I found I was enjoying myself immensely with absolutely no effort on my part. I felt…welcome, at their table, in their family. It was a wonderful feeling, and I luxuriated in it throughout the meal. About halfway through, Melinda made another surprising gesture.

"Lainey," she said, "I don't know if you're committed to the Academy dinner—I'm sure Constance wants you to attend—but we'd love to have you and your aunt join us for Thanksgiving. What do you think?"

I thought that was the most wonderful invitation I'd had in years, and I told her as much. But Dr. Stewart had already made sure we'd be at the Academy dinner, so I suggested we come for dessert instead.

"Any time you can join us at all would be wonderful," Melinda replied. "We can't wait to meet your aunt, though maybe I'll get the chance earlier in the week. Carter told me about his plan to take you shopping for…practice objects, and I think it's a good one. Plus it sounds fun. I thought I'd come with you at least once."

I was afraid I was about to ruin our enjoyable dinner, but here was the perfect opening to ask the few questions about the Perceptum I had left. I gave a silent apology before saying, "I think we'd both like that, Melinda, thank you. Though I hope I'm not keeping Carter, and you, from too much of your work…at the bookstore or, you know, your other job."

Jeff actually laughed, and it transformed him from not just handsome to intoxicating, in the same way that Carter's smiles transformed his face. I found myself smiling in response. "You don't have to worry about that, Lainey," he said. "You're more important right now than reading news clippings for the Perceptum all day anyway."

I looked at Carter and then Melinda. "Is that what you spend a lot of time doing?" I asked. That wasn't what I expected. Actually, I didn't *know* what I expected, but reading the news wasn't it. I supposed it made sense though.

Carter made a face. "Pretty much, yeah. It's…kind of boring, honestly. Not very sexy, either."

Melinda looked at Carter fondly, then back to me. "He loves it, honey. Don't let him fool you. Besides running and reading, there's not much else Carter likes to do. Except spend time with you, that is." It was the kind of statement that would make most boys roll their eyes or blush uncomfortably, but not Carter. He just smiled and winked at me. "But yes," she continued, "we read a lot, the two of us, looking for clues, I guess you could say. It *is* a little tedious sometimes, but we're a good team. I see the patterns—that's my gift, by the way, *Exemplar Aspicio* if you want the technical term—and Carter remembers the details. Jeff really does the hard part." He was, apparently, the Sententia investigator because he found things. Literally. That was a *Venator's* gift.

I thought it must be quite expensive to travel so much. "I hope this isn't rude to ask," I started, "but…how do you pay for all of the Perceptum work you do? You don't have to do it yourselves, I hope."

"No," Jeff answered. "And it's fine to ask, Lainey. You won't insult us. The Perceptum pays the expenses."

I considered that for a minute. "How? I mean…well, where do they get the money? They're not a business, right?"

"No," Jeff said again. "They're definitely not a business, not in the traditional sense, but the Perceptum has plenty of funding to continue its mission long into the future. They established an endowment long ago and most members still contribute to it, depending on their means. Council members are actually required to pledge a percentage of their earrings."

I seized on Jeff's words and pushed forward into my *real* questions. "What exactly *is* the Perceptum's mission?" I asked carefully. "I understand about…recognizing and trying to prevent harmful Sententia activity. But…what if the person isn't interested in the Perceptum? What then?"

Carter chimed in this time. "They don't necessarily have to be. No one's forced to join, and we don't hand out membership cards. There's no secret handshake either, in case you wondered." He was joking, but there was more here. I *knew* there was more behind all of this.

"Okay…" I stalled, thinking furiously about how to put words to my sense of foreboding about the Perceptum. "So they don't have to join the Perceptum…but what if they're not interested in *discretion* either? That's the motto, right?"

And there it was: hesitation. I knew then that I'd tapped the root of my fears. Carter said slowly, as if measuring his words, "If an individual isn't interested in that…the Perceptum tries to convince them of its importance."

"And what if 'convincing them' doesn't work?" I demanded. Carter looked away and Melinda looked at me sympathetically. Jeff was the only one who maintained a level gaze. And that was the moment I knew the truth. If the person couldn't be convinced with words, the Perceptum convinced them in another way, maybe the *final* way. "Oh my God," I whispered.

Jeff's gentle voice confirmed my fears. "If persuasion doesn't work, and the individual resisting discretion is deemed a danger to exposure, then the Council may vote to eliminate the problem."

Holy. Shit. Holy F-ing SHIT. So they *killed* people? Killed people. Killed. People. My brain kept stuttering over my first thought, so that's what came out of my mouth. "Holy shit," I breathed. "You...you *kill* people?!"

Melinda leaned across the table and smoothed her hand over where I didn't realize mine were tightly gripping the table. "No honey, *we* don't kill anyone. We do research. And Jeff does absolutely everything he can to keep it from getting to that point. But the Perceptum...well, the Perceptum has had it done in order to protect us all. And I believe that wholeheartedly. I wouldn't be part of the organization if I didn't, and I wouldn't let my nephew either."

"But...but..." were all the words I could form at that moment. Melinda had sat back down in her chair so it was Carter who reached out to me this time. He brushed his warm hand across my suddenly cold cheek and, to my surprise, I didn't flinch. I looked at him with what I was sure were wide, frightened eyes.

"If you knew what most of these people were doing, you might not be so outraged," he said.

"Please," I practically begged him, all of them, as I looked around the table, frightened and skittish. "Please tell me *anything* that will help me be less freaked out by this."

Even more quietly than usual, Jeff answered my plea. "The last man to be executed was a Thought Mover who was using his abilities to do many disgusting things, but most offensively, to rape women without their remembering. He got three of them pregnant, and one he liked so much, he raped her several times. She thought she was going crazy and killed herself."

I gasped, and my brain reeled again. "That's...that's *horrible,*" I said, though it kind of went without saying. I tried to feel guilt that the man hadn't gotten a fair trial, but mostly I had a mingled sense of horror over what he'd done and relief that he wouldn't be able to hurt anyone else. "But why," I wondered, "...why didn't you contact the authorities? Send him to jail or whatever. Something *legal.*"

"Thought Movers are nearly impossible to keep in jail, Lainey," Carter said. "And besides which, he'd never have been convicted in the first place. Most of the others, the ones in recent history, are nearly as bad," he added, and Jeff confirmed this. He related a few more stories of the malicious people using their gifts to do pretty terrible things.

Somewhat ironically, these stories of bad people were making me feel better. I was still freaked out, couldn't help but be afraid of a group that behaved as its own judge, jury, and executioner, but I also couldn't dispute that I'd have wanted these people stopped too. If it were in my power to do something to stop them, I'd have tried to do it. Maybe not *kill* them, but something.

Most of all, I believed Melinda when she said she wouldn't be part of the Perceptum if she thought what they were doing was wrong. She was a *good* person, through and through. I knew that instinctively. I had to trust that if she believed there were no other options, then maybe there really weren't. But I had something more to understand.

"But why is being discreet so important?" I asked. "Why do we have to hide our abilities? There are millions of Sententia, or so you've told me, and...and we could do so much *good.*"

Everyone nodded, as if I finally asked a question they'd been expecting. Carter answered. "You're right. We could, but people wouldn't let us...because people fear differences. If we used our gifts openly, even for the greater good, we'd be persecuted. Historically, we were. They burned Sententia as heretics and 'witches' at the stake." He shook his head decisively. "No, I know it's hard to accept, but I believe in the Perceptum's efforts: anonymity is our greatest weapon. With it, we *can* do the good you're talking about. Plus," he added, "some people aren't at all *interested* in the greater good, including some Sententia. Unfortunately, being cognitively gifted doesn't automatically make you a good person. Sometimes it makes people *worse.*"

I needed more time to think about all of this—years more time, I suspected—but what Carter said did make sense. I realized that, much like this afternoon, somewhere in the middle of our conversation I'd taken hold of Carter's hand under the table and was holding it rather tightly between mine. Unconsciously, I had reached for his support and he'd apparently given it without hesitation.

Melinda lifted the tension in the room with a tiny, sweet chuckle. "Well, so much for our light dinner conversation," she said, then sighed. "I'm sorry, Lainey. This all must be so overwhelming to you. Carter's told me how amazingly you're taking it all, and if anything, I think that was an understatement. Why don't I go get dessert and give you a few minutes to…process." With that, she rose, and Jeff followed her back into the kitchen.

Carter was looking at me with concern and maybe a little admiration. It made little lines in the middle of his forehead and I wanted to reach up and smooth them out. Instead, I squeezed his hand and he smiled, erasing the lines for me.

"That…must have been hard for you," he said, words that qualified as possibly the understatement of the year. I think he realized it though, because he gave a glum little laugh and looked down at our entwined hands before asking softly, "Do you want to go home?"

"No," I said firmly, and I meant it. I think I surprised him, because his head snapped up to look at me. It was almost comical and exactly what I needed. I smiled and went on. "No, I definitely don't. I want to stay here for a while longer with you and your family because I trust you all to tell me the truth and help me work through all this if I need it. Mostly though, I want to put this out of my mind and enjoy dessert. Did I smell brownies?"

Now he laughed a real laugh, not loudly, but not with sadness either. "You really *are* amazing, Lainey. I think I've told you that before, but it bears repeating."

"I know," I replied. "But thanks for reminding me."

WE FINISHED DESSERT—I *had* smelled brownies, *and* they were topped with vanilla ice cream and caramel sauce—and coffee, with no more talk of the Perceptum or Sententia or distressing things at all. I felt somewhat relaxed and definitely reassured by the time I needed to head back to campus for curfew. Carter insisted on walking with me, which I knew he would. I would have asked him to do it anyway, if he hadn't volunteered.

By mutual, unspoken agreement, we took the long way, walking slowly and saying little, fingers twined. It was even colder than when I'd left for dinner, but I found it helped clear my head. I tried to focus on nothing but what I was doing that very moment: slow steps on the sidewalk, my and Carter's breath puffing in and out around us, his hand warm in mine. First bell rang as we crossed the street but it was otherwise quiet, most everyone already gone for the holiday. Carter and I were about as alone as we could possibly be on campus, and I stopped us under the giant oak tree between the buildings before we reached my dorm.

I thought maybe he knew what I wanted, from the way his pretty eyes were watching me, glinting with what I thought was a blend of hope and…desire. But he said nothing, just waiting. I said nothing either, watching him too, taking in the moment, his tall frame outlined by moonlight from behind. The cold air practically sparked between us, thick with anticipation.

I waited, not because I was unsure, but because I had an unshakeable feeling that this was…momentous. Special. More important than any other time either of us had done this before. There would be no going back from what I was about to do, I knew for certain. I took a step toward him, until I was close enough to feel the heat from his body and feel my own warm in response.

"I wanted to give something back to you," I said, looking up at him. "Something I stole from you the other day." Recognition instantly sparked in his eyes, chased by delight. Unlike before, I was not tentative or quick, and I did not aim for his cheek. I reached up and kissed him, once gently, and then again, as his arms slipped around my waist and the rest of the world fell away.

KISSING CARTER WAS…electric. I'd thought his smiles were intoxicating, but they were nothing like this. This was dangerous. Addicting. Like a drug I never knew I wanted but now couldn't imagine going very long without. I had no idea how much time we spent there under the oak tree, only that it was not long enough. When we finally broke the kiss, both of us breathing heavily, I found I was up against the trunk of the tree, holding Carter's strong body firmly pressed against mine. I had no recollection of when we got there but I knew that I liked it. We looked at each other, not moving away or speaking, for at least a minute. My breathing did not slow.

"Lainey…" Carter whispered, and he bent and kissed me again, his hands slipping under the edge of my sweater and onto the small of my back. I gasped as his cold fingers reached me and Carter gave a small groan in response. It was just about the sexiest sound I'd ever heard and though I wouldn't have thought it was possible, I pulled him even closer and lost myself in utter bliss.

When we finally pulled apart again, Carter rested his forehead against mine, saying, "God, you have no idea how long I've wanted to do that."

"Probably as long as I have," I teased.

He pulled back and looked at me. "Really? Then what took you so long?"

I stretched up and kissed him once more. "Wasn't it worth the wait?"

"Absolutely," he breathed. "I only wish it hadn't been quite so close to curfew. You missed second bell. I don't want to let go of you, but you should probably go inside before we get caught. Because I'd like to do this again. Very soon."

I laughed and untangled my arms from around him, stepping away from the tree. I instantly missed his warmth and his weight. He ran his hands down the back of my coat, which I could only imagine was covered in bits of tree bark, then took my hand and walked me up to my door. We kissed a final time, before he tore himself away and was down the porch stairs before I had time to protest or stop him.

He turned back around to face me and called softly from there. "Good night, Lainey. If I don't leave now...I'll try not to leave. I'll call you tomorrow." And with that he was gone.

I watched him disappear around the neighboring building and thought that I'd been right: there would be no going back from that. And hell if I wanted to, either.

Smiling hugely to myself, I took my keys out of my pocket as quietly as possible, hoping Ms. Kim was asleep or maybe not here yet. As I was about to step inside, I heard what sounded like someone hurrying off the porch from the side exit. I looked around quickly but saw nothing.

"Carter?" I hissed. Nothing. "Hello?" I said, a little louder.

I hurried around to the side of the porch and scanned the grounds in front of me. I supposed it could have been an animal, but wouldn't an animal have run as soon as we came close? I was about to turn around and head inside when a flash of movement finally caught my eye. Just as she rounded the corner of the library, I saw moonlight glimmer off a fall of short, blond hair over a set of petite shoulders in a dark coat.

I was certain it was Jill.

Chapter Fourteen

I woke the next morning, far earlier than I wanted, to the sound of my phone ringing. I glanced at the clock and groaned, but then scrambled to answer. It wasn't my aunt, as I'd expected, but Carter.

"I was asleep, you know," was how I answered, though it didn't come out nearly as irritably as I'd wanted it too. I sounded a little giddy to my ears. Damn it.

"Good morning to you too," he answered with a laugh. "Come outside."

"WHAT? I just woke up."

"Well, I just ran seven and a half miles. Come outside. Please?" he added.

"You're crazy," I said, but in reality I was delighted by the idea that Carter was waiting for me outside my building at early o'clock in the morning.

"About you," he replied, and it wasn't even sarcastic. I gave an excited little shiver at the thought. "Just come down. I don't care about your bed head. I thought this might be the only chance I got to see you today and I didn't want to miss it."

"Haven't you heard how girls like it when guys act all aloof and barely interested? You're not playing very hard to get. I may get bored of you."

I could practically see his dangerous smile through the telephone and I wished my room overlooked the front of the building. "Come outside and I promise that won't happen," he said and hung up.

I went outside.

But not until after I brushed my teeth.

ON THE WAY to breakfast, I made a call I probably *should* have made the night before, if I hadn't been so exhausted. It was early, but I knew no excuse would keep Amy from killing me if I didn't call her immediately and share the news. I'd had to keep so much from her lately, it felt good to finally have something big I *could* share.

"Lovely Lainey," she answered groggily. "I miss you too, but you didn't have to call so early to tell me. What's up? And it better be quick."

"It's quick," I replied. I was glad she couldn't see my stupid grin through the phone.

"Shoot."

"I did it," I said seriously.

"Define 'it,' Lane. What did you do? You're not sick again, are you?"

"Not even close."

"Spit it out, girl!" she said with a mix of amusement and exasperation. "I'm feeling all suspenseful here, and this is not very quick, by the way, so it better be worth interrupting dreams about my wicked hot boyfriend..."

"How about I tell you maybe I've got a 'wicked hot boyfriend'?"

Silence. "Come again?"

I laughed. "I kissed Carter, Ame. For real kissed him."

And then she screamed. I held the phone away to save my eardrums, until I heard her muffled voice, except she wasn't talking to me. "WHAT?...No, Mom, chill. I'm fine. It's Lainey. She did something freaking awesome...Yeah, exactly! I'll totally tell her. Lane? Lainey?" she said, louder now. "Ok, I'm back. HOLY SHIT. So, for real? Tell me everything. Immediately and in exacting detail. And my mom says 'way to go!' which sounds like something only an old person would say, but she means well. Anyway. DETAILS. Now."

So I told her, as much as I was willing to share, which was far less than she was hoping for.

"Jesus, Lainey, you're killing me. I've been dying to hear about this from anyone for approximately four years, two months, nineteen days, seven hours, and thirty-eight minutes, and all I get is barely more than 'it was great'?! Why oh why did I have to get Miss 'I don't kiss and tell much' as a roommate? I mean, seriously, Lainey, a girl has needs. Help me out. I tell you everything."

"Not because I ask you to!" I said on a laugh. "If you look up 'over-share' in the dictionary, your pretty face is pictured next to it. I mean your *mom* knew what you were screaming about. But I don't know what else to tell you. It was awesome. Imagine your best kiss ever, multiply it by ten, and subtract anything he might possibly have done wrong. And I can count his stomach muscles even through his shirt. There. Does that help?"

She giggled. "A little. But I already knew that, about the ridiculous abs, I mean. Let's just say that track meets were popular events the last few years. I only wish he'd been on the swim team...yeah, anyway. So it really was that good? You're not exaggerating?"

"Not even a little bit. I can't think of how it could have been better, unless maybe he hadn't been wearing a shirt."

She breathed a very un-ladylike word. "I always knew it. He does everything well. The boy really is perfect. It's not fair, but at least he's for you. Alexis is going to flip the F out. I can't wait!"

I pushed open the door to the dining hall then and grabbed a tray. "Try not to tell the whole school before you come back from break, okay?" I told her. "I mean, it's not like we're getting married or anything. We just…hooked up."

She snorted. "Right. That's all it was. Please, Lainey. I'm a genius, remember? Of course you're not getting married right *now*, but you will. Someday. I just…know. I don't need Brooke Barros to tell me this fortune. I can feel it. You two are…something special. But I will restrain myself from spreading the good news, because honestly? I can't wait to see everyone's reactions in person."

AMY WAS RIGHT about our being special, though it wasn't exactly how she thought. Maybe she was psychic too, because as soon as I looked around the mostly empty dining hall for anyone I knew, I saw Brooke Barros sitting by herself at a small table and waving at me.

"For someone so tall and thin, I can't believe you don't eat like a bird. I expected to see nothing but coffee and grapes on your tray," she said good-naturedly as she eyed my breakfast of coffee, scrambled eggs, toast, and grapefruit, pretty much what I ate every morning.

I laughed. "Not me. Swim practice usually makes me starving by breakfast time, though I guess I don't have that excuse this morning."

"I like it," she said. "Most of my friends survive on air and caffeine, so I always feel a little strange when I sit down with, you know, *bread* on my plate." She gave a mock shudder and I laughed again. "I just sat down. Would you like to eat with me?"

That was a surprising gesture. Brooke and I were friendly enough when we saw each other on campus, but I wouldn't have expected her to invite me to hang out with her. I'd always wondered what Brooke was doing with Alexis and those girls, but I figured it had much to do with looks, family, and money, all of which Brooke had in abundance. She was easily the prettiest girl in the sophomore class, with her chestnut hair, brown and gold eyes, and bow-shaped lips. She was also, I was certain, a Sententia. I wondered if she knew about me.

"I'd love to, thank you," I said and took the seat across from her. "Speaking of most of your friends…they don't like me very much. I'm a little surprised—in a good way—you asked me to sit with you."

She waved the idea away with elegant, manicured fingers. "Eh. Who cares what they think? Actually, they're just jealous of you. Well, specifically, *Lex* is jealous of you. You know, if it weren't for rooming with Amy, and the whole Carter thing, I suspect Lex would have tried to make you part of the group. Not that you probably would have been. Your look is dead on, but I don't really think you have it in you."

"Well thank you…I think, anyway," I replied. "I'm pretty sure that was all a compliment."

It was her turn to laugh, a tinkling little sound that I envied. I thought my own laugh was not nearly so feminine. "It was. Nothing about you says 'rich bitch' or 'rich bitch wannabe' so I'm pretty sure you'd have turned Lex down, flat and final."

"I don't think there's anything about you that says 'rich bitch' either, you know," I said honestly.

More of that tinkling sound. "It's in me, don't worry. I was born and bred to be one. Alexis and I actually grew up together. Her mom and my mom lunch together, our dads talk about money together. That kind of thing. And don't get me wrong, I like my friends. They're not all bad, even if sometimes I want to throttle them. But really, I'm friends with Lex because I want to be, not because I feel like I *have* to be. Maybe that's the difference. She'd probably be pissed if she knew I was making friends with the enemy, but she's not my social director."

Wow. Brooke was…kind of awesome. I was rapidly developing a serious girl crush on her. "Don't take this the wrong way," I said, "but I think I might love you a little bit."

She snorted, and even that she did gracefully. "Ha! Thanks, but I'm pretty sure you don't swing my way. There's a certain Northbrook graduate who'd be more than a little disappointed if you did."

"I have no idea who you're talking about," I lied.

"Yeah, ya do," she said, an amused smile turning up the corners of her mouth. "Lex likes to tell people that he's gay, but she says that about any guy who turns her down. Not that many do. I don't think so though."

"He's not gay." I was going for nonchalant, but then I ruined it by blushing.

Her eyes widened. "Oooh. That sounds like you've *personally* confirmed it. Yeah?" She seemed almost as excited as Amy was.

"Maybe," I demurred, and she laughed.

"Nice! I heard that rumor from some seventh grader the other day…but Amy swore to everyone that she'd be the first to know and *she* didn't, so…" she looked back at me, eyebrows raised in question.

I smiled. "It's a…recent development. But, uh, would you mind keeping it to yourself? I don't think we're really, um, putting a label on anything, you know?"

"Secret is safe with me, don't worry. I kind of like being alive, and if I were to go spreading that story before anyone else, I'm not sure who would kill me first: Lex or your roommate."

She stopped and leaned toward me then, a more serious look on her face than I'd seen so far. "Your other secret is safe with me too, honest. Everyone suspects—you *are* Legacy after all—but, oh, I'll just tell you. I sense desires…I can tell what someone wants most at any given time, and when you sat down you were wanting to know if I knew. And so, now I do. But I don't know what your gift is."

I swallowed my toast and looked around hastily. Her voice had been low, but I didn't feel reassured until I saw that we were practically alone in the dining hall. I also didn't feel sure in talking about my gift at all, but I decided to take the plunge and tell her. I swallowed again. "I, um, well, it's kind of creepy," I started, then stalled out.

She shrugged. "It's totally okay, Lainey. You don't have to tell me about it. I just wanted you to know that you could, if you wanted to. I'm a good secret keeper. I have to be. You *really* don't want to know what some people desire most sometimes."

I hadn't thought about that. Yuck. Brooke was probably inundated with things she'd rather not know. "Yeesh. You're probably right about that! But I...I want to tell you. It's just weird to me. I didn't know anything about this stuff before a few days ago, and I'm a little unsure how I feel about it. Plus, like I said, it's a little creepy. I should just spit it out. I...Carter calls me a 'Grim Diviner' which sounds a little better than saying I sense, well, death. How people died, or how they're going to die."

She gave a sympathetic frown. "Oof. Yeah, sorry, that is a tough one. I've sensed some people *wanting* to die, though most of the time they don't mean it, but knowing that they're going to, that's a different story. So you really didn't know anything about what we are before recently? How did you end up here, as a Legacy no less, if you didn't? I've never heard of anything like that happening before."

"Honestly? I don't know. I mean, I know how I got here, but I don't know where the Legacy comes from. It's anonymous. So I'm clueless, but grateful. I like it here, and I guess I belong here too, so it worked out."

"You're so *mysterious*," she joked. "Owner of an anonymous Legacy...able to bag Carter Penrose within moments of arrival...Seriously, I think we'd all like to know your secrets."

So would I, I thought.

      ❧   ❧   ❧

MY AUNT'S ARRIVAL was a whirlwind of hugs and tears—from her—and chatter and laughter, followed by a surprising personal welcome from Headmaster Stewart, who escorted us to my aunt's even more surprisingly plush guest suite. *She's* definitely *angling for a donation,* I thought to myself, but the suite was, well, sweet. After she settled, we bundled up so I could give her a full tour of the campus.

It hadn't snowed yet since I'd been at the school, but it was definitely becoming winter. There was a bite to the air and the bare trees rattled in the chilly breeze. Even so, campus was beautiful on the clear, brisk day, and I enjoyed sharing the school with my aunt. As I told her about it, showing her all my class and favorite buildings, answering her questions about my teachers, schoolwork, and activities, I realized that I really did love it here. The stress of the last few days had slowly eased out of me since the night before, and I was simply happy. Apparently, that was obvious.

My aunt reached over and squeezed my gloved hand. "You're so happy here, Lainey," she said. "I can see it in your eyes, and hear it in how you talk about this school. I miss you so much, but now…I can't imagine wanting to take you from this place. I only wish I could meet some of your friends while I'm here."

That was a wish I'd planned to fulfill. "Actually…" I said, "there is someone I'd like you to meet."

She gave me a knowing, eyebrows-raised-in-interest look. "Is it a boy?" I nodded, and she laughed the girly laugh that sometimes made her feel more like my sister than my mother. "Well, this must be an interesting one, because I don't remember your mentioning a boy in any of our recent weekly conversations."

I just smiled. She'd never know just how interesting he was.

I led her across the street, first to the coffee shop for something to warm us up and then finally to the bookstore. It was getting toward closing time and there were only a handful of customers on the first floor. Carter was behind the register, paging through a newspaper, when we came through the door. The bell jangled and he smiled broadly when he saw us. My aunt leaned close to me as he headed around the counter.

"Well," she said softly, "I sure hope this is him. My my, Lainey, he's a pretty one."

I laughed and tugged her forward. Carter met us halfway between the counter and the door, where he swiftly pulled me close and kissed me on the cheek. "Hi," he said enthusiastically, with another of those beautiful smiles. Beside me, my aunt couldn't keep herself from matching him smile for smile.

"Hi," I returned, while my aunt offered a little "hello" of her own, and then I made my proper introductions. "This is my Aunt Tessa. Auntie, this is Carter Penrose. He and his Aunt Melinda own the bookstore. He graduated from Northbrook last year."

"It's so nice to meet you, Ms. Espinosa," Carter said earnestly, shaking my aunt's hand. "Lainey's told me so much about you these last few weeks, I'm glad to have the chance to meet you in person."

Aunt Tessa gave Carter an approving once over and then turned to look at me before saying, "Well, Carter, it's nice to meet you too. Please call me Tessa. I wish I could say how much I'd heard about you from Lainey, but you're actually quite a surprise. Fortunately, I like surprises, and you look like you might be a delightful one. I take it you're dating my niece?"

He laughed, and I swore that charm, rather than blood, flowed in his veins. "I am if you and she will let me," he replied.

One glance at my aunt told me she was already as smitten as I was, but she said with mock-seriousness, "I'll take it under consideration, Mr. Penrose, and get back to you by the end of the week."

ೋ   ೋ   ೋ

THE WEEK THAT followed, despite my initial disappointment about being stuck around campus, turned out to be one of my best holidays ever. It took not the whole week but approximately twenty more minutes before my aunt was giving me an enthusiastic endorsement. Much as I expected, it took approximately ten minutes less than that for Melinda and her to become fast friends. I honestly couldn't have hoped for things to go any better.

Our shopping trip was not only fun but successful, ending with a tally of five practice items (bought covertly by Carter), one spectacular vintage coat (purchased excitedly by me), and zero migraines or passing out. True to his word, Carter helped me actively seek out pieces that triggered my gift without fainting or experiencing the vision. To my surprise, it was almost simple. Knowing what to expect, and most of all, knowing that I wasn't actually crazy, I was able to relax and blank my mind, letting only a hint of the tell-tale dizziness develop before I'd snatch my hand away from whatever caused it and point it out to Carter.

We endured the pomp of the Academy Thanksgiving and then had a wonderful evening with Carter and the Revells. Jeff's mother, Evelyn, on top of being a delightful woman, made the best pies I'd ever tasted. On the way back to campus from their apartment, drunk on pie and good times and, uh, a little extra wine, I decided it was the perfect time to do a little investigating. Or, more precisely, my mouth did.

"Auntie, was there anything special about my dad?" I randomly blurted out. In retrospect, my brain concluded it was a harmless question and maybe my mouth was on to something. Maybe Aunt Tessa knew a little about his Sententia abilities without really *knowing* about them.

She glanced sideways at me but gave an easy smile before saying fondly, "Of course there was, honey. Your father was a wonderful man."

"But…like what?" I pressed. "What was special about him?"

After a few paces to think about it, she said, "Well, I guess most of the things that made him so wonderful I've told you about before…he was kind, and always generous, very handsome too." She giggled at that, and I surmised she was maybe a little tipsy too, before she went on more seriously. "He was funny…not at all jaded, the way so many people who come from backgrounds like his tend to be. He was obviously a gifted investor, especially for someone so young, but…it was almost odd, his success. This might sound strange, but I always thought of him as the *luckiest* man I knew."

Honestly, that didn't sound strange at all. It sounded Sententia.

THE NEXT DAY, with the added help of a few aspirin, I endured our breakfast with Headmaster Stewart in much the same way as the dinner the night before: smiling often, saying little. As predicted, Dr. Stewart angled for a donation, and my aunt happily assented. To my surprise, however, in addition to a monetary donation, she offered a permanent sculpture installation, which she would complete over the summer.

Dr. Stewart actually smiled when she said, "Thank you, Tessa. That's a generous donation the Academy would be proud to accept," which told me she was beyond excited about it. All the talk of donations got me thinking the headmaster could probably answer some lingering questions of mine.

"Dr. Stewart," I said, "I was wondering if you could tell me a little bit about my Legacy?"

Unfortunately, I was wrong. She set down her teacup and ultimately raised more questions than she answered. "I'm afraid 'a little bit' is all there is to tell, Miss Young. Your Legacy was anonymous. Beyond that, I can tell you its size, which is quite substantial," she replied.

Aunt Tessa was possibly as curious as I was and she asked the next logical question. "Do you know when it was established, Constance? I think Lainey and I have both wondered whether Allen, her father, was responsible for it or not."

"I would assume not," she said, "unless he was a very wealthy and forward-thinking young man. Lainey's Legacy had been waiting to be claimed for forty-four years."

Forty-four years. Since the year my father was born.

Chapter Fifteen

As campus came back to life after the holiday week, word spread quickly about the tragic death of Ashley Thayer, exactly as I had predicted it in what seemed like practically another lifetime ago. Few students were surprised when we were all assembled at the Chapel on Monday morning for her memorial service, myself least surprised among them. I sat in the darkest corner I could find, weeping silently for a girl I didn't know but whose death I bore witness to before anyone else. For the first time of an incalculable many, I would wish I could have found some way to prevent it.

Word spread equally quickly about Carter's and my new relationship, and I suffered many speculative looks, whispered conversations, and more than a few of my classmates asking me to share details. Despite my remaining as closed-lipped as humanly possible, by the end of the next day, I was pretty sure there wasn't a single person on campus who hadn't heard. The camps seemed divided mostly between the envious and the encouraging. No one was openly unfriendly, save for one.

She caught up to me after class and was, surprisingly, alone. I almost felt the hostility before she fell in step beside me. I'd been expecting this, though I thought it would come earlier in the day and as a much more public spectacle.

"So, I hear congratulations are in order. You finally did it, huh?" Alexis said. Her tone was friendly. *Almost.*

I sighed. I kept my voice as level and calm as possible. "I guess so. And I don't want to fight with you, Alex."

"Oh, don't worry," she said. "I don't want to fight with you either. It's actually funny. You think you've won some great prize…Carter Penrose, the beautiful, perfect boy every girl is dying to have, right? What a laugh!"

Okay, this was unexpected, especially coming from Alex, who'd seemed to want him more than anyone. I glanced at her quizzically but said nothing.

"So it's true! You really have no idea."

Maintaining my cool was difficult, but I kept trying. "You're right. I have no idea what you're talking about. Could you just get whatever you want to say over with before I get back to my dorm?"

She laughed again and came to a stop, completely dropping the veneer of friendliness. "Poor Lainey. Sure, I'll make it quick and painless for you. Why don't you ask your new boyfriend *exactly* why he never really attended classes here. And after that, ask your roommate how many girlfriends her buddy has gone through in the last few years. You're the flavor of the month, Lainey; you just don't know it. But I'll give you a tip before I go: don't get too comfortable in those handsome arms. They'll only be around you until he realizes it's going to take too long for you to give it up." And with that she turned and walked away.

SPEAKING OF THE devil apparently works, because mine was sitting on the porch steps when I arrived at my dorm. He jumped up when he saw me and pulled me to him so quickly that I didn't think to stop him. Honestly, I didn't know what to think. Alexis's ugly words were on constant replay in my head. I didn't want to believe them, but thanks to her gift, it was so easy to believe anything she said. But I also didn't believe she'd flat out lie to me. Couldn't anything in my life be simple right now?

I realized Carter was still holding me tightly and also talking. "...take my break, before it gets crazy at the store later, and see how your day was."

"I..." was all I managed to squeak.

He stepped back and looked at me closely, frowning. "What happened?"

"I just talked to Alexis."

"Whatever she said about you or us doesn't matter."

I fidgeted. "Actually...it was mostly about you. And what I don't know about you."

His face darkened and he looked like he wanted to spit. It was kind of how I felt too. "Let's go for a walk and figure this out. Forget all about Alexis."

He grabbed my book bag and then my hand, leading me off the steps and toward the gates. We started walking down Main Street, past all the shops and the bookstore, until he turned abruptly and, for the second time, tugged me onto a path into the bordering woods. Somehow they had become our confessional.

"Okay," he finally said. "Tell me."

I didn't want to. In fact, I wanted nothing more than for the words, and maybe even their speaker, to disappear completely. But the longer I kept them in, the more they seemed to resound in my head. I settled for simply repeating her terrible speech calmly and as closely to what she'd said as I could. Carter listened quietly and then sighed. He let go of my hand to run his through his hair and across his face, as if he suddenly had a headache. He looked angry but also a little dejected.

"Oh my God, it's true!" I gasped. *That* got his attention. His face darkened even more and he reached out to take me by the shoulders.

"No it is absolutely *not* true," he said vehemently. "You are not 'the flavor of the month' and it kills me that you might have thought that for even a few seconds, let alone the last ten minutes."

"So she was lying then," I said, but didn't entirely believe it.

He looked around us quickly, and then tugged me to the ground and sat cross-legged facing me, grabbing both my hands. He looked down at them while he said, "She wasn't lying either," then returned my gaze sadly. "Just...saying things in a way that would make me look bad."

I stared at him for a second and then decided to warm my hands in my own pockets. "Okay...so please make yourself not look bad."

He started at the beginning and I listened, with what I hoped was an open heart and mind. I couldn't believe that everything I thought I knew about Carter was disingenuous. But I didn't want to be a fool either.

"My never going to classes is just coincidental," he said. "But the *why*...well, it mostly has to do with my dad dying. He died and I was an orphan and it hurt. So I looked for as many ways as possible to make it not hurt. When I was fourteen, I found a girl who was looking for the same thing." He paused and looked at me, and I understood without words. Really, I should have known where this was going all along.

"You're telling me that in, what, in *eighth grade*...you...?" I wasn't quite able to complete the thought aloud.

"It was between eighth and ninth but, yeah, I...lost my virginity."

Okay, wow. I never thought of myself as a prude, but I suddenly felt like one. Having sex before high school kind of...shocked me. Intellectually I knew kids did, but I'd never entertained the idea that my boyfriend, or whatever Carter was, was one of them. Fourteen was only two years younger than I was, but it seemed like such a long two years. I also knew I was blushing furiously and damned my pale skin for always giving me away.

"I'm not proud of it," he went on, "but I won't deny it either. I wish I'd waited, but well, I didn't. And I haven't waited. With other girls too, I mean. I've been with…a few more since then." He looked down at his empty hands and said morosely, "Honestly, for a while, with anyone who'd have me."

Given his appearance alone, I imagined the list of the willing was long. So far none of this was making him look better and I said so.

"I know," he sighed, "and I'm sorry. A million times over. But I haven't lied to you yet, and I don't plan to start now. I'm not perfect, Lainey. If you expect me to be, I promise I will only disappoint you. And I don't want to. Disappoint you, I mean, though it seems like that's what keeps happening. If you didn't want to be with me, I'd understand. And probably deserve it."

I was mulling that over when his low voice started again, as much as if he were thinking out loud as talking to me. "I knew Alex would be jealous of you, but I never thought she'd try something like *this*. I suppose I should have known better, especially since she knew you'd believe her." He cursed and shook his head. "You know, I've never really talked about this with anyone but my Uncle Jeff, and that was only after I finally admitted to myself what an ass I was."

"What did he say?"

He laughed sadly. "Not much, which should be no surprise. Actually, the first thing he did was, well, haul me off to the doctor's for every test imaginable…I was always safe—I might be an idiot, but I'm not stupid—but he insisted it was the necessary thing to do, and the responsible one."

I had to agree with that. As my initial shock began to dissipate, I gave silent thanks to my aunt for being such a great mother. She'd been talking frankly about sex with me long before I'd been remotely interested in it. Without her, I imagined this conversation would have been impossible.

Carter continued his quiet confession while my mind churned. "After that…he told me it was time to grow up, wise up, and think farther ahead than tomorrow. It's advice I remind myself of every day. And then…then he talked about my aunt. That probably sounds strange, right? But it wasn't. He told me about what it was like to love my aunt, and that someday I'd find someone I could love the same way. *That's* what would take the hurt away. I remind myself of that daily too."

He stopped then, and I let my thoughts tumble in the resulting silence. Facing difficult realities was starting to feel like a daily occurrence. It felt like I'd had more than my share of challenges already. Obviously Carter had too. But life and love were never going to be easy, and I admitted that maybe I *had* been thinking Carter was practically perfect. Maybe that was unfair. Or maybe he only had to be perfect *for me,* flaws and all. Ultimately, I kept coming back to one simple, important question. So I asked him.

"All I want to know is this: will you wait for me?"

His smile was sad but genuine. "You don't get it, Lainey. I've been waiting for *you* for years. I'll keep waiting as long as you want me to."

ON OUR WAY back to campus, I finally remembered the bizarre connection that started the whole conversation. "What's the coincidence?" I asked.

"Hm?"

"It was the first thing Alexis said," I reminded him. "This—somehow—has something to do with your not going to classes here. You said it was a coincidence."

"Oh, that," he said. "It's true, that there's a connection, but it really is a coincidence. Sententia gifts…well, sometimes having sex can jumpstart developing gifts. Bring them to full strength. We don't know why, exactly, a chemical reaction in the brain or an incomplete connection that's sparked…"

"I take it you were sparked?"

He laughed softly. "I woke up and all of a sudden I could remember…*everything*. It was a little overwhelming at first, to put it mildly. I'd always found school pretty easy, but that seemed like struggling compared to what I can do now. What I could suddenly do then. I started at the Academy for my freshman year, but it only took a few weeks to realize that sitting in class all day was pointless. In that year, I finished what would have been most of my entire four years' worth of education."

"Wow. My brain hurts just trying to imagine that. But…why didn't you go to the Academy in seventh or eighth grade?"

"Because the Penroses are scholarship students, not Legacies. It was part of my family's original agreement with the Perceptum, but the school was only the equivalent of a high school then, so we're only invited starting in the ninth grade. I didn't graduate from the Academy right away, though I could have, because I didn't want to give up my high school years *entirely*. So I did advanced projects, things like that, and mostly played sports and had a little bit of a social life within the Academy other than serving my classmates at the bookstore." We'd reached the Academy's gates and he stopped outside of them. "Speaking of which…I really have to get back. I'm sorry."

"It's okay," I said. "Unlike you, my homework is going to take me a few hours." I started to take a step toward school, but instead he pulled me back into his arms, so tightly I almost couldn't breathe. He didn't kiss me though, just held on.

"Lainey…I *am* sorry," he said, as he tucked my head under his chin. "I don't deserve you, but I'm grateful you'll still have me."

AMY FOUND ME later sitting on my bed, staring absently at the wall, not doing my hours of homework.

She looked at my vacant expression and threw herself down next to me. "What are you doing, deeply contemplating my excellent choice of paint color? What's up with you?"

I told her the whole story, starting with Alexis's accusations right through Carter's sordid history. I didn't hesitate before I decided to share *everything*. Amy might have loved gossip, but she didn't like to spread misery.

"God, I hate that bitch," she said when I was done. "I mean, seriously. Hate her. I've always known she was a bitch, but she's outdone herself this time. Jealousy is *so* ugly."

"Did you know?" I asked her. Alexis had intimated that she did, and so far there'd been some truth to everything she'd said.

Amy sighed, her perfect eyebrows dropping down over her eyes. "Ah, sort of, I guess. No, don't be pissed at me. I didn't know *all* the details…I figured Carter wasn't a perfect angel, and yeah, I knew he'd had his fair share of girlfriends. More than fair share, obviously. But honestly, even if I'd known the whole gory truth, I'd still be happy you were with him. I *am* happy you're with him. I mean it. None of this changes my opinion of Carter. Mistakes in his past or not, he *is* a good guy and he's my friend. I'm glad you didn't dump him. I think I'd have punched Alexis in the mouth if you did."

That image made me laugh and it felt good. "I might still do it myself, so don't steal my thunder."

Amy joined in my laughter and gave me an impromptu hug. "You just being you is enough to ruin her whole day. You don't even need to punch her." I lapsed into silence again until I found Amy's arm creeping back around my shoulder. "Okay," she said. "What's really bugging you? It's obviously more than Carter's past. Can I have three guesses what it is?"

I was having trouble articulating to myself what was wrong, or, to be honest, I didn't *want* to spell it out. "Go for it," I told her. I should have known she wouldn't need three guesses. She wasn't guessing at all.

"Now you're worried about the sex thing. Because you've never done it and he has, lots of times, and you're afraid you either won't be good enough or he really will get bored of waiting until you're ready. How'd I do? Pretty close?"

Yeah, that was a bulls eye. "Is it so obvious? How did you know?"

She sighed again. "Because I've been there, Lane. That was me, two years ago, except the guy really was a first class jerk and I was just a naïve freshman mooning over the upperclassman. Fourteen really isn't all that young," she added softly at the end.

I found myself shocked again. I knew she wasn't a virgin, but I'd never asked about any of the details. "I...never thought you'd have been naïve about anything. What happened?"

"It is surprising, isn't it? As for what happened...I honestly thought I'd be the girl who got the guy and kept him. No surprise, but I wasn't. Like an idiot, I gave it up way too soon, and like the skilled player he was, he kept on with me just long enough afterwards that he didn't look like a complete ass to everyone else."

Now it was my turn to hug her. "I'm sorry, Ame. That sucks. I don't know what else to say."

She waved her hand. "Ancient history. I hated myself for a little while afterwards, mostly for being so stupid—some genius, huh?—but it hardly feels important anymore. He's gone to college and gotten a fat beer gut, and I have a fabulous, sexy boyfriend who I actually think loves me. What's to feel bad about anymore?"

Her boyfriend *definitely* loved her, no doubt. I would have been embarrassed to ask my next question to anyone else. "Have you...been with anyone else since then?"

"Yeah," she replied without hesitation. "Two guys. Neither one of them are Caleb, by the way. Not yet, anyway." I knew that, because she told me *everything*, and I was certain would tell me that happy news as soon as it happened. "Neither one is from Northbrook either. And I mean, it's not like I'm whoring around or whatever. I wish my first had ended up being more special, but I don't regret the times since."

As was often the case, I envied Amy's positive attitude, and despite my previous life as a world traveler, felt infinitely less sophisticated than her. My next question I actually *was* embarrassed to ask, but I went ahead and asked anyway, softly, my trademark blush lighting up my face. "What's it like?"

This time she laughed at me. "That depends. Do you want me to tell you it's all magic and rainbows, or do you want me to tell you the truth?"

I couldn't help but laugh too. "The truth, please."

"Well," she said, "I'm sorry to be the bearer of bad news, but at first, it might not be real great. It might even hurt a little. But there's a reason people seem to enjoy it so much...it just takes a little while to understand. After that though, well, sometimes it can be magical. And being with someone who respects you really helps."

"Thank you," I said. "For understanding. And especially for being honest with me. I appreciate it."

She bounded up off my bed and over to her desk, pulling out books as she went. "My pleasure," she said. "Who else is going to tell you the dirty truth?" Then she giggled. "Hopefully I put you off the idea completely."

"This whole day has put me off the idea completely."

She laughed, but I wasn't exactly joking.

THE FALLOUT FROM my showdown with Alexis was...a little ugly. The day after our disastrous confrontation, she came into the bookstore with her friends, a bold move if you asked me. I doubted she noticed I was there because I was at the end of the counter, talking to Melinda. Carter was in the storeroom, but I think he must have heard her before he saw her. His face was already stormy when he came up the back stairs.

"Carter..." was all I got out before he walked straight past me and into the lounge area. I didn't want to move—actually, I wanted to disappear—in case she saw me, so I stayed where I was and tried to remain inconspicuous. Melinda gave me an understanding smile and squeezed my hand. She also gave a little shrug, as if she knew this was coming and couldn't stop it. I willed myself not to watch, but I found I couldn't help it. At least it was brief.

Carter walked directly up to Alexis—she hadn't even had a chance to sit down—and pointed to the door. "You need to leave."

He wasn't polite, he wasn't quiet, and he didn't apologize.

Much to my amazement, she played coy. "I'm sorry?" she said, offering up a dazzling smile I was sure would have distracted any other guy.

Carter was not having it. "What the *fuck*, Alex! You're not stupid, so don't pretend to be. You. Need. To. Leave. Either that, or apologize—and mean it." If the whole room hadn't been watching already, they were absolutely riveted now.

I was sure she wasn't used to being called out, pretty much ever, and it deflated her almost instantly. She looked down and fiddled with the strap on her bag, her words coming out in a faint stammer. "I...I'm sorry, Carter. It was just a joke, you know? I'd have told her that the next time I saw her."

Carter actually laughed. "I was wrong. Maybe you are stupid, or you think I am. It wasn't a joke, and you and I both know it. And I'm not looking for an apology for *me*. Lainey's right over there"—he gestured to where I lurked at the counter, with a truly mortified expression on my face, I was sure—"so you can apologize now, and *mean it*, or you can go."

He turned abruptly and walked toward the counter, leaving her gaping at his back. The murderous look she gave me was followed quickly by what I thought were genuine tears—Carter couldn't see her, so they weren't for his benefit, and certainly not for mine—before she ran out the front door, leaving her friends standing dumbstruck. After a few unsure moments of glancing between us and the door, they picked up their bags and followed after Alexis. The rest of the room erupted into excited whispers, and I hid my face in Carter's shoulder, both embarrassed and secretly pleased.

A few days later, I ran into Brooke, again, alone in the dining hall. Winter activities started after Thanksgiving, and because I couldn't sing or dance or debate and, despite my height and Coach Anderson's heavy recruitment, wasn't interested in basketball, I had joined the volleyball team. I missed my excuse for getting up early—swim practice—so I decided to do it anyway. I went to breakfast by myself, using the time to read a book for fun or finish up some homework. Until I found Brooke, anyway. Then I used the time to gossip about the enemy camp.

Strangely, I'd already seen more of Brooke since break than I had the whole first part of the year, since she also played on the volleyball team. *Kicked ass* on the volleyball team was more like it, because though she might have been small, she had a wicked serve. But despite that I saw her every afternoon, we never got to talk privately.

"What on earth are you doing here at this hour?" I asked, smiling as I dropped my bag into an empty seat.

"Waiting for you," she said, and laughed that delightful laugh of hers. I ran off to fill my tray before I settled back at the table for the first of what would become our weekly breakfast dates.

She gave me a sympathetic look and said, "So obviously I, uh, heard about what happened." It was a vague statement, but we both knew exactly what she was talking about.

"It's not a big deal," I said, and she laughed again.

"Lainey, seriously? It's the biggest deal here all year! Lex has a good game face, but she's never been so embarrassed. All I can say is it's a good thing you're not going out for the drama production, or I swear she'd bust a vein."

Brooke really had a keen ability to make me smile, rivaled only by Carter's and Amy's. I appreciated it immensely. "I kind of feel like I'm already *in* the drama production, if you know what I mean."

"Totally," she agreed. "That's what's killing Lex the most. She thought she'd orchestrated this great scheme, and it completely backfired on her. But that's her tragic flaw—we're doing a drama unit in English, right?—arrogance. She can't believe that *everyone* else doesn't think she's as amazing as she thinks she is, because, with her gift, most of them do. You probably hate her, for good reason, but I just feel sad about it. She can be great if she wants to. I just wish she weren't so spoiled."

"I...don't hate her," I said, and realized it was true. "Not really. I mean, I don't really *like* her either, but definitely not hate. I...think I feel sad for her too."

Brooke snorted, but delicately, like she did everything except play volleyball. "I promise not to tell her that! She probably would bust a vein then."

"Well, even I wouldn't wish that on her..."

"For such a pretty girl, she does get ugly sometimes." Brooke paused, sighed, then brightened again. "But I have a great idea! Let's not talk about Lex anymore and you tell me *all* about dating Carter Penrose, yeah?"

I laughed and then I told her, just a little bit.

Chapter Sixteen

Naturally, I tried to spend as much time with Carter as possible, even if it was only studying in the bookstore lounge some evenings—not always the most conducive place for *actual* studying—and I began a ritual of having dinner with his family on Sundays. We also began a ritual of meeting on Wednesday evenings for my official Sententia practice sessions.

The third floor of the library housed the Academy's Special Collections—its historical documents and donated artifacts. It was also closed to the student population in the evenings, making it the perfect location for our needs, private and neutral. Most of the floor was divided between displays for the collections and a space for class meetings and guest lectures, but the back half featured a handful of library tables and a few stacks of Academy and local history books. This was where Carter and I sat, staring at a box of cutlery.

An expensive box of antique silver cutlery, to be exact, and one that was making me lightheaded and nauseous. It was the week before Christmas and our third Wednesday meeting. I had done pretty well at my previous practice working with a wooden stool from which I'd seen clearly how a man toppled off of it and broke his neck. It was awful, of course, but I was able to watch the vision three times without passing out, and one time I was able to keep myself from having the vision at all. My head ached when I was done, and I was exhausted, but I felt like I'd accomplished something.

Carter had wanted to work with the same object, to have me try to prevent the vision consistently, and possibly read more from it, but I said no. I wanted to work on the not passing out first and foremost, and, well, there were only so many times I could watch a man die before I wanted to take a break from his tragedy. So instead, I was waiting for a vision of someone else's likely tragedy. But it wasn't coming. And I was *trying* to have it.

"I just feel sick again," I said in frustration.

Carter picked up my hand from where it rested on the mahogany lid of the silverware set's box and kissed it gently. This was one of the problems with our practice sessions: staying on task. I was easily distracted and my tutor was the distraction. "You aren't actually sick, are you?" he asked.

"No. I feel fine otherwise. Now. This set is definitely *something*; I'm just not seeing it."

"Maybe you're not close enough to whatever piece was involved." He opened the lid so we could see the dully gleaming forks and knives and spoons. It was an enormous set, in a heavy case with a lid that flipped up and two drawers of specialty and serving pieces. I felt bad that Carter had had to lug it all the way over to the library, but since I found him distracting enough in this setting, I *really* didn't think practicing in his apartment was a good idea. Especially since his aunt was still at work.

"Try again," he suggested.

I dutifully rested my hand over the stacks of silverware, closed my eyes, and concentrated on opening my senses. *My own personal death senses*, I thought glumly. I couldn't exactly focus them yet, not specifically in the way I could concentrate on hearing or touch or taste, but I *could* tell when I was resisting them. The pressure in my head increased. Carter believed that was why I so frequently fainted and had migraines, because I was fighting the gift, making my brain shut down in order to protect itself. If I worked *with* the gift, and felt my way through the visions, I shouldn't have those problems. Unfortunately, this time all I felt was more dizzy. The vision would not come.

I sighed. "Still nothing. Just dizzy. If I keep up with the dizzy much longer I'm going to pass out just from that."

Carter thought for a moment. "Maybe you'll need to find the specific piece that was involved. It's obviously not the case. Probably not any of the pieces your hand was touching directly either."

I sighed again and began to repeat my process, picking up pieces of silverware one by one. I started with the sharp knives, thinking they were the most obvious choices, moved on to forks, and was halfway through the teaspoons when my dizziness spiked.

Out of instinct, I dropped the spoon, watching it clatter across the table. Resisting was a hard habit to break, but at least it gave me a moment to prepare myself. I took a deep breath and picked up the spoon again.

Dizziness washed over me, but I gritted through it and concentrated on the vision. It's hard to know what to expect when you're about to see someone's death, but what happened next was completely outside of any scenario I'd considered. In my vision, an aristocratic young woman sat down at an elegant table, stirring the contents of a pretty teacup with the spoon I now held. She looked up and said something—what, I'll never know, since I had no audio during these visions—to a handsome man sitting across from her. He looked like he'd walked out of an old painting of British men on a foxhunt.

He was also cleaning a rifle of some sort, so maybe he *had* just returned home from a foxhunt. Wherever he'd been didn't matter compared to what happened next. He opened his mouth to respond to the woman when the gun bucked wildly in his hands. A split second later, most of the woman's face exploded.

I dropped the spoon again, looked at Carter in shock, and promptly blacked out.

WHEN I CAME to, I was looking up at the library ceiling, my head resting in Carter's lap. His hands stroked my hair and the side of my face. My head was positively throbbing, even more than usual after one of these incidents.

Carter saw my open eyes and gave me a small smile. "You had to fall off your chair away from me, didn't you? You hit your head before I could catch you. Sorry." I tried to sit up, but the edges of my vision got blurry. Carter gently pushed me back down. "Easy there," he said. "Why don't you just lie still for a little while, okay?"

I groaned. "Please don't tell anyone! My aunt, I mean, mostly. I'll have to stay here for all of Christmas break if she hears I passed out again."

"I won't tell her," he said, laughing. "Promise. Though it is tempting. Would make my birthday a lot better if you were around."

I couldn't believe I'd overlooked it, but I realized I didn't know when Carter's birthday was. "It will be your birthday while I'm away? Damn. When is it?"

He nodded. "It will be while you're away. I was actually born on Christmas Day."

"That kind of sucks. I bet you always get screwed on presents, huh?"

His eyes took on a sad cast that confused me. "It does suck," he said, "but it's also the day my mom died, so that sucks more."

I clapped my hand over my mouth in both surprise and embarrassment. "I'm so sorry," I said and then repeated, grabbing his free hand with mine and giving it a squeeze. "I had no idea."

"It's okay." He was quiet for a moment, looking across the room and stroking my hair a little more. "It's been almost nineteen years...I've kind of gotten used to it. But yeah, Christmas has never been my favorite holiday. My father always told me I was the best gift he ever got, which I think is what most parents say to their kids, right? I believe he meant it, but I guess I was an expensive gift. I cost him his wife." I didn't know what to say to that, so I just held his hand tighter. He looked back down at me and smiled a little. "I don't know when your birthday is either."

"February eighteenth," I told him. "I should have come on a holiday too. Aunt Tessa tells me my mom was due on Valentine's Day, but I insisted on waiting a few days more."

He laughed lightly. "You've always been stubborn, huh? That's right around the Winter Ball...a good time to celebrate."

I had already heard talk of the famed Winter Ball. Apparently Northbrook didn't hold a traditional prom in the spring, like most high schools, because the school year ended earlier here and because, well, they seemed to like doing things differently. So they chose to have a formal ball in the slowest part of the year—the deep of winter.

I hadn't given it too much thought, but I supposed I was looking forward to it. I'd never been to any school dance before, but having seen other events put on by the Academy, I had every expectation the Winter Ball should be lavish. I supposed I should nail down my date in advance too.

"Will you go with me?" I asked Carter. I honestly didn't know the answer. I thought he would, but I didn't get the impression he'd ever gone to anything but sporting events when he was an actual student.

He smiled. "With you? Yes, absolutely. It will be my first Winter Ball," he added, confirming my suspicions. I told him it would be mine too, my first dance of any kind. "It'll be fun," he promised.

ꙮ   ꙮ   ꙮ

TRUE TO HIS word, Carter told no one about my fainting in the library, and I was free to get away for three glorious weeks in sunny Mexico with Aunt Tessa and her family. Christmas for me meant beaches and bikinis, not snow and scarves. I'd never experienced a white Christmas and, except for Carter's birthday, I wasn't disappointed to be missing one this year either.

The fourth week we had off I spent with Amy in Boston. I liked Amy's mom and Amy clearly loved her even if they were almost complete opposites. Mrs. Moretti was very balanced and mellow, and though they looked similar, everything about Amy was just...*more*. Amy was prettier, curvier, bubblier, more spontaneous, more hotheaded, and, well, more my best friend. I had no idea how much I'd missed her until I was back in her company.

The Morettis' house was *amazing*, an enormous three stories of Victorian perfection, a few miles outside the city proper. Of course, I was forced to make that observation in only about two minutes, because Amy took me on the fastest tour of a twenty-room house that was humanly possible before dragging me into her giant third-floor room, locking the door, and flopping into one of two chairs by the windows overlooking her back yard.

"Your house..." is so beautiful, I started to say, but Amy cut me off completely.

"Thanks, I know. So we did it. Finally," she said excitedly.

"Er." She'd changed the subject so abruptly, I had no idea what she meant. I didn't have time to ask before she went on.

"Me and Caleb," she clarified. "We *finally* had sex!"

Of *course* that's what she meant. I smiled hugely at the not-exactly-surprising news. I knew I didn't need to say much because, like everything, she wanted to tell me about it. The hardest part was getting her to spare me some of the details.

I stuck with single-word responses so that I could at least express a complete thought before being interrupted again. "Great! When?"

"Christmas Eve. And twice last week." I, naturally, blushed, but there was little point in trying to stop her. "But the first time was Christmas Eve. I drove out to his parents' house to meet them—his town is only about half an hour from here—but then they had to leave to go to some party, and his brother was already gone, so yeah, Caleb and I had the house to ourselves. They're really nice, by the way, his parents. I think they liked me, I guess probably until they find out what I did to their youngest son after they left…"

I hoped they wouldn't find out, not any time soon anyway, because I was sure they wouldn't want to hear about even half of what Amy proceeded to tell me. Caleb had been a virgin, apparently, but certainly wasn't anymore.

After the big reveal, I got another, more formal tour of the house, and it was as beautiful and impressive as I'd thought it was but hadn't had time to appreciate. We spent most of the week hanging out, doing homework, and going to parties at her local friends' houses in the evenings, where we talked, laughed, and occasionally had a few drinks of whatever alcohol the hosts had managed to steal from their parents or get their older siblings to buy for them.

This, I imagined, was what most sixteen-year-olds did on their school vacations. It was foreign to me, but fun. The more time I spent doing normal things, the more I realized that I really wasn't normal at all, in a way that had nothing to do with the absolutely-not-normal secret ability I was carrying around. I had grown up on the move, with adults as my most constant companions. Sometimes I felt like I was twenty-six, maybe even thirty-six, instead of sixteen. I related this discovery to Amy while we did something else I'd never done before: shopped for dresses with a girlfriend.

"Lane, relax," Amy said, holding up at least the twentieth dress in front of me before putting it back on the rack with a shake of her head. "You're perfect. People like you because you're not a typical sixteen-year-old. That's why *I* like you. I mean, that's not the *only* reason, but it's part of what makes you so fabulous. You're smart and fun and sexy as hell. So what if you've spent more time reading books than gossiping on the phone, or more time at fancy art receptions than going to the mall." She waved her hand at the racks around us. "No one cares. Neither should you."

I wanted to argue that I'd spent plenty of time in Saks, which is where we'd started our quest for the perfect Winter Ball dresses, but mostly I went with my aunt or by myself. That didn't exactly make my case.

Instead I said, "I think some of the kids I met last night cared. I swear, I could barely talk to them, and I don't usually have trouble talking to people I don't know. I mean, I grew up having to do it on an almost daily basis. Everyone last night was just so…normal, I guess."

"God, would you get over the 'normal' thing? There's no normal. You're not abnormal. Just different. We're all different. And those kids at the party aren't normal either. They're…average," she said, and then giggled. "Is it really so upsetting that you can't figure out how to talk and flirt with average guys? You've got me. And *Carter*. What on earth could those so-called 'normal' guys have to say that could intrigue you?"

I couldn't help but laugh with her, and silently thank my lucky stars or whatever it was that had given me such a great friend. "You're right. There is no normal. I don't know what I am, but it's not normal. And I guess neither are you. And that's okay."

"Hells yeah!" she said, then added, "And neither is *this*." She held up a black dress in front of me. But it wasn't just any black dress. It was, I couldn't deny, *the* black dress. It was short and strapless, with a sweetheart neckline and intricate folds of expensive satin that looked like they'd hug everything just right. I was in love. And afraid to put it on.

"I...I've never worn anything like that," I stammered. I'd worn plenty of dresses to art events and galas with my aunt, but never anything quite so...drop dead sexy.

Amy rolled her eyes before laying it over her arm along with the few dresses we'd picked out for her. "There's a first time for everything, Lainey."

It fit even better than I'd imagined.

Chapter Seventeen

The return to campus after winter break was a flurry of both snow and activity. I was quickly back in the routine of classes, sports practice and matches, work hours, homework, and friends and Carter whenever I could fit them in. Sometimes it seemed as though the most alone time I had with Carter was during our weekly practices.

I was steadily improving, quickly even, I thought. The more I used it, the more I learned not to fight my gift. I hated having to witness death after death, was sure I would always hate it, but I found by accepting it was part of being me—like it or not—and that the visions were inevitable anyway, I was able to control my abilities, rather than let them control me. I secretly practiced all the time, whenever I had the opportunity or a handy object. The only thing I avoided practicing on was people, for obvious reasons. I'd already witnessed one of my classmates' deaths this year and had no interest in seeing more.

Though it had been somewhat dangerous, I'd risked having an "episode" and practiced while I was on break. It had helped me, actually, because I was relaxed, without classes or homework or anything to worry about. Exercising my Diviner sense was easier than usual, and after the third week in Mexico, I felt my risk of passing out or developing a migraine was pretty low. Unfortunately, that wasn't the only risk involved. A few days after I'd arrived at Amy's, I was nearly caught.

"What are you doing?" Amy had asked me, one eyebrow arched in curiosity and a little bit of suspicion, as she stood in the doorway to her bathroom, tightening the belt on her bathrobe.

I was so startled, I squeaked and dropped the gold and opal ring I'd been holding. Thankfully it landed on the dresser and only skittered a little across the surface before I caught it. I'd been so intent on letting the vision of Amy's grandmother's death play out, I hadn't heard the door open.

"S...Sorry!" I stammered, wracking my brain for an excuse. "I've seen you wear it before and I just love that ring. I think it must be an antique."

In fact, I knew it was an antique, simply by looking at it, but also because it had most definitely belonged to Amy's grandmother and she'd most definitely been wearing it when she'd died. Normally, such a simple death—she'd passed peacefully in her sleep—would amount to a split-second awareness on my part, barely a vision at all. But after concentrating on replaying it like Carter had coached me, I'd seen more. None of it was particularly interesting—an old woman brushing her teeth, putting on her pajamas, and climbing into bed—but I'd never before been able to force more of a vision to develop. I was fascinated by the truest form of morbid curiosity.

Amy made a sad sound. "Yeah, it is. And I love it too. It was my grandmother's. She died last year."

"I'm sorry," I said. "It is beautiful though. You're lucky to have it to remind you of her."

"I am, I guess. I always think of her when I wear it...but what's with you?" I gulped, probably audibly, but before I had to ask what she meant, she was continuing her thought. "I mean, I swear that's the third time this week I've seen you touching something like...like you're meditating on it or something."

"I..." and I blushed, I could feel it, but it gave me inspiration for my excuse. "This is lame, sorry, but I love antiques—you know that, right?" She rolled her eyes at this. Everyone knew I loved antiques. "Well, sometimes I like to imagine stories about their history. I guess I do it more obviously than I thought I did."

This excuse worked because it was the tiniest bit true. I did that. Sometimes. Much to my relief, Amy seemed to accept it. She smiled and then laughed at me as she came over to the dresser where I was standing. She picked up her grandmother's ring, turning it over in her hand. "You really are strange sometimes, Lainey, but I love that about you. If you want, though, I could tell you a little about my grandmother. Then you wouldn't have to imagine this ring's history..."

I listened gratefully to her stories about her grandmother. She seemed like a wonderful lady, and I was happy to let Amy talk about her, but I was even happier to have gotten out of my predicament. In my eagerness to explore my Sententia abilities, I'd been reckless with guarding my secret. I was afraid of what Dr. Stewart would say if she found out I'd slipped up.

"It's harder for you, because this is all so new to you," Carter said. We were in the library for our first official practice after break and I finally admitted to my almost screw-up with Amy. "It gets easier. The hiding. Becomes second nature, really, the longer you do it." At this, he shifted uncomfortably in his seat and then stood, pacing near his chair. "About being Sententia, I mean..." He trailed off before sitting back down abruptly. "In a way, we all have to live two lives. You'll get used to it," he promised, and, in a gesture of affection I never tired of, reached over to brush his hand through my hair, distracting me completely from his odd behavior of a moment ago.

I wasn't entirely sure I would get used to carrying my secret, but I supposed I had no choice. What I *was* getting used to was my gift it-self. I improved noticeably every week. If I wanted to, I could stop myself fairly regularly from having a vision, which was an important skill, but at the same time, having the visions wasn't as burdensome as it had been in the past.

This week we'd gone back to the wooden stool, and, much like when I'd been holding Amy's ring, I'd been able to regress my vision to see several pertinent scenes leading up to the man's unfortunate accident. Not in a time-lapse replay of his last days or moments, but a replay of scenes that had some relation to the impending death. With Amy's grandmother, I hadn't initially seen the connection. Now I real-ized how in each scene, she'd rubbed her chest a little, the only indicator of what was to come. If I were a detective, these would be the clues I uncovered.

This development was a major breakthrough, one I was proud of and knew I'd continue to explore, but it had made me tired of practice for the night. Thankfully, my favorite distraction was sitting across from me, and still had his hand resting warmly on the side of my neck. I put the stool on the table and climbed out of my chair and onto his lap. His eyes flared in a tantalizing way as his hands circled my waist to steady me.

"I can get used to this too," I said, brushing my fingers over his lips before I kissed them.

At almost the exact moment our lips touched, we heard the eleva-tor bell ding across the room. Carter hastily slid me from his chair onto my own, as I reached for the stool and pulled it back into my lap. The elevator doors glided open, revealing Dr. Stewart striding into the room. Just as hastily, we stood up to greet her.

"Ms. Young, Mr. Penrose. Hard at work, I'm pleased to see," she said, coming to a halt in front of us and looking us both up and down suspiciously. "How are your studies progressing?"

Carter jumped in immediately. "Lainey's progressing amazingly," he said, giving the headmaster a full-wattage smile I knew would do nothing but piss her off. "She's come even further than the last time we spoke. Right before break." If possible, his smile grew, and I knew it implied the...*which was the last time we met, so why are you here asking this question?* that he'd left unsaid.

I had to stifle my own smile, since I could see how Carter irritated her, but as always, she was collected and straight-faced. She turned her direct scrutiny on me, where I stood, stupidly holding the stool.

"Do you agree with Cartwright's assessment? Are you progressing 'amazingly'?" Even if her face didn't sneer, her words certainly did. Sometimes I really disliked the headmaster, but respectful—and honest—were the keys to living with her while a student.

"I'm not sure I'd describe it exactly that way," I replied, "but I do think I've come a long way." I recounted to her everything I'd been able to do.

"Impressive," she said when I finished, though she didn't honestly sound impressed. It was better than condescending, at least. Then she surprised me. "It's time for your first test." She held out a short length of rope I hadn't noticed she'd been carrying.

I glanced at Carter but all he did was give a minuscule shrug. I held out my hand to take the rope and was nearly knocked over by a wave of dizziness. A *strong* wave of dizziness. And I hadn't even touched the rope yet. This time I glanced at Dr. Stewart, but she simply stared back. I knew this couldn't be good, but I took a deep breath and reached for the rope again.

Almost as soon as my fingers touched it, I was overwhelmed by visions of deaths. I saw men, women, even children swinging from the end of the rope. Somehow, gruesomely, the headmaster had gotten hold of a length of rope from a gallows. These might not have been the most grisly deaths I'd witnessed, but the problem was that there were so *many* of them. The visions came so quickly I could barely process them. In fact, I *couldn't* process all of them.

I dropped the rope and quickly followed it to the ground.

LIKE THE LAST time I'd been in this room, I found myself waking up on the floor with my head in Carter's lap. This time, however, I was looking up not at the ceiling but at Headmaster Stewart's disapproving face. As I opened my eyes, I heard Carter saying "…happy now? Did you *want* that to happen?" before his face—a solid mixture of concern and anger—briefly replaced Dr. Stewart's in my line of sight. I took his words as an indication that I'd only been out for a moment or two, which was actually another improvement. He saw my eyes open and softened.

"Hey," he said. "You're awake. That was quick." His hand gently brushed my hair, just like last time, and I'm sure I saw Dr. Stewart's disapproving look deepen.

I smiled at him weakly. "That was a tough test."

"Yes, it was," Dr. Stewart confirmed. She conspicuously failed to ask if I was all right, I noted, but I honestly didn't think she'd wanted me to pass out. If I had to guess, she seemed disappointed that I hadn't handled it better. "And it appears as though you'll need more practice before we can consider your 'migraine problem' cured."

Carter looked at her almost murderously, but I broke in before he could say something to further damage their already strained relationship. I knew it wouldn't do me any good to say something flippant either, so I swallowed my anger and said, "You're right. I do need to keep working. I really need to be able to do this without passing out."

"Indeed. I'm sure that's enough practice for this evening, but I'll check in again shortly. Are you able to leave?"

I pushed myself into a sitting position and fought off the headache I could already feel blooming. What I wanted to do was finish out one of the only private hours I got with Carter, but any weakness was surely something a woman like Dr. Stewart would exploit, and hell if I was going to show her one. "Yes, I'm ready."

I picked myself up off the floor as gracefully as possible, with Carter's help. He kept his arm around my waist and grabbed both my backpack and the stool before we left. Then the Headmaster escorted us out of the library and ordered Carter home with a stern, "Good night, Mr. Penrose," before I could get a proper good night for myself. To my further dismay, she insisted on walking me to my building herself.

"Much to my surprise, your progress is satisfactory," she said as soon as Carter was out of earshot.

"Thank you." As far as compliments went, it wasn't much of one, but it was more than I'd been expecting.

"I was hesitant to let you work with Mr. Penrose at all, even more so in light of…the developments in your relationship, but it appears as though you are practicing as I instructed."

"We are," I said, and it was the truth. As tempting as it was to blow off practicing and fool around with Carter, I *needed* to get a handle on my Sententia gifts. And I wanted to, as quickly as I could. It would make my life easier in general, and I knew mandatory practice wouldn't last forever. I'd get that hour a week back eventually.

"And so you will continue, so long as I see regular improvement. If at any point I don't feel you're developing control at an acceptable rate, your practice sessions will continue with me personally."

Thankfully it was dark out, so I'm not sure how much of my uncontrollable grimace she was able to see. "I understand," I replied, which seemed safe. Her threat made me nauseous, but at least my reply was a simple truth. I didn't think I would learn any better if I were constantly nervous about performing in front of her, but I didn't say that either.

She then made me more nervous by saying, "The Perceptum President has been asking about you personally, and I expect that you will do nothing less than impress him. I have guaranteed it myself and will see that it happens."

"O…Okay. I won't let you down," I finished lamely.

"Don't," she said. "Good night, Ms. Young." And with that she turned and left me at my front porch. I didn't know why the president of the Perceptum would be interested in me, but I knew for sure I didn't like it.

THE NEXT DAY, I hurried over to the bookstore after volleyball practice to talk to Carter about what Dr. Stewart had told me. I found him behind the counter, reading something as always, and talking to Jill.

Jill. I'd barely seen her since the night I'd caught her, or so I'd thought, running away from my porch. The night Carter and I had started dating. Carter had suggested I try to make friends with her, but I was finding that an impossible task. I may have been paranoid, but I swore she was actively avoiding me.

Without swim practice, we had no classes in common and didn't share work hour duties. That left seeing her around campus, which only happened occasionally at meals, or at the bookstore. Jill was there frequently, as was I, but aside from small friendly gestures, I was entirely unable to interact with her. Whenever I came in, she seemed to have something to do anywhere but where I was. I could barely say hello to her, let alone befriend her, and especially not ask her if I'd seen her that night.

This time, however, I was unavoidable. They were pretty relaxed at Penrose Books anyway, and there were all kinds of perks when you're dating one of the owners. I walked right behind the counter to talk to Carter, essentially trapping Jill at the register.

"Hi," I said, hugging Carter quickly. I leaned around him and added, "Hey, Jill."

"Hi," she practically whispered, and then busied herself with the register. I gave Carter a look that said I-keep-trying-but-this-isn't-going-to-work. He just gave a little shrug.

"What's up?" he said out loud. "Not that I'm not happy to see you, but this isn't a time you usually come over here. Your hair is still wet." He moved his fingers from around my waist to run them through my damp hair from my post-practice shower. I wasn't sure which touch I preferred, and was momentarily distracted while trying to decide.

I shook my head—seriously, I *had* to figure out some way to spend more time with my boyfriend—and said, "Uh, I had something to tell you."

I dropped my voice even more, and told him about my conversation with Dr. Stewart the night before. I didn't worry about Jill overhearing, since she undoubtedly knew more about the things I was talking about than I did, but I didn't want anyone who wandered up to hear something they shouldn't.

Carter listened, studying me with his trademark thoughtful look, and then, when I finished my story, he glanced back at Jill. "I wouldn't worry about it," he said, his voice pitched as low as mine. His response wasn't exactly the reassurance I was hoping for.

"But why would he or she ask about me? I'm no one."

Carter laughed, and Jill, I was sure, inched closer to us. She was definitely listening. "You're not no one, Lainey," Carter said. "You're a long-lost Legacy with a unique gift and a mysterious past. I'm sure he's just curious about you and…I wouldn't worry about it is all." He glanced over his shoulder at Jill again. Something was clearly up and I didn't understand it. He grabbed my hand and suggested, "Why don't we go upstairs and talk about this there?" That was a plan I could totally support, but I didn't get the chance to agree.

"Carter!" Jill squeaked from behind him. We both turned to look at her. She blushed, instantly and deeply, a problem with which I commiserated. "You need to help me bring up the new books before my shift ends, remember?"

"You're right. I'm sorry." He turned back to me. "Come over for dinner tonight? Aunt Melinda won't mind. We can talk after."

"Can't," I said. "I have study group for Chem. And homework." Much to my disappointment.

A dangerous smile played over his face and his voice dropped. "I could teach you chemistry…"

It was embarrassing, but I giggled. I couldn't help myself. "I'm sure you could, but I don't know how much that would help me pass my test. Besides, I already said I'd go."

"Tomorrow then," he said. "I'll see you tomorrow." He leaned down and gave me a quick kiss, then hugged me close. To my surprise, he whispered in my ear, so low I almost couldn't hear him, "Don't worry about this. Really. It won't be a problem."

I turned his words over as I left. He clearly meant what he said, but I wasn't convinced. Somehow, I was sure that this would not just be a problem but a big one.

Chapter Eighteen

I didn't get to talk to Carter privately the next day either, but I did have a surprise conversation with someone else. I was headed back to my dorm after last class—I had only an hour before we had to leave for a volleyball match—when she caught up to me.

"Lainey," Alexis called. Her voice wasn't loud and, most surprisingly, it was not bitchy, superior, or angry. Like the last time she found me on campus, she was alone. "Wait. Please?"

I nearly stumbled from shock at the last word. I debated ignoring her, but decided I was too curious to find out what she wanted. That might have been stupid, but I couldn't imagine what she'd try next and I really wanted to know. Call it morbid curiosity. I guess I was naturally prone to it.

We were in a fairly open stretch of the grounds, between the auditorium, and the main part of campus. The grass was covered in crusty snow, but it was the fastest way to Marquise House, practically the other end of campus. Alexis looked as great as she always did, if you considered having hair, makeup, and clothes that seemed effortlessly put together paired with a killer body and a flawless face "great." Which pretty much everyone did, myself included. It was hard not to envy Alex a little whenever I looked at her, so long as she wasn't talking to or glaring at me.

Of course, if her "please" had made me stumble, her next words almost made me pass out. "I…I'm sorry," she said. The crazy part was it sounded like she meant it. I knew it was easy to believe anything she said, but I was pretty sure I *actually* believed her. "I shouldn't have said what I did."

"Wow," I replied before I could stop it from coming out of my mouth. Actually, I wasn't sure what else I'd have said anyway; I was too surprised to think straight. I looked around and saw that, yes, we were alone. Her chic but practical boots crunched a little on the snow as she shifted around uncomfortably. For the first time in, oh, probably ever, Alexis looked…awkward. Unconfident, even.

Then a little of the girl I knew and, well, not hated, but really didn't like, returned. Her spine straightened—it was difficult to say which of us was taller—and a little of her haughtiness came back to her face. "Look, I get it. You don't have to accept. It's not important."

"Well, I do accept," I said, "but I'm not sure why you're bothering. If it's not important." I turned and started to walk away.

"Wait!" she repeated, and tentatively touched my arm. I looked back and saw her features deflate again. "It is important. I…I'm not good at this."

"If you did it more often, it wouldn't be so hard," I said. I couldn't help myself.

She glared, briefly, but then abandoned it. "You're right, okay? You're right. But I'm doing it now. And I mean it. I'm sorry. I was a bitch and it was stupid and I won't do it again, okay?"

"Okay. Thanks." I hesitated, since this seemed like a genuine apology and really, I didn't want to be fighting with anyone, Alexis included, but I decided to ask my question anyway. "Don't take this the wrong way, but why are you apologizing now?"

"Because I have to!" she nearly shouted, and I swear tears started to shimmer in her gorgeous eyes. Color me more shocked. She got her voice back down to normal levels before she went on. "I miss going to the bookstore, and Carter...won't talk to me, and my friends don't know how to act, and I don't have any other way to fix this. And Brooke, she likes you. She...she said I should grow up and apologize like a big girl—she said that to me!—but so I am. I'm sorry."

If this wasn't so unexpected, and Alex didn't look so miserable, I might have laughed. But I didn't. Even I didn't want to prolong Alex's misery more than I had to, it was so painful to see. I silently thanked Brooke for standing up for me—and for being so damn funny—and let Alexis off the hook. "Okay," I told her. "I believe you. Thank you."

She nodded, and I practically felt the look of relief that came over her face. "I...Will..." she floundered, but I knew what she wanted to say.

"I'll tell Carter," I said. *That* was the important part.

I probably should have been a bitch right back to her, let her suffer, but I didn't have the heart for it. I'd tell him, and she and her friends would come back to the bookstore like they were never gone. I wasn't sure it would repair her and Carter's friendship, but at least I could put an end to some of this silly drama. Besides, if I was being honest, it was the teensiest bit more rewarding to see Carter actively choose my company over hers. So maybe I was a little bit of a bitch, just on the inside.

As predicted, Alexis and her crew returned to hanging out at the lounge almost as if nothing happened. Carter didn't exactly welcome her back with open arms—I'd probably have smacked him if he did—but he was friendly to most of them and polite, if not entirely warm, to Alex. I could tell she wasn't completely happy with the situation but was certainly happier than before. She'd even taken to being polite, but definitely not warm, to me, which was exactly how I treated her. There was a lot of that going around.

Jill continued actively avoiding me, except for a sudden appearance as a Sunday night dinner guest with Carter and the Revells. She still didn't talk to me, though she was almost animated in her interactions with the others, Carter especially, but she did stay the entire time I was there until it was time for us to go back to campus. I was beginning to think that, except for our official hour on Wednesdays, I would never get alone time with Carter again.

"She's in love with him," Amy said one night as we sat in the bookstore lounge.

Since there were at least two or more candidates for "she" in the room, I honestly had no idea who she was talking about. The "him" was obviously Carter.

"Jill," she clarified. "It's obvious." The girl and boy in question were currently behind the counter, in quiet conversation. She did look happy, I had to admit.

"Maybe," I said. I thought I should give her the benefit of the doubt. "She's like one of the family though."

"Whatever. She's in love with him. Even easier for her if she's 'one of the family.' And she was the closest thing he had to a girlfriend in the last year. Must be tough for her to see him with you."

I didn't know what to do about that. It wasn't like I was going to give him up. I shrugged, and glanced at where Alexis and her friends were perched in a chatty group. "I guess I'm lots of girls' boyfriend stealer."

Amy gave an effervescent giggle and looked over at Caleb who was sitting next to her, head in a book and earbuds on loud, oblivious to our conversation. "Just keep your eyes off my boyfriend, Heartbreaker, and we'll be fine."

I laughed, but I was only partly paying attention. What Amy had suggested—about Jill, not her boyfriend, of course—had crossed my mind before, but I'd never thoroughly considered it. So I studied Jill across the large room…as she studied Carter while he did something store-related. It looked like he was checking off an inventory form. If I was honest with myself, I could see that she studied him exactly the way *I* liked to study him, when he wasn't looking, and especially when he was doing something simple.

Carter was a lot of fun when we were hanging out, but he was also very, very serious about so many things and he worked—at one job or another—all the time. Seeing him do something relatively easy and stress-free, like stack magazines or whatever he was doing at the moment, was the best time to watch him. It was almost as good as when I caught him out jogging. Jill looked like she enjoyed the rare opportunity as much as I did. So yeah, she was probably in love with him. And maybe so was I, I realized, though it seemed too early for me to be making declarations like that.

Melinda distracted me from having to think about *that* by emerging from the back and taking over whatever task Carter had been doing. Almost as if he sensed I was watching them, he looked over and caught my eye immediately. I nearly blushed for being caught, if not for the enticing smile that spread across his face. He raised his eyebrow at me in a question and then looked pointedly upstairs. I gave a fleeting thought to the homework open on my lap before stuffing it in my bag and rising from the couch. I looked over at Amy to give some excuse, but she was already grinning at me.

"I get it," she said. "Later. I won't wait for you at dinner either." Even Caleb winked at me as I headed toward the counter.

I exchanged greetings with Melinda (who responded fondly) and Jill (who barely responded at all) before Carter said, "Lainey and I are going to go make dinner, Aunt Mel," and tugged me through the door and up the back stairs. I just had time to see Melinda smile at us as we went.

"So what's for dinner?" I asked once we got up the two flights into their apartment, but I barely got the words out before Carter was kissing me.

"Pizza," he said finally. "I'll call for delivery when it's closing time downstairs."

I'd been in Carter's bedroom before, but never when we were alone in the apartment. In fact, this was the first time I was ever really alone with a guy and a bed. It scared and excited me in equal measure. I discovered that I liked my hands on Carter's skin—it was warm against my touch and soft over the taut muscle underneath—and then surprised myself by urging his t-shirt over his head. It landed with a faint thud on the floor below us.

After some time, I realized with a bit of shock that my jeans were unbuttoned and Carter's hands were around my back, below my waistband. It's not that I minded—honestly, I kind of liked it—but all of a sudden I was nervous. Getting carried away was almost too easy. With my nervousness, Alexis's ugly words crept back into my head, and that's when I needed to stop. Self-doubt had to be my own tragic flaw, which you'd think if I recognized I could stop, but that's easier said than done.

I disentangled us and righted all of my clothing, though I let Carter's t-shirt stay on the floor. I looked up at his handsome face, and it was difficult to say the next words when he was shirtless and looking at me the way he was. We were both breathing a little heavily, which I hadn't noticed before, but I guess once you get nervous, you become hyper-aware of everything. I took a deepish breath and made myself go on with my resolution. "I need to..." I said, but Carter brushed his hand over my lips before I finished.

"It's fine, Lainey," he said. "You're in control here."

I gave him a little smile and let out that breath before laying my head down on his bare chest. That was another new experience, an innocent one, but turned out to be highly enjoyable. His arm was around my back and he began to run his fingers through my hair the way I loved. I thought I'd worn it down every day since I'd started dating him just for this opportunity.

I wasn't sorry for stopping us, not at all. I *wanted* more, wanted Carter, but the wanting was easy. Every time he touched me, I wanted him to touch me more. But my body and my heart and my brain were not all ready for the same things. The last one was going to take a lot longer to be ready for everything than the first two, and in this situation, I needed to rely on it.

I looked around Carter's room while we lounged. It housed a queen-sized bed, large dresser, one comfortable chair, and a small closet. His bathroom was across the hall. The room had most of the things I expected a typical nineteen-year-old boy's to have, namely a TV, stereo, and video game systems, but it was also full of books—stacked *everywhere*—and lacking in posters of women or sports. It was also, except for the books, surprisingly neat. I hadn't asked him if he cleaned it for me, because I didn't think so. It seemed natural for him. I didn't think Carter could relax if things were messy.

As we lay there together, I mused over how I'd always thought alone time would be easier to come by at a boarding school, without parents around to monitor us, but that was turning out not to be true. At all. Between Carter's jobs and the long list of demands on my time, being alone was something we had the benefit of only rarely. In fact, this was the first time we'd been entirely alone together since Dr. Stewart had freaked me out with her comments. I seized on that advantage.

"Now would finally be a good time to tell me what's going on with Jill," I said.

He stiffened and sat up to look at me, confusion clear on his face. "What? *Nothing's* going on with Jill. Why would you think that?"

"Not between the two of you, silly. I *know* nothing's going on there. But something is up with her. Maybe it's just the fact that she's in love with you."

He frowned and tried out my seemingly foreign words for himself. "In love with…Lainey, what are you talking about?" He honestly looked like he didn't understand, and Carter was pretty much always honest. Acting clueless was not in his nature.

"Oh, come on!" I said, and I sat up too. "You're the most self-aware guy I've ever met. How can you not realize how she feels about you?"

He thought about it for a minute but said, "That's just not possible."

I snorted. "It's *totally* possible. It's a fact. It's such a fact that she's been willingly putting herself in my company—something she avoided completely before, by the way—to keep us from being alone together."

I didn't know if I'd realized that was what she was doing before I said it, but it seemed obvious now. Whenever I was around Carter, she was suddenly nearby, the complete opposite of her previous behavior. Ever since the day she'd overheard me trying to talk about Dr. Stewart's proclamation.

Carter was not convinced. "That's not it, Lainey." I shook my head, but he went on. "No, I mean it. It's not what you think. She's my cousin."

"You might think of her that way, but it's obvious she doesn't feel the same."

"No, she really is. Sort of." He ran his hands through his hair in his typical show of frustration. I knew he did it without thinking, and usually when he was uncomfortable, but I secretly liked it. It tousled his caramel-brown waves in a way that some guys spent hours at a mirror trying to do intentionally. Even so, I reached up and pulled his hands down, smoothing out his hair. I might have liked it, but I knew he didn't. Neatness really did come naturally to him. He relaxed a little and went on, pulling me back down to the bed with him. "She's...I think she's been hanging around because she heard you talking about her father."

It was my turn to be confused. "Huh?"

"She never asks about him, but I know she likes to hear about him—*tries* to hear about him—even if she won't say so."

"You've lost me. Who's her father, and when was I talking about him?"

"Who is he? He's a lot of things, but mostly I think of him as my uncle's brother."

Okay. "Doesn't that make him your uncle?"

"Well, no, not really. I'm a Penrose, not a Revell. Aunt Melinda is my father's sister." This conversation was rapidly giving me a headache totally unrelated to my usual ones. "Besides, he's not a Revell either. He's Uncle Jeff's half-brother. But he's still Uncle Dan to me, even if he's technically not. Kind of like your Aunt Tessa. Anyway, Uncle Dan is an Astor. He's also Jillian's father."

"Wow. That's a fancy family name," I said. I'd definitely heard of the Astors before. I also noted that Jill's name was *not* Astor. "I think my aunt might have done a commission for an Astor."

"It wouldn't surprise me. They tend to appreciate fine art."

"I'd tell her you said that, but she doesn't need to like you any more than she does already. I mean, I think she likes you more than I do." I smirked at him, but he leaned over and gave me a swift kiss to wipe the smirk off my face.

"I doubt that," he said with zero trace of sarcasm. And he was right. I hated him. He leaned in again, but I resolutely kept us on track.

"So is he? One of the fancy Astors?" I asked. "You don't talk about him much."

"That's true, we don't. But he's definitely one of the fancy Astors. In fact, he's not just Uncle Dan; he's *Senator* Daniel Astor."

Wow. A senator. "For real? As in senator in the U.S. Congress, right?"

"The very one. He's the senior senator from the fine state of Montana."

"So why does Jill have to listen in on conversations about her own father? She's obviously not an Astor, but still...and what does this have to do with anything I said?" Though suddenly I knew. "Wait. *Your uncle* is president of the Perceptum. And Jill's father." And a senator, too. Jesus Christ.

He smiled. "Exactly. Which is why you don't have to worry about him asking about you. But Jill...well, you're right. She's not an Astor. At least not by name. Her mother and my uncle never married. Actually, I think her mother *refused* to marry him and refused to let him be an active part of her life. Jill doesn't talk about it and she hasn't had any contact with him since she was young, except for being his Legacy here. I asked Uncle Jeff once, but he didn't talk about it either. *Nobody* talks about it."

Carter shifted on the bed and pulled me close to his side. I snuggled contentedly—really, I could get used to simply lying next to him—then said, "So she really doesn't talk to him? I...well, I can't imagine having a father and not talking to him." After all, neither Carter nor I could talk to our fathers if we wanted to.

"No, she doesn't. At least she tells me she doesn't. The way she listens for our conversations about him, I believe her. I think she's starved for the idea of him, and maybe his attention, but she hates him a little too. And respects her mother too much to contact him. When she graduates...I don't know. I think she'll talk to him."

"Why don't *you* guys talk to him?"

He shifted again, fidgeted really, absently wrapping a strand of my hair around his finger. "I never said I didn't talk to him. Just not *about* him…"

Which meant maybe Uncle Dan wasn't entirely popular with the rest of his family. "I take it he and his brother don't get along?" I guessed.

"You're right," he said, smoothing my hair. "Uncle Dan…is a good man. I think so. But they're very different, my uncles. Both take after their own fathers. I know Uncle Dan didn't understand when Uncle Jeff joined the military instead of going to college. He thought he was wasting his brains and…putting his gifts to the wrong use, I guess. Plus there's Jill. My aunt and Uncle Jeff, they don't say this, but I think they're angry with him over her. They couldn't have kids, and have had to settle for, well, me. And Uncle Dan *has* a daughter but he's not part of her life. It's not completely fair, because I think Uncle Dan wants to have more contact with Jill, but anyway…When Uncle Dan became president of the Perceptum, it brought them back together a little, gave them some common ground. He usually visits once a year now."

I could tell by the light in his eyes that Carter looked forward to those visits more than he let on, but all I said was, "So your uncle, the Senator, is also your uncle, the President, in a way. That's amazing. He's a pretty important guy."

"True. He followed his father's footsteps in both his positions, by the way. He's also kind of my uncle, my boss."

I laughed a little, but then fell serious. "So why is he asking about me?"

"Relax, Lane," he said and somehow, miraculously, pulled me closer to him. His hand slipped back around my waist. "He's just interested in you, because of all the reasons I said the other day, and because *I'm* interested in you."

"So you've talked about me? To him?" For some reason, that made me more nervous than Dr. Stewart talking to him about me.

"Of course. I talk about you to *everyone,*" he said, giving my side a light squeeze. "So yeah, I've told my Uncle Dan about you too, and he's asked how you're doing."

"But why is he asking Dr. Stewart too?"

Carter sighed. "He probably didn't. She's always trying to impress him, so now she's probably trying to impress him with *you,* the Mystery Legacy. I've told you, she's a political animal as far as the Perceptum is concerned. I think she'd like to serve on the Council, and Uncle Dan's nomination would mean almost an automatic seat. Plus, he's a highly eligible bachelor and maybe the second best thing to my Uncle Jeff, in her eyes anyway."

I knew he was being serious, but I couldn't help but laugh. The idea of Dr. Stewart playing political *and* romantic games was too much for me. "Well, whatever she's doing, I don't think it will work. *Any* of it. I might not know your uncle, but for one, she's a total shrew, and for another, I'm not that impressive."

"You've impressed me plenty," he said, and I liked the husky tone in his voice.

I shoved him playfully, but he dragged me back. "And Jill is *not* your cousin," I said. "Not really. You're not related at all."

"It doesn't matter, Lainey. She thinks of me the same way. And I only think of you. Let's not talk about Jillian or any of this anymore. There's nothing to worry about." He pulled me up on top of him and for a minute I forgot everything else completely. Until we were interrupted, that is.

"Carter?" came a tentative voice from the kitchen. I froze. In our haste, we'd left the door to his bedroom open and I, at least, hadn't heard anyone come in the back door. Carter actually groaned before kissing me once and sliding me back onto the bed.

"Melinda wanted me to see if you needed help with dinner," Jill called.

I honestly doubted Melinda had sent her up here, but it didn't matter. She was here now and alone time was over.

Carter stood and grabbed his shirt off the floor as he walked toward the hallway. After a second, I followed. He was pulling his shirt over his head when he reached the kitchen, which made my face flame with embarrassment, and I swept my hair over my shoulders to try and cover it up. Even if I hadn't been sure—despite his protests—that Jill was in love with him, making this extra terrible for her, she'd still caught us fooling around, and Carter had just given evidence to that fact. Sometimes I forgot that, though I felt like a high school girl in her boyfriend's parents' house, Carter was technically an adult, and also at least half owner of this house. And he pretty much never felt embarrassed about anything.

"Hey," he said. "Thanks, but I was just going to order pizza. Are you staying for dinner?"

Jill's deep blush matched my own. If anything, with her blond hair, she looked even redder than I'm sure I did. In a sort of anti-motion to what I'd done, she nervously tucked strands of her short locks behind her ears. "I…I guess, yeah," she stammered. "I told Melinda I would. Want me to call? She'll be up in a few minutes."

I hadn't realized how long we'd been upstairs, but the clock over the kitchen window told me it was indeed past closing time at the store. Dinner hours were open at the Academy, and I was sure Amy and our other friends were already gossiping about my conspicuous absence. I weighed my options, but a slightly awkward pizza dinner with Carter, Melinda, and Jill was probably better than the mocking I'd get from my friends. I went back to Carter's room and grabbed my homework while we waited.

That night, as I was lying in bed, I caught myself wondering about what it took to be Perceptum President. Something special, I bet. I drifted off to sleep with a lingering question: what was Daniel Astor's Sententia gift?

Chapter Nineteen

Y ou look awesome," Amy said. "Carter's going to flip."

"Thanks," I replied, smoothing my hair for at least the fiftieth time. "*Everyone* is going to flip when they see you."

"You think?" With a giggle, she twirled around in the center of the room.

"I'm *sure.*" And I was. It was the night of the Winter Ball, and Amy looked practically unreal.

Her dress was a blush pink that looked almost like skin, in a material that was gossamer but clingy in the right ways, with a deep show of cleavage pretty much no other girl on campus could come close to matching. It looked like she was wearing a designer gown and absolutely nothing, all at the same time. I didn't know how that was possible, but there she was, pirouetting in front of me. Her hair was gathered in a loose and wavy fall from the back of her head, and her lovely face looked, well, lovely. Quite honestly, I was in awe. I couldn't stop looking at her.

I wasn't sure they'd let her into the ballroom, she looked so sexy, but she assured me she wouldn't be the only one. Northbrook had no real dress code—the wealthy parents apparently wouldn't stand for it—and the Winter Ball was, as Amy put it, the least proper night of the year. I'd been worried about my own dress being acceptable too but, much like the first time I'd met her, I felt subdued in comparison to Amy. And that was saying something, because my dress was one of the sexiest things I'd ever seen.

It fit me right off the hanger like it'd been made for me; the complex folds gave me the appearance of a shapely waist with a hint of curves, instead of my normally straight and narrow middle, and the neckline made my average chest look nearly ample. Not like Amy's, of course, but good enough to be noticeable. It was short to begin with, and with my long legs and the heels Amy and I had picked to go with it, it looked even shorter.

The muted shine of the black satin matched my hair almost perfectly. I'd planned to wear it up, since I almost never did, but Amy insisted it had to be down. As usual, she was right. The long, straight curtain of it made a great contrast against my skin and complemented my dress. I was a picture of pale and dark—dark high heels, long pale legs and arms, long dark hair and short dark dress, dark lined eyes— and I admitted to myself that I looked good. Okay, maybe *really* good. I'd honestly never felt so beautiful. I couldn't stop fidgeting.

Amy, naturally, noticed everything. "Relax! You clearly need more of this," she said, before pouring more champagne into the glass I was holding.

She'd produced the bottle, and one that was already empty, along with real crystal glasses, after we'd returned from the hair salon. Classes met only in the morning on the day of the Ball, and campus was a flurry of excited girls and limousines for the rest of the afternoon. Group by group we were chauffeured to beauty appointments and last-minute fittings with tailors, then back to campus to dress for our big night. The guys were much more relaxed about the whole thing, and I had hardly seen any of them around the entire day. I would not see Carter until he met us to leave for the Ball.

I sipped the champagne and tried to do as Amy said. I had no idea where she'd gotten it—for such a small town and closed campus nothing seemed very hard to get around here—but I was grateful. It was bubbly and sweet and made my stomach feel fluttery in a much better way than the nerves I was having trouble calming.

"I…" I started, but was immediately cut off.

"Yeah, you've never done anything like this before, I know. Relax, Lane," Amy said, in her form of exasperation, which was more like she thought I was funny. "You seriously need to learn yoga or something. You look wicked hot, Carter's going to fall over when he sees you, and tonight is going to be super fun. You don't have to have done this before to enjoy it. I promise." She drained her own champagne then refilled *both* of our glasses.

I blushed, embarrassed and frustrated by my inability to loosen up, and I didn't tell her that my aunt had been trying to get me to do yoga with her for years. "You're right. I'm sorry. Okay, relaxing now." I lounged back on my bed and sipped some more of the champagne. As always, thank God for my roommate. She provided a fine distraction.

"I won't be back to the room until way late tonight—or well, early this morning—so don't wait up, at least not for *me* anyway," she announced while giving her hair one last primp in her mirror. It was almost time to go.

I was, as ever, the naïve innocent. "What? Why? What time does this thing end?"

She gave me another exasperated-but-not-really look from the mirror. "Lane. Seriously. Why do you *think* I won't be back until early?"

Again I blushed. Of course. "But…But where are you going to go?"

"Caleb's room. You know he has a single."

"But…how?"

This time she sighed, and it was clearly all she could do to keep from laughing at me. "It's not *that* hard to sneak into someone's room if you want to, but tonight, pretty much anything goes around here. *Everyone* is in a good and look-the-other-way mood, if you know what I mean. The only important thing is being back in your own room before the sun comes up. Otherwise sneaking back gets a little trickier."

As almost, but not really, an afterthought, she added, "It's not very hard to sneak someone *into* your room either, you know. I put some condoms in your nightstand…"

I nearly leaped off the bed in shock, though honestly, I wasn't sure why. This was, on the scale of shocking things she'd said to me, near the bottom of the list. Still, I was mortified. "Amy! That's…not going to happen. Not tonight anyway." I opened my nightstand and, sure enough, there was a small package of condoms, decoratively tied with a bow. I shoved them to the back of the drawer.

Now she did laugh, a sound almost as bubbly and irresistible as the champagne. "Hey, that's fine. Just, you know, want you to be prepared. It's a good night for sneaking and…other things. I put those in there *last* weekend, by the way. You obviously don't use that drawer very often."

"Last weekend" was my seventeenth birthday. Amy, Caleb, Carter, and I had gone on a real double date, meaning at an actual restaurant, off-campus. It had been, in a word, great. But not great like that. "Amy, geez. I'm not going to need these for…a while." I didn't want to put a timeframe on it, because I had no idea when I'd be ready. "And I think *you're* the only one who's pressuring me."

I pretended to be outraged, but the effect was ruined when I couldn't stifle a giggle at the end. I blamed the champagne and, true, I'd felt a little lightheaded when I jumped up from the bed. I hoped dinner was served right away at the Ball.

She looked surprised, and I didn't think she was pretending. "Really? I mean, I know we talked about how you weren't rushing or anything, but…well, I thought it was a done deal by now. Everything about you and Carter is…serious, you know? Then I was in the library on Wednesday night a few weeks ago but couldn't find you anywhere. You're so private about those things, I figured you'd made up an excuse and that was your alone time with Carter."

For a second, all I could think was *Shit!* I'd told Amy I volunteered to help with a project at the library on Wednesday nights. As far as deceptions went, it was pretty small and, so I'd thought, a good one. Probably foolishly, I *didn't* count on her looking for me, but Amy sometimes came to the library in the evenings, like every other student. In a way, she was right too. The hour or so of our practice actually *was* my private time with Carter…just not *romantic* private time. Mostly. My champagne-fogged brain was having trouble coming up with a response.

"Hey, it's cool, okay?" Amy said while I fumbled for a new excuse. "And I'm *not* trying to pressure you, honest. But…well, if you're not with Carter, where on earth are you on Wednesday nights?"

"I…I am at the library," I finally said. "I'm usually on the Special Collections floor sorting things, so you wouldn't see me if you looked for me." I decided to throw in a little more truth to make it convincing. "And sometimes I am with Carter. But it's *not* how you think. He just comes to hang out. We don't see each other all that much, you know, and the librarian doesn't mind if he's there. Sometimes he even helps me. It's pretty boring, but I don't mind the work."

She looked sideways at me, like she was a little skeptical, but it wasn't in the way I thought. "So you give up an hour of what could be play time with your boyfriend to help sort boring books or whatever at the library? Maybe you *are* trying to become Saint Elaine."

My laugh was genuine, since I was *so* not close to being a saint—lying was, after all, part of my daily existence—and I was relieved that I'd gotten out of another near screw-up with my roommate. Keeping my secrets from her was an on-going problem. "I'm not *that* good," I said, with enough implication in my voice to make her smile slyly.

"Thank God," she said. " 'Cause if there's a boy out there worth not being good with, it's Carter. Speaking of…" Her phone had begun to buzz at almost the same time mine did. The guys were waiting downstairs.

MARQUISE HOUSE MADE for a great entrance. The final turn of the staircase opened into our dorm's grand entryway, complete with a glittering chandelier that before tonight I'd seen lit only once. I went up and down these stairs many times a day, but tonight it felt new and special. Amy's natural flair for the dramatic had us descending like queens, slow and stately, and to great effect. The looks on our dates' faces were worth every second we took to reach them.

Carter's eyes were as large as I'd ever seen them, and I heard him utter a barely audible, "Wow." I'm not sure he meant to say it out loud. Caleb, I noted with amusement, had nearly the same reaction. Not that I wasn't impressed with the two of them either. They cleaned up quite nicely, I was not surprised to see.

Carter looked shockingly good in a modern-cut tuxedo with tie that emphasized his broad shoulders, slim hips, and somewhat untraditional good looks, all of which was complemented by his seductive smile. I wasn't sure how the rest of the night would go, but I admitted that the beginning of it had been worth all the hours we'd spent getting ready. Finally seeing Carter miraculously cured my nerves, replacing them with a sense of anticipation and excitement.

Caleb wore a more traditional tuxedo that suited him well, complete with a bow tie, matching pocket square, and what I thought might even be a pocket watch. He looked like a classic Hollywood movie star, and I could see that Amy was entirely enamored with him. They presented us with flowers—a corsage for Amy, a bouquet for me—and after a few required photos with Ms. Kim, we were off.

If it weren't for our driver, whom Amy and I had met that afternoon, standing next to it, I'm not sure how we'd ever have found our limousine. The entire campus main drive was filled with them, nearly end to end. It was an amazing thing to witness. Even at the biggest art galas I'd attended with my aunt, I'd never seen anything like this.

Amazingly, another bottle of champagne appeared in the limousine, adding to our festive mood. I couldn't believe we could get away with it, but then I guessed what Amy said was true. As long as it wasn't obvious or immediately life-threatening, everyone really did turn a blind eye on the night's activities.

Thankfully the newest bottle was split between the group of us— instead of just Amy and me—and after another glass, I felt amazing. Relaxed and excited and happy. I snuggled up to Carter and kissed him, rather boldly, as we rode in luxury to the dance. Carter was surprised, but obliging, and my friends were both shocked and amused.

"You should give Lainey champagne more often," I heard Caleb say, and I laughed. Tonight was going to be incredible. I was sure.

THE HOTEL HOSTING the ball might have been fancy, but the ballroom itself was insane. It was opulently decorated in white and silver, with the tiniest touches of pale blue for color, and the entire room twinkled. I'm not even sure how the effect was achieved—a combination of candles, white lights, crystal chandeliers, and, just maybe, all the champagne I'd drunk—but the results were breathtaking. A true winter wonderland had been recreated indoors, all for our amusement. For the second, maybe third time tonight, I was in awe.

"So this is what I was missing the last four years," Carter said.

"This is way better than last year," Amy agreed, though I think she was looking at Caleb more than the decor.

The Ball was limited to sophomores, juniors, and seniors, and nearly all of them were there. To my surprise, even Jill had come, and I thought she looked like she was actually having fun. She was lovely in a simple sheath dress of royal purple that flattered her petite frame and her coloring. Her blue eyes were always impressive, but the purple of her dress made them riveting. She was with another sophomore, a shy boy I'd seen around campus a few times, who seemed like a nearly perfect match for her. It was clear to me that he was hoping tonight was more than a friendly date. However much I wanted to believe Jill returned the sentiments, I couldn't be convinced.

As the last dinner dishes were cleared away, it was time for the real party. The room buzzed with excitement for the announcement of the Winter Court. The nominations and voting had taken place over the last month, but there was no drama and no surprise when Dr. Stewart herself—in a severe dress that, I wouldn't have thought this possible, made her look taller and thinner than ever—read aloud the winners. Naturally, Alexis was crowned queen.

She was beautiful enough on a normal day, but this was clearly her element. Her one-shoulder, floor-length dress was undeniably designer, with a smattering of beading that glittered artfully in the light and a slit that went to almost illegal heights. It was both elegant and seductive, and also a perfect, unexpected shade of winter white, a color you'd think would have clashed with all the white and silver decorations, but it did the exact opposite. It stood out in a way that made me think the whole room had been designed to complement her. Maybe it had.

Lightly tanned, with naturally pink cheeks and lips painted a dramatic shade of red, she was so luminous, it was almost impossible to look away from her. Her dark brown hair fell in waves from the crown of her head, and her dark eyes danced with the reflection from her sparkling tiara. Yes, Alexis had been born to be Winter Queen.

Amy, too, was elected part of the court. With her own unique beauty, not to mention her cleavage and miraculous confection of a dress, I think she drew almost as much attention as Alexis. The Court members started off the dancing with their dates, and I leaned back from my chair into Carter's arms while we watched the couples glitter and sway on the dance floor. I was also surprised to see Alexis had come with Garrett. Maybe his affections were finally being returned. They certainly made a good-looking couple, and seemed intent on each other during their dance.

"Are you enjoying yourself?" Carter whispered to me as his fingers traced lightly along my arm. It was a fairly innocent touch, as far as touches went, but I shivered in response.

"This is *fantastic*," I whispered back. "I can't believe you never came to one of these."

"I was just waiting for my date to get here," he said and kissed me lightly on the cheek.

I was in heaven.

For a little while anyway. Then, almost literally, my own personal hell broke loose.

Chapter Twenty

Soon enough we were all dancing—the floor was packed and barely fit everyone—and though I'd never done much of it before, I found it came naturally. All you needed was good music, some rhythm, and a bottle of champagne to start the night, all of which I had. After what seemed like hours but was probably only one, I finally took a break to go to the restroom and catch my breath. Instead of the opulent but crowded bathrooms in the main foyer, Carter and I slipped out to a quieter set through a side door behind our table. Unsurprisingly, the corridor was deserted.

When I came out of the women's room, my date was missing. I waited for a minute before deciding he must have gone back to our table. But he wasn't there either, or on the dance floor. In fact, he wasn't anywhere I could see in the ballroom. At about this time, I also realized that I'd misplaced my lip gloss, so I went back into the corridor to search for it and my date.

I found my lip gloss where I'd left it on the bathroom counter, but no Carter. The hallway was still empty. I was about to head back to the ballroom when I heard what sounded like crying. I thought it was coming from some kind of service entrance around the corner from the bathrooms.

As I was walking toward whoever it was to make sure they were okay, I also heard a familiar voice say, "She'll break your heart, Carter, she will. Please. You know how I feel."

There was only one Carter in the vicinity of Northbrook, and there was only one person bold enough to try something like this on a night like this. I rounded the corner to find a girl in an exquisite ivory dress crying lightly and standing way too close to my boyfriend, her pale hand clutching his arm.

Carter sighed and started to say, "Alex, you know I don't..." but that was all he got out before she leaned in even closer and kissed him. On the mouth. With tongue.

Carter, thank God, looked a combination of shocked and angry, and was already pushing her away when I squeaked in outrage. They both turned toward me in surprise. Carter's face was frantic, and Alexis...looked devastated, beautiful—honestly, even all sniffly and mauling my boyfriend the girl was gorgeous—and practically murderous.

"What the hell are you doing?!" I said, looking at the two of them as I stalked forward. To my surprise, I didn't shout. My voice was low and dangerous and I barely recognized it.

"Lainey, I—" Carter began, but it wasn't him I was worried about.

"Not you. *You,*" I said, and pointed toward Alexis. I'd expected her to make another play for Carter at some point—it just wasn't in her to give up—but I'd never dreamed it would be so soon after our delicate truce or, of all nights, tonight.

Alexis sniffled again. After seeing and hearing her pleading, I believed she was truly interested in Carter, as more than a conquest, and that she was upset about his rejection. For half a second I also believed she was going to admit all of this to me and apologize. But as the saying goes, old habits really do die hard. She stiffened and glared at me. "I'm seducing the guy who should be my boyfriend. Do you mind?" she hissed.

I couldn't stop myself. I slapped her.

She recoiled in shock, her own hand covering the spot where mine had cracked across her cheek, before she turned and ran around the corner out of sight. For my part, I stared at my hand like I didn't recognize it. I'd never hit someone in anger before. I'd never even considered it. And for all my years of kick boxing and martial arts, I had no idea why I'd slapped her instead of punching her in the mouth. I'd been trained to do it, had dreamed of doing exactly that, but when the real opportunity presented itself, I'd missed it completely.

Carter reached for my hand and went into rapid apology mode. "Lainey, I'm so sorry. I just…thought I'd listen to her, she was so upset, and then…I never expected *that*. I *didn't* encourage her, I swear. I…"

I let him go on for a while, mostly because I was still in shock, but also because honestly, it was a little amusing to see him so thrown off balance. Eventually I came to my senses.

"It's okay," I interrupted. "Well, it's *not* okay, but I'm not mad at you. You probably shouldn't have listened to her, but that's just you being too nice to everyone. Especially her."

His relief was instantaneous. "I'm so sorry," he repeated and wrapped his arms around me. I wiped the remnants of red lipstick off his lips and then briefly covered them with my own. "I can't believe she did that," he said.

"I can. I'm having a harder time with the fact that her tongue was actually in your mouth, but I can believe she did it."

He reddened in embarrassment but then glanced down at where my hands were pressed against his lapels. "I also can't believe you hit her."

"That one I am surprised about," I admitted. "I...didn't even think. I just did it. I'm sorry I did, sort of, but maybe it will finally get her to leave you alone."

"Maybe," he said, but I'm not sure either of us believed it. "Let's go back. Forget this and have fun."

I was in complete agreement, though I was certain I wouldn't forget it for a long time. I think we both knew that Alexis wouldn't tell anyone what had happened; she might get some sympathy because I'd hit her, but overall it was too embarrassing for her. It was definitely no coincidence that she'd run into him in the side bathroom hallway and decided to pour her heart out. She had to have been watching for an opportunity to get Carter alone, and she also had to have been planning this.

At first I'd been unable to understand why she'd done it tonight, a night during which she was the absolute star, but I finally realized that *was* why. Tonight was *her* night. Maybe she thought she could make it perfect by winning Carter away from me. On top of that, as she'd breezed past me around the corner, I noticed a distinct smell of alcohol mixed with her perfume. Like most of us, Alex had been drinking, and whatever she'd had was stronger than the champagne I'd filled up on.

It dawned on me that maybe the champagne had been a major culprit in my violent reaction. Even with dinner, I reluctantly admitted that I was still a little drunk. Maybe more than a little. I sent Carter to get me some water as soon as we got into the ballroom, which gave me a chance to fill my roommate in on what had happened. Amy was appropriately outraged, but also thrilled by the fact that I'd hit her. Caleb was equally impressed.

"That stupid bitch!" Amy nearly shouted. "I hope you left a mark on her too-pretty stupid face!" I wondered if Amy wasn't a little drunk too.

Carter returned with my water. It was cool and very, very welcome. I already regretted all the champagne, and I was afraid I would regret it more tomorrow. As I sipped gratefully, I looked around the room and was surprised to see Alexis had already returned. She looked almost as if nothing had happened. Her cheeks were a little redder than before, and maybe her eyes were a little red, but I saw her gesturing to her ankle and limping up to her date. Garrett bent down and gently lifted her foot, moving it around as if it were something almost too precious to hold. She sniffled a little, and he practically picked her up and set her in a chair.

So this was how she'd cover up her tears and red face. It was a brilliant plan, and with her Heraldic gift, I'm sure Garrett was utterly convinced she'd tripped and twisted her ankle. Probably even without her gift. As I watched, he leaned over and kissed her tentatively. In response, she threw her arms around his neck and kissed him back, in a very good simulation of what she'd just done to Carter. I made a little gagging noise.

"Unbelievable," Carter muttered, following my gaze to where Alex was making out with her replacement guy. Carter shook his head, and then said hesitantly, "I, uh, ran into Jillian while I was getting your water. She asked if she could have a dance, and I couldn't say no, but…after what just happened, I thought I should warn you first. Do you mind?"

I actually did, a little. I'm not sure it was rational, but I suddenly didn't want any other girl except Amy within touching distance of him. Maybe not even Amy. Realizing how ridiculous that was, I gave my brain a mental slap. I would not be *that* kind of girlfriend. So I said, "Of course not!" Then I added, in what I thought was a hysterical joke, "Just try to keep her tongue out of your mouth, okay?"

He laughed. "That shouldn't be a problem."

When the next slow song came on, Carter went to find Jill. I welcomed the chance to sit one out because, honestly, my head really needed it. Amy, Caleb, and most of the other couples at our table were taking a break too. I drank some more water while I watched Carter lead Jill onto the dance floor.

I'd expected Jill to be a somewhat stiff and awkward dancer, but together they looked surprisingly comfortable. As always, she seemed to relax around Carter. They made an amusing couple, tiny, petite Jill dwarfed by Carter's broad frame. He was well over a foot taller than she was. I found myself smiling as he spun her expertly—really, she was probably a better dancer than I was—and she laughed in response. My ridiculous fears from earlier rapidly evaporated. Until the song ended anyway.

As the music transitioned and couples started to leave the dance floor, Carter leaned down to give Jill a hug. She must have said something, but it looked like it was too quiet for him to hear. He frowned slightly as he leaned down closer. I saw his lips forming a question when, without warning, for the second time in less than an hour, a girl who was not me leaned in and boldly kissed my boyfriend on the mouth.

I froze. In fact, I'm pretty sure the whole room froze. I think we were all too stunned to move or react or do anything at all. This included Carter. I hadn't been surprised Alexis would kiss him, but this was *Jill*. And it was in the middle of the Winter Ball, in front of practically the entire school. I'd known that she loved him as way more than a cousin, but never in even my craziest moments did I imagine she'd so publicly declare it.

I also couldn't imagine what had given her the courage to do it. Maybe it was their effortless dancing, or the magical atmosphere of the ball, or his gentle hug. Hell, maybe she'd had too much champagne too. Whatever it was, though, it had led to her mouth on his stunned, half open lips, and—I'm not even sure how I could see this, but I did—her small tongue tentatively slipping between them. Suddenly my joke from a few minutes ago was not funny but terribly prophetic.

Beside me, her jaw hanging open in utter disbelief, Amy said, "Holy shit! Apparently it's kiss-your-boyfriend night and we didn't get the memo!" She looked around as if there might be other girls in line for the honor. I was almost afraid there were. I even noticed Alexis gaping.

Without thinking, I shot up from my chair, just as Carter regained his senses and stumbled backward from Jill. He looked completely dazed, both reaching toward her and touching his lips in total confusion. Jill turned and sprinted from the room, slipping out from under Carter's hand on her shoulder.

Lightheaded and dazed myself, I too stumbled. And of course, in the most ridiculous of coincidences—though by that time, I probably shouldn't have expected anything less—a helpful server happened to be on hand to catch me as I fell backwards. The moment he touched me, I saw that he was going to die, and soon. He had no idea he had cancer. His might not have been a very grisly death, but my champagne-and-shock-addled brain was already too overwhelmed to handle the surprise.

"I'm so sorry," I cried, then promptly fainted in his arms.

MY FIRST WINTER Ball became the stuff of legend. I'd felt popular-by-proxy since I'd arrived at Northbrook, and had then gained further notoriety by my own antics—namely dating Carter, nearly "dying" at the bookstore, and causing Alexis Morrow to be banned from said bookstore—but because of the level of witnesses and the sensational nature of the events, I was instantly catapulted to a new stratosphere of recognition after the Ball. *Everyone* wanted to know how I was feeling, how I dealt with my "condition," and, most importantly, how I felt about seeing my boyfriend being French-kissed by his "ex-girlfriend."

I didn't bother correcting people that Jill wasn't ever his girlfriend, and I couldn't imagine the level of attention I'd have gotten if people knew I'd actually seen it twice; it was already ten times worse than the day after my first collapse or the day my relationship with Carter went public. I'd learned to enjoy gossip since coming to the Academy, but the negative side of that is learning to hate being the subject of it.

If I felt bad for myself, I felt a million times worse for Jill. I wasn't mad at her, not really, just sorry. I didn't like pitying someone, but I couldn't help it, even if she'd brought the attention upon herself. I couldn't fathom why she'd done what she did at the Ball, but she certainly wasn't talking to me about it. In fact, she wasn't talking to anyone.

Carter had tried, repeatedly, but she was avoiding him as effectively as she'd previously been avoiding me. She hadn't quit the bookstore, but she wouldn't stay within five feet of Carter when she was there and she stopped attending Sunday dinners completely. If I'd thought she was isolated by nature before, now she was in a self-enforced solitary confinement. For my part, I left her alone—I didn't think it would help if I tried to approach her—and I encouraged everyone else to do the same. With time, I prayed this would blow over, or that something more sensational would take stage.

The only other item remotely worth any attention was the new 'It Couple' on campus: Alexis and Garrett. Carter and I had held the title for a while, but we'd become relatively old news by this point. Apparently Alex hadn't dated an Academy boy since her freshman year, and Garrett had never really dated anyone, so this was big news for the queen of campus. I was intrigued to discover that the last fellow student she *had* dated was the same senior Amy'd gotten tangled up with her freshman year; I had a feeling that's where some of the their animosity came from.

I wished I could be happy for the new couple, but it was difficult. I wasn't sure that Alexis wanted more than someone to distract her from her failed attempt on *my* boyfriend, and I was afraid Garrett's heart would end up broken. Speaking of, I was also bizarrely concerned about *Carter's* heart. I couldn't shake from my head what I'd overheard Alexis say to him the night of the Ball: *She'll break your heart, Carter. She will.* Would I? Why did she think that? And why the hell couldn't *I* stop thinking about it?

I was sure she meant it, just as I believed her feelings for Carter were more than surface-deep. The worst part was that this time her Sententia ability had nothing to do with my shaken confidence. She'd been too far away from me that night for it to have had any effect. No, something about her words struck a nerve of doubt, all on their own merit.

But I kept these worries to myself, for now. I didn't *think* I would break Carter's heart or, at least, I had no intention of it. The depth of my feelings for him grew on a daily basis. What I felt for him was love, plain and simple, even if I wasn't ready to say so out loud yet. In fact, the way in which I became absorbed with him was incredible. It should probably have been frightening, but I wasn't scared to fall in love with Carter. Instead, I was fascinated, excited, and eager to see how much further I *could* fall.

I was also convinced he felt the same way, maybe even more so. Where I was reserved by nature, Carter was not. He was passionate and intense about whatever he believed in. Luckily for me, he believed I was the one for him. And I believed it too, so I did my best to push away my nagging fears and, as Amy said, enjoy where I was right now.

Chapter Twenty-One

As a distraction, I threw my attention into something else: discovering my heritage. It had been months since I'd thought about it, there were so many other demands on my brain, but I decided that knowing where I'd come from would eliminate one question in my life. That could only be a good thing.

During one Wednesday session, I had a stroke of genius.

"What if my dad's parents, whoever they were, went here?" I said to Carter as we were packing up to leave the library. "That's possible, don't you think?"

"One of them must have, at least," he replied. "Otherwise why establish a Legacy? It would be an unlikely thing to do if they hadn't been a student here first."

I got up from our table and started to wander while I thought. I was walking between the stacks of Academy history when I saw them. "Hey! Aren't these all the old yearbooks?"

Carter joined me and surveyed the dusty spines in front of us. "Looks like it to me." I trailed my fingers over the yearly records of Academy students—every year since the school's inception was lined up in neat row after row—and stopped on one from the year my father was born. Carter tilted his head at me in curiosity. "What are you thinking?"

"I don't know…just, what if I can look through these and see someone who looks like him? It could be a clue or something to go by. I know it's a long shot, but…"

"Let's give it a try anyway," he suggested. "Why not? It might be a long shot, but we don't have anything to lose but a few hours of time together. I can afford that."

It amazed me that he seemed excited to spend time looking through dusty old yearbooks, just because it would be with me, but I think he liked the challenge of the mystery too. He wanted to figure it out as much as I did. We went back to the table and began flipping pages. Not knowing where else to start, I picked the book under my fingers, from the year of my father's birth.

It was actually fun, looking at all the unfamiliar faces and imagining who they were today, or which of my classmates they were like, seeing how styles had changed or not changed. We finished the first book without any luck, but it wasn't late and we were having a good time, so we picked up the one next to it.

Turned out my silly idea was a good one. Except that our search shouldn't have been for my *father's* face.

We were nearing the end of the second book, in the middle of the senior class portraits, when I stopped in surprise. There, smiling back at us from the second row from the bottom, was an almost exact likeness of…me. I pointed at her and stared for a minute. She really looked just like me, except for a subtle difference in the shape of the eyes. Otherwise, it could have been a picture of me taken yesterday; her long, dark hair was even styled the same. We both leaned over to read the corresponding name printed on the side of the page. The small text read: Virginia Lillian Marwood.

Carter inhaled sharply. "Is it possible?" he said aloud, but I was sure he was talking to himself.

I tapped his arm. "You know who she is?"

"Yes, though obviously I'd never seen her before, or I might have known who you are too…" he trailed off and recommenced staring at the page.

"Um, so who is she?"

He turned back to me and said, "She is—was—the last Hangman. Now…maybe that's you."

Hangman?! I was not encouraged by that. "Wh…what do you mean?"

But he was back to muttering to himself. He stood up and started pacing. "It could be…half the gift makes sense anyway…but there has to be another."

I stood too and moved into the small path he was wearing in the carpet next to the table. He nearly bumped into me. "Hello? I'm still here, and kind of freaked out. What do you mean, Hangman? Who is she?"

"Sorry! I…just can't believe it." He put his hands on my shoulders and guided us back to our chairs.

"Well…maybe it's nothing."

Carter gave me his measured look. Okay, it probably wasn't nothing. "The resemblance is way too strong to be a coincidence, don't you think?"

"I do. But you've scared me, so I'm pretending maybe there's nothing to worry about."

He shook his head. "No, you don't have to worry. It's just, well, you're special. Even more than we already thought."

"What does that mean?"

"The Marwoods were the last documented Hangmen. Virginia Marwood was, we thought, the last of the last and she disappeared the year after she graduated. I don't know anything else about her, but I'd heard that much at least. We're always on the lookout for evidence of another."

I felt like I was missing something. "So they could do what I do? Predict deaths?"

He shook his head again. "Not exactly, no. If that were the case, I'd have known immediately who you were. You must get that, well, *part* of that, from whoever is your grandfather. It has to be. No Lainey, they didn't predict anything, but they did deal in death. The Marwoods are exactly what I said. They're hangmen…executioners. *Carnifex* is the Latin."

Okay, this was *not* good at all. He said I didn't have to worry, but honestly, this was about the freakiest thing I'd heard since this whole crazy thing started. And that was quite a distinction, considering. "Can you spell this out for me, please? What, exactly, is it that they could do?"

He ran his hands through his hair, the international sign, as far as Carter's signs went, that I was right; I *should* be worried. He reached over and grabbed my hands. "You can do it too," he said. "At least I'm guessing you can. With Thought, Lainey, they—you—can cause death. That's what they could do. All of them."

It was my turn to gasp. If Carter hadn't been holding onto me, I would have fallen off my chair. *"WHAT?!* That…that's impossible."

"It's not," he said gently. "It's no less possible than anything else we can do."

I felt like I might hyperventilate. Or something. Maybe pass out, which I usually tried to avoid, but might welcome at that moment. Anything but believe what he'd said was true. Since my arrival at Northbrook, I'd learned many things that defied belief, and many things that frightened me, but none more than this. So instead of coping, I asked a stupid question. "Why didn't you tell me people could do that?!"

He actually smiled. It was a small one, and it made me blindingly angry for a second, until he brushed his hand lightly across my cheek and I came to my senses. I definitely wasn't thinking straight, but how could I, in light of what I'd learned? "Because we didn't think anyone could anymore."

"How?" I asked. "How does it work?"

"I don't know," he said, then held his hands up quickly. I'm sure my frustration was obvious on my face. "I'm sorry. It's just...how do any of our abilities work? It's Thought. And there hasn't been anyone with that gift for more than forty years. The limited evidence we have says a Hangman can stop a person's heart and that it's completely natural."

I digested his words and then I laughed, a completely inappropriate laugh, but I couldn't help it. "Amy was right. I really am a heartbreaker," I said, before I dropped my head onto my arms resting on the table.

Carter's warm hand traced light circles over my back. I practiced some of my auntie's yoga breaths and tried to come to terms with this new revelation. *If I think hard enough, I can kill someone.* Just thinking about thinking about it scared me. What if I did it by accident? Could I do it to myself? Suddenly all the times I'd jokingly thought in my head, *I'd like to kill that person!* took on a whole new, frightening meaning. What if I actually *could*?

"You have to touch the person," Carter murmured. "My guess is it needs to be skin to skin, though I don't have any evidence of that, just a good hunch." Suddenly I envisioned myself wearing gloves for my foreseeable future. My skin was, apparently, a deadly weapon. Carter went on, almost as if reading my thoughts. "It's not a simple thing, to use a gift with impetus. It's impossible to do it accidentally or casually.

Nearly impossible," he amended. That was a small relief, at least. Maybe I could reconsider the gloves.

"It's not like your visions, where the object sometimes forces its history—or future—on you. That's just a sense. No, this gift…you're essentially a Thought Mover, but you can only move one thing: a Thought of, well, death. It takes conscious effort and a channeling of the gift. It's almost a physical sensation, actually. You can feel it, when you exercise the impetus, kind of like electricity in your veins. So I've been told, anyway," he tacked on at the end.

"So I don't have to ask you never to touch me again?" My voice was muffled by my arms and the table, but I was sure he could hear me. Maybe my mind wasn't in exactly the right place, but that was the most miserable thought I'd had in relation to this whole miserable scenario.

"I don't think that will be necessary," he said with a chuckle. "Unless you decide you want to kill me, in which case, I'd appreciate a little warning and a chance to discuss it."

It was almost amusing how Carter could be so serious about things except for when it was time to be serious. I ignored his joke and asked, "Can I do it to myself?"

He inhaled sharply, exactly like he had when he'd seen the name Marwood on the page, and his hand stilled on my back. "NO! Why would you even ask that?"

I turned my head slightly to look back at him. "It's something I need to know. I…wasn't considering it. I just want to know what I'm dealing with."

Carter released his breath slowly. "As far as I know, none of us can use our gifts on ourselves."

"That's good to know."

We were quiet again except for the sound of my yoga breathing. I wasn't sure if it was helping, but it gave me something to concentrate on. Of course, I should have known the worst of the news hadn't come yet.

In his most soothing voice, Carter said, "You might not like what I tell you next." Before I had a chance to react, he continued. "The Council will be very interested in this. I'll...have to tell my uncle." He paused. Dan Astor was already interested in me, so I wasn't sure why this was a big deal, but then Carter dropped the real bomb. "At least one of the Marwoods worked for the Perceptum almost since its inception. Up until Virginia disappeared, anyway."

That got me to sit up. I hadn't been able to shake my fear of the Perceptum despite numerous reassurances. "By 'worked,' you mean..."

He nodded solemnly. "They did what their gift allowed. They were...the Council's executioners."

I BEGGED CARTER not to tell anyone. I was not beneath bribery, of a sort, so I kissed him until he agreed. Or compromised, anyway. It wasn't exactly what I was looking for—which was not telling anyone, ever—but he promised not to talk to his uncle about it until we tried a little more to confirm my father's parentage. I contemplated completely dropping the subject, but Carter wouldn't let me, and I didn't honestly want to. Even if the truth was distressing, I thought I wanted to know it. With that in mind, I finally made a call I'd not exactly been putting off, but hadn't made until it suddenly became a priority.

"Lainey!" came my Uncle Martin's rich voice from the other end of the line. "What a pleasant surprise! I didn't expect to hear from you so soon after your birthday. What's going on? Have you found a piece you'd like to purchase? You haven't used much of your investment budget lately..."

Talking to my uncle always made me feel like a little kid talking to Santa. I felt warm and happy knowing he was there for me even if I only saw him maybe once a year. Whenever we spoke, I almost always asked for something, and he always tried to give it to me. I knew he had many, many clients, but I was pretty sure I was the only one he considered family. Usually my unexpected calls to him had to do with one of the other weird clauses my dad put into my trust fund, giving me a special budget every year to use only for investments. My chosen market was, naturally, antique furniture.

Carter was next to me and I idly ran my fingers over his as I spoke. We were sitting in front of the fireplace in the bookstore lounge after the store had closed. I was nervous to make this call, not because I didn't think my uncle would try to help me, but because I was generally afraid of what I'd learn. The combination of dim lights, soft couch, warm fire, and Carter helped me feel more relaxed. I took a deep breath and got to the point.

"Unfortunately not, Uncle Martin. There's not a whole lot of time for me to go shopping up here. But I don't mind! You know I really like it at the Academy. I...never knew what I was missing before."

"So what can I do for you today, or maybe you were just missing your family, called to hear a friendly voice?" He said the last part with a smile, I could tell. Uncle Martin knew me well. It must have been obvious I needed something.

"I..." I started, and then stopped. I'd never asked questions like this about my father before, and I didn't exactly know how to start. Carter gave my hand an encouraging squeeze and I cleared my throat. "I was hoping you could tell me some things...about my father."

Uncle Martin made a thoughtful noise. "I'm going to guess the question means something different this time than when you've asked it before," he said.

"I guess, yeah. You're right. I...was hoping you could tell me about where he came from."

"I've always wondered when you'd ask," he said. "It surprises me it took until now. I knew it would be sometime soon; with the unusual nature of your school placement, you were bound to want to find out where it came from."

"Do you know?" I asked. "You said it was anonymous, but I thought maybe…"

He laughed a little. "Thought maybe telling you about it was another clause in your trust, like offering your place at the Academy? Unfortunately not. What I said earlier was the whole of my knowledge, even if I wish I could tell you more." I think he could sense my deflation over the phone line. "I'm sorry, Lainey. I do so hate to disappoint you. But I'll tell you what I do know. It isn't much. Your father was…very private about his past. He liked to say his real life started when he turned eighteen and nothing before that mattered. He put himself through college, made a fortune on nothing more than his own wit and maybe a little good luck, and then met the loves of his life: first your mother, then you."

I smiled at that. Not remembering them myself, it was sometimes hard to imagine how much my parents probably loved me, but I had evidence enough to believe it wholeheartedly. Uncle Martin continued, "His childhood, I gather, was not a happy one, but I like to believe it made him the strong, self-reliant man he was. I think you've inherited those traits, by the way, even if your childhood has been one of more joys than sorrows. I know he was born in Boston, but if he ever learned who his birth parents were, he never told me. He was adopted by the Young family before he was one year old. The rest you already know."

I stammered out my thanks, but was mostly depressed by his lack of information. I didn't know where else to turn if he couldn't help me. Aunt Tessa knew even less, and that was the extent of my list of people to ask.

Carter, thankfully, was there to make the obvious next step obvious to me. I gathered he could hear most of Uncle Martin's part of the conversation. He scribbled something on the edge of my notebook and raised a questioning eyebrow at me. *His adoptive family?* is what he wrote.

I felt foolish for not thinking to ask more about them. "What about the family who adopted him? Do you think they might know more? If you even know who or where they are."

"I don't know much about them, either," he said, but before I got too depressed, he went on. "But I do know where his adoptive mother lives. Or lived, in any case. Your father left a small sum to her in his will. Perhaps I shouldn't tell you this information, but, well, I understand why you want to know more. Her name is Chastine Young…"

Chapter Twenty-Two

T his is it," Carter said.

He idled in front of a modest, one-story house with faded white siding and a cracked concrete driveway. Okay, "modest" was a polite way to describe it. It was actually pretty shabby, as were most of the surrounding houses. The crowded neighborhood wasn't quite one where I felt unsafe, but it wasn't the nicest I'd ever visited. It was also where my father had grown up. We were in an urban area outside Boston looking at Chastine Young's house.

It had taken me two days to work up the courage to call the number Uncle Martin gave me. My father had had no contact with her from the moment he left home up until the day Uncle Martin called about her bequest in his will. She was also, I thought, my only hope, and I'd been desperately afraid she'd have moved or died or, worse, refused to speak to me. But after some initial surprise, she'd invited me, almost excitedly, to visit the next weekend. Maybe I'd inherited some of my father's renowned "luck" too, among all the other less-appealing things.

There were no spaces on the street by Mrs. Young's house, so Carter parallel parked a little ways down. As we walked back, I tried to imagine my father playing in this neighborhood when he was a kid, but I couldn't picture him in it. I had the feeling it had been run down for a long time, and my idea of my handsome, urbane father just didn't fit.

"Try to relax," Carter said and grabbed my hand.

He sounded so much like Amy always did that I laughed. "Please don't tell me to take up yoga."

We climbed the crumbling concrete front stairs and stood under the small aluminum awning while I gathered my courage. I took a deep breath and rang the doorbell.

A soft chime sounded from inside, and after a little while, the door cracked open in front of us. A tiny, aged woman peered at us through the screen. I had to work to hide my surprise. Chastine Young was far older than she should have been, with short, curly white hair and a slightly stooped back. She'd clearly lived a lot of life, if not necessarily years, and much of it not easy. I was ready to introduce myself, but it was fairly obvious I didn't need to. As soon as she looked at me, she gasped and put her hand to her mouth.

"Oh my word," she said quietly.

"H…Hi, Mrs. Young?" I stammered. I took another deep breath and went on in a stronger voice. "I'm Lainey Young—we spoke on the phone—and this is Carter Penrose."

"Oh my dear," she said, echoing her first words. "Just like Virginia…"

I glanced at Carter. Any doubts I was still harboring vanished. Carter had been convinced all along, but I'd held out the tiniest hope that it was a coincidence after all, that I was not the last Marwood.

She opened the screen for us and gestured inside. "Well, why don't you come in, Lainey? I suppose I'm your grandmother of a sort, and it's nice to meet you."

We followed her into a small, dim living room, filled with furniture that had seen better days many years ago. I thought it was possible my father had known this furniture. Everything in the room might have been worn, but it was tidy, and smelled faintly of lemon cleaner, as if it had just been dusted. Carter and I sat together on what served as the couch, but was no bigger than a love seat, while Mrs. Young fluttered by a doorway. "You wait here while I get us some tea—an old woman needs her tea—and then I'll tell you everything you want to know."

With that, she disappeared through a swinging door into what I assumed was the kitchen. I squeezed Carter's hand and he smiled back encouragingly. I was grateful for Mrs. Young's warm reception. It didn't sound as though her and my father's relationship could have been very good—he did leave her home and never once come back. We waited in nervous silence for her to return. Well, I waited in nervous silence. Carter simply memorized the small room and held my hand in support.

Mrs. Young returned after not very long, carrying a small tray with three steaming mugs and a plate of a few cookies. She set the tray on the low table in front of us and sat herself in the ragged chair to my left, placing her own mug on an end table between the chair and loveseat. The lamp that rested on it was the only light in the room. The curtains were half drawn over the picture window that dominated one wall and looked out on the small front yard. Carter and I both picked up our tea and took polite sips. It was weak, but warm and relaxing, extra sweet with sugar.

"Thank you," I said. "For the tea, and for being willing to see me."

"I suppose you've come to hear about Allen," Mrs. Young said as she peered at me over her own mug. She didn't seem like a woman who was afraid to get straight to the point.

"Yes, if you don't mind…" I told her about Northbrook, the mystery of my Legacy, and how we hoped she might help us understand where it had come from.

"I don't know exactly how your schooling came to be, but…well, it would probably be easiest if I just started at the beginning…"

I listened to her story in rapt silence.

"Allen is my greatest regret, in a long list of them," she said, pausing to take a brief sip of her tea. "He was a good child, special, but I…I suppose I was not a very good mother to him. For certain I wasn't. It's why he left here practically a boy and I never heard from him again 'til he'd passed. I am sorry about that, young lady. He was so young and you had to be, too. I'm sorry you didn't get to grow up with your own parents, either."

Mrs. Young had a soft Boston accent, almost charming in her old-lady voice. When she said "either," it sounded more like a gentle *ee-tha*. "You're the spitting image of Allen's real mother, you know. You could've been a ghost on my doorstep, except it's not the middle of the night and you're not holding a squalling baby. Her name was Virginia. Virginia Marwood. I hadn't seen her in years before she showed up that night, and that was the last time I saw her at all. She thought she was making a good decision, bringing her baby to me. I wish it had been true.

"We'd known each other since we were practically babies. My mother was the housekeeper for Virginia's family. Our lives were very different then—I was poor and she was not—but when you're children, the differences don't seem to matter. Virginia was happy enough to play with me, another girl only a few years older than she was. By the time we were teenagers, we were on very different paths, or so I thought. Virginia went away to a proper school—maybe the same one as yours—and I…I did finish high school, for all the good it did me, but I was not interested in learning. I was interested in…freedom, I guess.

"'Course, as soon as I had it, first thing I did was give it up. Got myself pregnant, and then, because I was a romantic, got myself married. I thought that was the right thing to do, and I stuck by that decision. At eighteen I had one baby, by twenty I had two, and it would turn out that by twenty-one I'd have three. Long time later, I'd realize that was two too many. I could barely manage one, and three tipped me right over the edge. But you came to hear about your daddy, not the sad story of my mistakes…"

She paused to sip more tea and nibble at a cookie. I discovered I'd practically been holding my breath the entire time, and gulped needed air while I glanced at Carter. He too sipped his tea, and though he looked relaxed, I could tell he was as fascinated by the story as I was. Mrs. Young cleared her throat softly and went on.

"Like I said, it was late at night when Virginia showed up at my door. I hadn't seen her since she left for her fancy school. I'm not even sure how she found me—I was long gone from my mother's— but she did. She was pretty as ever, just like you, Lainey, but she looked tired and, most of all, scared. Her son, your father, squirmed and cried in her arms, as if he knew what she was going to do. She was only eighteen, maybe nineteen, I can't remember for sure."

She shook her head sadly and smoothed the surface of the worn velvet chair cushion with her equally worn hand. "For all her good fortune, we ended up in the same predicament. Children with children of their own. I think she must've gotten pregnant before she graduated from high school, or not long after. Said she wouldn't marry the baby's father, as I had, and couldn't even if she wanted to. I never asked why, but I assume he was married already. He was older, she said, and important. And dangerous. She said she couldn't bring herself to end the pregnancy—that wasn't so easy back then, either—and she refused to tell the father about the child. In fact, she hadn't told anyone. When she'd gotten too big to hide her condition, she'd run away.

"Allen was only a few weeks old when she showed up here. She begged me to take him, raise him as my own. I asked why she'd picked me, another destitute young mother. She said she couldn't bear to leave him with someone she didn't know, but she didn't want his father to find him either. She thought Allen would be safe with me. She was wrong, though not because of whatever threat his father posed. But I couldn't have seen that then."

Mrs. Young stopped abruptly and rose, looking around as if she'd just remembered something. She bent stiffly and pulled an aged photo album from a stack under the coffee table. After flipping a few pages, she handed it to me. "Your daddy," she said and pointed to a picture of my father as a young boy. I'd have recognized him even though I'd never seen pictures of him as anything but an adult. He looked serious and sad, but still my father.

"Willie," she went on, pointing to another photo, "my husband, wanted to refuse. We had enough trouble with our own two babies and ourselves to take on one more mouth to feed. Until Virginia gave us her suitcase. It was full of money, a *lot* of money in that day. She said it was everything she had from her family and from selling all her nice things. If we'd take the baby, and promise to raise him, we could have it. We accepted."

I turned pages in the album as she spoke, seeing pictures of a much younger everything—this house, Mrs. Young, my dad with two little girls—and it was almost as if her story came alive before my eyes.

"For a while," she continued, "we were happy. We were able to buy this house and live well. Better than we should have. But the money didn't last as long as our promise, and though we never went back on it, I think your father's the one who paid the price. Willie hadn't wanted him to begin with, and once the money was gone…he treated

Allen almost as badly as he treated me. Our daughters were spared his hand—Allen and I were plenty enough to knock around—though not my foolishness. I never defended your father, and I barely raised my daughters. It's a wonder they love me, but they do, and I'm grateful.

"For all that, Allen grew up to be a good boy. He was a big boy too, taller even than you, young man"—she looked over at Carter—"and just as handsome in his way. He didn't look much like you, or Virginia, I suppose you know, except for your same dark hair. I imagine he looked like his father's family.

"When he got old enough, he was almost never home. He went to school, and when he wasn't at school he worked at any job he could find. That was another problem, because he refused to give my husband any of the money. Sometimes he'd sneak some to me, for his sisters, and I hid it away without a word. The little bit of time Allen was home, Willie would be on him about the money, or any other problem he could blame on him. Allen was big enough to fight back by that time, but for some reason, he never did. Not until the end.

"The day Allen turned eighteen—before he even graduated from high school—he came home to say he was leaving. He gathered up the few things he wanted to take while I cried and begged him not to go. He refused, not that I should have been surprised. I think he meant to be gone before my husband got home, but he didn't make it.

"Willie went after him right away—for taking off on his family, for upsetting me, for being a bastard child, anything you could name. I sobbed and sobbed, and for the first and last time, begged Willie to leave Allen alone. He didn't, and then he turned on me. That was the final straw. For all my failures, I think your father loved me too, and I think he knew that when he was gone, I'd be the only one left for Willie to hit. I wasn't sure how long I'd survive that, but it didn't matter.

"Allen turned on Willie and told him not to touch me, not to touch me ever again. Willie came back after him, and Allen grabbed his swinging fists and shoved him away. That was all it took. Willie stumbled, fell, and never got back up. We didn't know what to do, your father and I, it seemed so unreal. Eventually the doctors came and pronounced Willie dead of a heart attack and gave us their condolences."

She was crying now, not sobs, but slow, sad tears that overflowed her eyes and ran down her cheeks. She wiped them away absently. I imagined these weren't the first tears she'd cried in memory of my father and her youth. "In the same day, I lost my husband and my son. I cried many more tears that day, most of them from shame. More than loss, I felt relief, and some regret. Even if I didn't know how I'd go on, I knew I was better off without my husband. And Allen...I knew I deserved for him to leave, and he did, but not before giving me almost all the money I think he'd saved. I was amazed at how much it was, and cried even harder. He'd given me more than my husband had brought home in months of working. And that was the last time I saw him, Lainey. The rest of his life, you'll have to tell me about."

I couldn't respond for a moment. I'd never imagined my father's childhood was so...terrible. And I knew, without a doubt, what had happened to his adoptive father. I wondered if my father did, if he knew that *he* had caused the heart attack, but that was a question I'd never have answered. Regardless, Chastine Young's sad story confirmed everything I'd suspected before we came. I *was* the last Marwood, whether I wanted to be or not. I didn't realize that I was crying too, until Carter reached out and gently brushed away the tears on my cheeks. I hastily grabbed a napkin from the tray and blotted them away.

"I'm sorry, child," Mrs. Young said. "It is a sad story, and I'm ashamed it's all true. Allen's life got better once he left me, though, I know it did. You're proof of that. Perhaps you can lift my spirits by telling me about the man he became. Do you even remember him?"

I didn't, not really, but my aunt made sure I never forgot my parents. I told Mrs. Young what I knew, all the way up until their accident. I told her a little about my life too, though I glossed over exactly *why* I ended up at Northbrook, which brought us full circle.

I hadn't wanted to interrupt her story, so I finally asked the few questions I'd been saving. "Did you ever learn who his real father was?"

She shook her head. "I didn't, no. I've always wondered if he did, but he never told me. One day when he was maybe fourteen, I looked out the window and saw he was home from school. Except he wasn't on foot. He was getting out of an expensive car. A man who looked like a driver sat in the front, but I couldn't see into the back. Your daddy slammed the door and marched up to the house, shoving something in his pocket, and angrier than I'd just about ever seen him. I asked what was going on, but he told me it was nothing. He said if I ever saw that car again not to talk to them. I...I think whoever it was must have been his real father. He'd found him somehow. But either Allen didn't believe him, or he wanted nothing to do with him. Not sure it matters which. We never saw him again, and I don't know who he was."

Carter had been silent almost our entire visit, but he asked a question that sounded innocent enough, yet I understood the meaning behind it completely. "What was Allen like as a boy? Did he get along with the other children?"

Mrs. Young thought about her answer before speaking. "He was a sweet child, never complained much despite all the things he deserved to complain about. Never had problems at school either. He was a quiet, likeable boy. When he got older, he was bigger than all the other kids, which is what kept him out of fights, I think. And then...about the time he became a teenager, around the time I think he met his father, in fact, he became even quieter than before. I figured it was normal, for a boy who'd had his life, and for a teenager.

"But for all he seemed quiet and sad, everything else went well for him. His school grades were nearly perfect, and he always had at least one job or more, when jobs of any kind were not so easy to come by for a boy his age. It seemed like everything he touched turned to gold, everything except his home life. Even then, he almost always came home at the *right* time, avoiding Willie as if he knew where he'd be. Most of the time, anyway.

"The day Allen left, I knew he'd be fine, no thanks to me. Any high school boy who can save up more money working part time jobs than Willie brought home in a year was going to make something of himself. And he did. That lawyer who called after Allen died, he said Allen'd left me a 'small sum' of money in his will. Maybe it was 'small' by his definition, but it was a fortune to me. It's been enough to keep me here in my home in my old age, and to put some away for my other grandchildren too. Allen saved me twice with his generosity, so I guess maybe I did something right by raising him after all."

Carter nodded, as if he'd heard what he wanted to hear. I didn't bother to correct Mrs. Young that my Uncle Martin wasn't a lawyer. I didn't know how much my father had left her in his will, but I did know it truly was a small sum compared to how much he'd left me. How Chastine had described my father corresponded with my aunt's descriptions too. There was something special about my father, and it must have been his Sententia gifts.

"What happened to his mother?" I asked suddenly. "To Virginia." In all of this, I'd nearly forgotten about her.

Mrs. Young shook her head sadly. "She hung herself."

Chapter Twenty-Three

I was a Hangman. The last Marwood, the last of my kind.

My father had been the last before me, and his mother before him. Though horrible, the irony of Virginia Marwood's choice of suicide wasn't lost on me. Mrs. Young explained how she'd seen it in the newspaper, a story about the body of a young, unidentified girl found a few days after she'd seen her. They looked for her family, but not very hard, and though Mrs. Young wanted to contact the authorities, or at least Virginia's mother, to tell them she knew who the girl was, she couldn't do it without bringing too many questions about my father and breaking her promise to keep him a secret.

I walked around in a distracted fog for the next few days. I wasn't sure why being a Hangman was harder to accept than all the other bizarre things I'd come to accept in the months since November, but I was having trouble processing it. Maybe it was the nature of the new gift that came with this fact. I'd gotten used to being a Grim Diviner rather easily, because it was a concern of my daily existence, and because it was easier; that gift couldn't cause anyone harm but me.

Carter repeatedly told me not to worry, that I would never use the ability accidentally: the ability to stop someone's heart with only my touch and a thought. Or Thought. I was back to considering it in capital letters. I also believed Carter was likely wrong. My father had almost certainly used the ability accidentally. Maybe now that I knew what I could do, I never would, but it worried me. I could have, and that was bad enough.

Based on my abilities, and the similar comments about my father made by my aunt, Uncle Martin, and Mrs. Young—his luck, his seeming ability to avoid bad events—Carter was certain that my father and *his* father had been Diviners. Nothing else made sense. Without any real proof, we guessed that my father could sense possible outcomes, or even just bad outcomes, thus being able to avoid them. Whatever he'd been able to do exactly, it had translated in me to the ability to sense only one outcome—someone's death.

"I still don't understand how this works," I said to Carter at our next practice session. "Why can we do such different things, my father and I…you and your father and, well, I don't know what your mother could do?"

"My mother was dormant," Carter replied, not elaborating further. "And the rest of us, it's not completely different, what we do. It's all related. My father knew when he'd seen or heard something before. It's similar to what I can do, and my aunt, and what their parents could do. Same with you. You can do something similar, if not precisely the same, to what it seems like your father could do. Eventually it all gets muddled together." He thought for a minute, then said, "Think of the way you look like your grandmother. Did your father look like her?"

"Not at all," I said. "I never thought I looked like either of my parents, not really. I was always a little sad about that, by the way. My mother was very beautiful. My father was handsome too, but I'd have loved to look like my mother…My dad and I do have kind of the same eyes, only a different color. Otherwise, yeah, I guess I look just like Virginia Marwood."

"Who is certainly as beautiful in her own way as your mother must have been in hers," he said with a smile, and a brief kiss of my hand, but was quickly back to business. "So that appearance is in your family history, even if your father didn't share it. It's the same with Sententia abilities…they can skip generations, or express themselves in slightly different ways. It's the same with…regular people too. If your aunt had a child, he or she might inherit her artistic abilities but excel in a different area. Oil painting or something. Or nothing. Our abilities can manifest strongly, weakly, even not at all, in comparison to our parents' and families'. Sometimes parents who have average skills produce children who are exceptionally talented or vice versa."

"How…how can we be certain that I'm a Hangman then? It's not like I'm going to test it, and you just said I could be…average."

His smile was a mixture of amusement and sadness. "You're far from average, Lainey." I didn't think he was talking about only my Sententia abilities, and I blushed again. I couldn't help it. How was it possible I could learn to control an ability that allowed me to see the future, but I couldn't keep myself from blushing every time Carter said something remotely flirty? It boggled the mind.

Oblivious to my internal struggles, Carter went on. "I suppose we can't. There's a possibility you didn't inherit the death touch"—I shuddered at the phrase—"but since you did turn out a *Grim* Diviner, I'm guessing you've got it. I'd be surprised if you *didn't.*"

I sighed. Really, I should accept the idea and move on. But I couldn't, not when Carter reminded me of something I dreaded almost as much as the gift itself.

"I still have to tell my uncle," he said quietly, and I knew he didn't mean Jeff Revell.

"And I still don't want you to," I countered. I got up from the table and paced around in frustration. "Why can't it be a secret, Carter? I'm rare enough to begin with, or so you say. That should be enough. I will *never* use the gift. Not for anyone, and definitely not for the Perceptum."

He was quiet for a minute. "It's too important not to share," he said finally. "And I'm an Historian. I work for the Perceptum. I've made a commitment to share what I discover about the Sententia. I have to share this."

So *that* was the real reason. He felt bound by his job, which was a sort of promise. I didn't know how to react to that. I wanted to be more important than his work, but really, I'd only been part of his life for a few months. And it was more than a job to Carter. If I was from a special family line, so was he. He was a Penrose. Being Sententia and working for the Perceptum was practically ingrained in his whole existence. He'd even worked for them since he was fifteen, when he abandoned regular schooling. It was a breach of protocol, but between his incomparable ability and his uncle at the helm, it hadn't been much of a challenge for him to be accepted.

I thought this was our first real fight, though we weren't really arguing. Disagreement might have been a better term for it. It only took a few months for it to happen. I imagined what it would be like to be a regular couple, like Caleb and Amy, arguing about mundane things like sports and what movie to watch, and not have our relationship affected by being part of a secret world. On the other hand, my friends argued about things that ultimately seemed unimportant to me compared to, oh, whether or not I told a secret organization that I was their long-lost assassin.

I felt stuck, caught between wanting to be with Carter and wanting little or nothing to do with the world he inhabited so completely. This would not be the last time I had this feeling, I was sure.

"The Perceptum already thinks my family has died out, or disappeared, or whatever. Please can't we let them keep thinking that? It would be that simple," I said.

It was Carter's turn to sigh and start pacing. Between the two of us, the library's third floor carpet was in serious danger of being worn into paths. "It's *not* that simple for me, Lainey. I'm sorry."

I decided to try a diversionary technique. It had worked before. I stopped in front of him and wrapped my arms around his neck. "Do this for me?" I whispered. I didn't give him time to reply before kissing him soundly and enthusiastically. My plan, at least, was a lot of fun, and it worked. For a little while.

Carter finally broke away from me and stepped out of my reach, running his hands through his hair as he went. The caramel waves were an absolute mess tonight, a sign of how frustrated he was. "You're killing me here," he groaned. "It's not that I *want* to tell them; I just...I *have* to. Please understand. And don't ask me to choose between you and my family. Either way, I can't win."

The last part defeated me. I *was* asking him to make that choice, and suddenly I felt bad about it. Not bad enough that I was ready to acquiesce, but pretty bad. I decided to try for another compromise. "You're right. I'm sorry. But maybe we can wait a little longer...until we've figured out my *whole* family tree. This Legacy had to come from somewhere, and I think it had to have been my grandfather. My dad must have met him that one time." A new idea dawned on me. "He...he had to have known Virginia was pregnant too, even if she thought he didn't! Dr. Stewart told me the Legacy was established the year my father was born."

"That makes sense," he replied. "Chastine also said Virginia described the man as older and important. 'Important' usually means rich. He had to have come from money, considering the size of your Legacy endowment. And...okay. Yes, we can wait a little longer. But I have to tell them, Lainey. I can't not do it."

"I understand." I wandered over to the stacks with the Academy history, musing to myself. "It worked once, so maybe it can work again...let's look at the yearbooks from the first years Virginia would have attended the Academy. It could be one of the upperclassmen when she was a new student. Maybe we'll see something."

And with that decision, my whole world took another bizarre twist.

I stopped in the row by the yearbooks and scanned the shelves for a few years prior to Virginia's graduation. Carter was just walking up to join me. The years I needed were on a shelf above my reach, and I grabbed the rolling ladder that connected to the stacks. But it hadn't been attached correctly by whoever used it last. As I gave it a good tug—the ladders were old, and heavy—to move it down the rail, it detached from the top of the stack and came falling fast, straight at me.

But it didn't hit me.

It should have smacked me soundly in the head, but it suddenly, inexplicably, changed course and fell in the other direction, where it landed hard and cracked down the side. Carter was there, with eyes wide and flashing, just opposite where the ladder had fallen. And like that, I knew.

Carter Penrose had a secret of his own.

I stumbled backward and caught myself ungracefully on the shelves, tumbling over sideways before I, too, ended up on the floor. What the ladder failed to do, my own shock accomplished perfectly well, along with what I was sure would be a wicked bruise on my thigh. At least my head was undamaged. I flipped over and stared up at Carter, as wide-eyed as he was.

"You did that," I breathed.

He gave me the measured look I was certain he had patented. "I did," he admitted after a moment.

"What..." I couldn't form words to finish the question. But thankfully, I didn't have to.

So softly I could barely hear him, he said, "I can move almost any-thing."

"But…" I fumbled again. "But you're a Historian."

"I am. But that's not all I am."

Chapter Twenty-Four

He reached a hand out to help me up, but I stayed stuck on the floor. My brain whirled with a million questions, but landed on one thought: Thought. "You're…"

He closed his eyes and sighed deeply. When he opened them, they were sad, and scared, and maybe a little bit angry. "A Thought Mover, yes. Partially. But I can't pick you up except with my hand, so please take it." He reached down for me again.

I accepted his help, warily, but when I held his hand, he still felt like the same Carter I thought I knew before the ladder fell on me. Or *almost* fell on me, I corrected. Carter had saved me from a black eye, for sure, or maybe worse. Yet I still felt like I'd been hit squarely in the head.

He had me standing, but what I really needed to do was sit down. I stumbled my way back to the table where we'd been working and planted myself in my chair. I stared at my suddenly unfamiliar boyfriend. He followed me back to the table and sat down in his chair across from mine. Without thinking about it, I scooted a little farther away from him.

This was a revelation. Made all the more shocking because he'd kept it from me. I understood, academically anyway, that Thought Movers existed. That they could move objects, or a person's thoughts, with their minds. But seeing someone actually use an ability that, until a few months ago, I'd considered the stuff of science fiction, was amazing. Seeing it used by someone I loved, the same person who'd *hidden* the ability from me, was mind-scrambling. I couldn't understand it.

"How…" I trailed off again.

"Are you sure that ladder didn't hit you? You haven't finished a sentence in the last four tries." His tone was light, but it didn't match his expression. If possible, he looked even more miserable at this moment than after Jill kissed him.

I thought about smacking him for joking, but this was too serious for me to make light of, even if Carter was trying. Instead, I went for one more incomplete sentence. "Please," I murmured. "Explain."

He sighed again. "My mother was a Thought Mover. My father was a *Lumen*. I won the gene lottery and got both. Plus great hair."

"This isn't funny, Carter!" Angry, as well as confused, I shouted at him for the first time ever. "How can you make a joke about something like this? And why the hell didn't you *tell me?*"

The great hair got more of a workout. It was sticking in every direction, which actually *would* have been funny, if not for everything else that had just happened. "You're right," he said. "It's not funny. And I didn't mean to tell you at all. It's a secret, and if you weren't so damn clumsy, I'd have kept it."

I glared at him. I might have been clumsy, true, but this was so not my fault. He had no right to be angry at me for something that he'd done. I'd thought we were having it earlier, but *this* was our first real fight. I leaned back from him even further and crossed my arms. My own anger was helping clear my fuzzy brain.

"I didn't do this, Carter. You did. If you want to be angry at someone, be angry at yourself. And as for me, I'll be mad at you too." His
words clicked into place then, and it dawned on me that this secret was
not only from me. Color me shocked again. "When you said 'secret,'
you mean…*no one* knows? How is that possible?"

Carter's anger drained, replaced by agitation. He hopped up and
paced back and forth several times before abruptly dropping back into
his chair and looking at me. "My family knows, and now you know
too. No one else. I didn't think, when I saw that ladder about to hit
you. I shouldn't have done it, but now I have, and I can't take it back
as much as I wish I could, even if I'd be carrying you to the infirmary
right now instead. In fact, that would have been far more romantic
than what I'm about to do, which is beg you not to tell anyone, or," he
added very quietly, "force you not to, if I have to."

For a moment, I didn't breathe. Had he just threatened me? I
looked at his face, completely serious, and I knew that he had and that
he meant it too. I added scared to my list of angry and confused.
"But…why? They might be rare, but there are other Thought Movers,
or so you tell me. Why are you a secret, a secret you have to *threaten* me
to keep?"

"Because Lainey, I can move anything I've seen at least once before."

"I don't understand."

He rubbed his hands over his eyes, those beautiful blue eyes, and
like that, I *did* understand. There was something else he'd been keeping
from me, though it was a connection I should have made long ago. I
saw it the first time I met him, and several times since. When the ladder fell, I'd seen it again. When he used Thought, his eyes flashed, for
the briefest moment, becoming deep blue on the inside, with the light
blue line around the outside.

"Oh my God," I whispered.

He looked up at me sharply and smiled a bitter smile. "So maybe you do understand after all."

I went for the lesser question. Much like when I had the worst of my visions, I was starting to feel the blackness at the edge of my thoughts that signaled I was going to pass out. I needed to give my brain time to cope before it shut down completely. "Your eyes," I said. "Your eyes…invert when you do it."

"Yes. Though only other Sententia can see it."

"Why is that?"

"It's kind of like subliminal messaging, I guess, or a defense mechanism. A way that we can recognize each other. It's so fast, most people would never be able to notice it, or if they did notice, they'd write it off, think their eyes were playing tricks on them. Sententia are special. We can see it and recognize it for what it is."

"Do mine do it?"

"Sure, though it's hard to tell." His face softened. "They're such an equal mix of green and brown." He reached out as if to touch my hand or maybe my cheek, but I recoiled. I wasn't ready for affection.

"Why didn't you tell me about it? So that I could defend myself," I demanded. "It was your job to tell me about our world and I trusted you to do it."

Putting it like that wounded him, I could see it. His dejection was almost palpable by now. But instead of answering me directly, he asked, "How did you figure it out?"

"At the bookstore," I said, "the first time I met you. I saw your eyes, when your Aunt knocked over the box downstairs. But I guess she didn't knock it over. You did. I thought I was going crazy."

"Guilty. I was pretty sure she was about to say something you shouldn't hear, so…" he shrugged. "I stopped her." He took a deep breath. "I'm sorry. I didn't tell you because…well, I thought you hadn't noticed. You never asked about it. And I thought…if you hadn't noticed, didn't know about it, it would make it easier to keep my secret. I...I wanted to tell you, Lainey. *Everything,* I mean. I really did. You're the only person outside my family I've *ever* wanted to tell, even been tempted to tell. It's just...I've been keeping it secret for so long, it's second nature. I would have told you eventually though, I swear." He shook his head. "God, when am I going to stop having to apologize for my screw-ups? I can't do anything right when it comes to you."

I mulled that over. It wasn't exactly true. Carter did most things right in our relationship, as far as I was concerned. But at the same time, we had been in this position a few too many times, me on one shore of Carter's ocean of regret. Secrets really were the epicenter of most harmful things, I thought. I hoped we'd finally exposed all of the ones between us.

I ran my palms over the smooth surface of the oak table. It suddenly seemed enormous, like a giant, comforting shield. I wanted to put my head down on it and not think, but that wouldn't get us anywhere. The dark, fuzzy feeling had dissipated, so it was time to face reality. It seemed like I was doing a lot of that today. I looked at Carter closely. He was on edge and uncertain, the complete opposite of his usual cool and confident. I wasn't sure if he was more worried about his secret or about me forgiving him. Probably it was a tie.

Finally, I asked, "When you said you can move anything you've seen once, you meant anything, *anywhere,* didn't you? You don't have to be near it, or looking at it, at the time?"

He nodded infinitesimally.

"Oh my God," I said again. "How far?"

"As far as we've tried to test it. I don't think there's a limit."

I nodded, like what he said made perfect sense, but my brain was working feverishly to rewrite its definition of *possible.* If anything should be impossible, this was it. "What did you mean by 'almost any-thing'?"

"I can't move things anchored by God." I raised my eyebrows at him. "Fancy Perceptum talk for alive," he clarified. "I can't move any-thing that's rooted by life. But pretty much anything else is fair game…rocks, boxes, old library ladders…"

I thought about these limitations. I already knew it was quick, sim-ple movements—changes of intention—that Thought Movers could produce. Earlier, he'd changed the direction of the ladder from knock-ing me out to cracking on the floor. But even small changes of intention or direction could produce big consequences.

Finally I asked, "Could you move an airplane?"

"It wouldn't be easy, but yes, if I've seen it or parts of it that might matter, like the control panel. And there's no one in it."

So no crashing airplanes out of the sky, at least. "Could you stop bullets?"

"Possibly. If I've seen them."

"Could you *fire* bullets?"

He hesitated and looked away. "If I've seen the gun."

I repeated my new favorite phrase. "Oh. My. God."

"So do you understand? Why this has to stay a secret?" He stared at me adamantly, then added, "Do you understand what would happen to me if it doesn't?"

I nodded. The possibilities of his power were practically limitless. And awesome. And frightening. "There'd be no end to how people would try to use you. To be a humanitarian. To be a weapon."

"Yes, that's possible," he agreed. "But it's not what I meant."

"What could be worse than that?"

He gripped my hand and I let him, his intensity was so absorbing. "Don't you see, Lainey? If the Perceptum knew about my abilities, they wouldn't try to use me. They'd send *you* to find me."

"You…you can't be serious," I stammered. How could anyone want to hurt Carter? How could anyone think that *I* would hurt Carter? I realized he was holding the hand the Perceptum would send to hurt him, if they could, and I snatched it back.

"Deadly," he said with a wan smile. "And that's not even a pun, so don't get angry." He sighed before saying, "Every once in a while, maybe once a generation, a person comes along whose gift is too powerful to exist…This time, it's me."

I shook my head. Now I understood how he'd been willing to threaten me. Carter's very life hung in the balance of this secret. And his own *uncle* was head of the Council. There's no way he'd let that happen, would he?

I was outraged at the thought. "How could your uncle do that to you?!"

Carter shrugged. "I don't think he would. But this is why there's a council. They're supposed to be objective, not emotional…I'd have to pray for a tie vote, where the President is the tie breaker."

I'd already feared the Perceptum, but now I hated them. I could recognize how they thought what they did was for the greater good, but I couldn't support them, especially not when Carter himself was at their mercy. And I didn't trust them. The Council was made up of human beings, and humans were fallible. We'd already talked about how being Sententia didn't necessarily make someone a good person. I was sure that applied to Council members too. Plus, power corrupts, right? For all I knew, the Council was *more* prone to temptation, not less.

Of course, maybe I wasn't giving them, the whole organization even, a fair chance. I didn't know. All I was certain of was I would do whatever was in my power to keep Carter safe. I'd have kept his secret anyway; knowing the severe consequences of not keeping it made it easier to do.

"Does…does your uncle not know? Your Uncle Dan, I mean. If he knows…" I trailed off. If he knew, wouldn't the Perceptum already know too?

I was surprised by his response. "He does know. And no, he hasn't told the Council," Carter added quickly. "It could get him voted out of the presidency, but he hasn't told them. I guess he loves me enough to risk it."

"Why did you tell him at all? I thought you hardly ever see him."

"Because I had to talk to someone!" he nearly shouted. The extreme intensity was back. This time I reached out and took *his* hand. It was a big gesture from me, considering how he'd been threatening me a few minutes before. But for perhaps the first time, he needed *me* to support *him*. He gripped my hand tightly and managed to give me a small smile.

In control again, he continued in a more subdued voice. "I was thirteen, which is hard enough, when I did it the first time. It was the silliest thing. I was down in the store, getting ready to go to school, when I realized I'd left my TV on. I thought about turning it off. I was late, and I didn't want to run back upstairs, and I…I *felt* it. I hadn't just thought about turning it off; I'd *Thought* about it."

He cleared his throat, and I squeezed his hand to encourage him to go on. "I told you before how there's a physical sensation to using Thought in that way—God, I've almost slipped up with you so many times before; it would have been so much easier if I'd just told you the truth. Anyway, it's difficult to describe. Like electricity, maybe. But it's real and I felt it then. Just like that, I knew I was a Thought Mover. And what I knew about them scared me. I *shouldn't* have been able to use Thought to affect something so far away. *That* was not right and I was in trouble."

"Your uncle?" I prompted. He'd started this story with needing to talk to someone, and his Uncle Dan had been it. I guessed I knew what that meant about him, and about Carter's mother, but I wanted to let Carter tell me the whole thing.

"Yeah, my uncle...There was no one else. Obviously my mother was gone—she really was dormant, by the way; I didn't lie about that—and my dad didn't know how to help me. He was more freaked out than I was. My grandfather—my mother's father, I mean—was already gone too. Besides which, they'd lived in Canada and kind of hated me...pretty much thought my dad stole their daughter and then I killed her. Anyway, despite their differences, Uncle Jeff thought his brother was who we needed and he trusted Dan to help and protect me. And he has."

"So your uncle...and I guess your grandmother too, they're..."

"Thought Movers, yes." Carter confirmed. "Uncle Dan is particularly strong, which is why Uncle Jeff thought he'd be most helpful. But we've never told Grandma Evelyn, so she won't worry."

"Your uncle...he can move objects too?"

Carter shook his head. "No, he's limited to thoughts. Not that it's much of a limit for him."

The very gift I'd thought was most incredible, and fearsome, until I'd learned about my own, and now Carter's. "Can you...?" I breathed.

He shook his head again. "No. Just objects." He looked around and then gestured to a dictionary on a pedestal a few feet away. As I looked, a few pages turned, and then the book closed entirely.

I shivered. This would take a lot of getting used to. "So your uncle helped you understand your gift, how to control it?"

"Yes. It would have been a lot harder without him. That was probably, no, *definitely,* the worst week of my life."

"I'm sorry," I said. "If it's any consolation, this has probably been the worst week of mine."

He squeezed my hand, and then looked down sadly. "Yeah...but at least your father didn't die this week, too."

I gasped. "Oh, Carter! That was all the *same week?*" I didn't know what to say, so I went with the always-appropriate standby. "I'm sorry. I...I can't even imagine."

"Don't try," he replied.

My heart won out over my head at that moment, and I leaned over and threw my arms around him. He scooped me up and onto his lap, where I stayed silently for several minutes. Finally I murmured into his shoulder, "If you can keep this secret, why can't you keep mine?"

He ran his hands slowly over my back. "Because you're not in danger from it," he said. "And because I promised Uncle Dan I would never keep anything from him. I owe him a lot, maybe my life. If I thought telling him could hurt you, I *would* keep it a secret. I swear I would, Lainey. But you'll be fine. I'm sure of it."

I only wished I were too.

Chapter Twenty-Five

March slowly became April. Those were difficult weeks for me, and I found myself as depressed as I thought I'd ever been. And it wasn't only me. My dark mood was reflected all over campus, even in my usually upbeat roommate. The months of late winter and early spring were by far the longest we'd endure, and people were dragging.

When I wasn't counting down the minutes until Spring Break, and my much-needed escape from campus, I spent my time hiding. From everything. Carter and I, well, we didn't exactly "take a break," but we did dial it back a little. I'm not sure if that helped or hurt my mood, but it was necessary. I was under too much stress and he was, unfortunately, a minor reason and major reminder of it. Thankfully, he gave me as much room as I needed with little argument. I think he knew arguing or pushing me in any way would have ended our relationship almost instantly. I saw him only at the bookstore and only when I was with my friends.

The library's third floor became my sanctuary. The reason I *usually* visited it—my official practices—I put on hiatus, hopefully indefinitely. I wanted the break, it was true, but mostly I felt I was ready. I had developed solid control over my Diviner abilities, incident at the Winter Ball notwithstanding. Besides, how could I possibly find myself in *those* circumstances again anyway? And I would continue to get better at using my abilities over time, like everyone else my age did. I was a little amazed and a lot proud at how quickly I'd caught up to my peers.

So instead of practice, or hanging out with my…well, I wasn't sure what Carter was anymore, I spent my time alone with my problems. It was easy to ignore the things causing me such heartache when I was surrounded by other people. Distractions were nice sometimes but weren't helping me come to terms with all the things I needed to accept. From the time I started learning about Sententia, I'd taken most of my strength from Carter's support. And I'd appreciated it, I had, but if I couldn't bear these burdens on my own, I'd never truly be able to live with them. This was the key to getting over my depression, I was sure. Sometimes you had to work *through* the darkness.

After stopping official practices, the next decision I made was to abandon, at least temporarily, maybe permanently, the quest to find my grandfather's identity. Almost overnight I went from being desperate to know to desperately afraid of it. I couldn't handle what might be one more shock or disappointment. Also, I'd lived for seventeen years without knowing. A little more time—or never—probably wouldn't hurt me.

And it didn't. It took me a week of hard thought to realize it was the right decision, but when I finally did, I felt relief. Why *did* I need to know anyway, besides curiosity? My Legacy wasn't going anywhere, no matter who it came from, and I felt sure that if whoever had established it were still alive, they'd have come forward by now. My father too, I believed, hadn't been interested in whatever his father had offered him the one time they'd met, and he'd turned out fine. More than fine. I surely would too.

To my surprise, the thing I most dreaded—telling the Perceptum about my true identity—also turned out to be an enormous source of relief. I realized too late to save myself the hours and days of worrying that I couldn't possibly keep what I'd learned a secret. The deadline for it becoming at least semi-public knowledge was imminent, as soon as Dr. Stewart invariably tracked me down and asked what I'd learned during my visit to Chastine Young's. I'd had to get her permission to take the trip off campus in the first place, and despite my best efforts, I couldn't come up with a creative way to avoid telling her. Obviously, I couldn't lie to her either.

I was stuck, and with that my choice became simple. A few days before Spring Break, I finally relented. Other than never telling anyone at all, it was perfect timing. Carter promised his uncle would let me tell Dr. Stewart myself, and right after that, I'd leave with Amy for a long getaway in Mexico where my cell phone, conveniently, would not work.

So I gave Carter the go-ahead and held my breath.

And nothing happened. All my anxiety was for nothing. As relayed through his nephew, Daniel Astor was shocked but pleased by the discovery and looking forward to meeting me eventually. That was it. Carter had told me over and over not to worry about him, or the Council, and though I couldn't entirely shake my distrust of them, I felt a little foolish for being so fearful of their reaction.

Dr. Stewart also was shocked, along with outraged that I hadn't told her immediately, and irritated that she couldn't be the one to deliver the news to Daniel Astor herself. I only assumed that last one, but I would've put money on my being right. I pushed my luck that night by also requesting to be officially released from my practice sessions. She didn't have to know that I'd already quit them unofficially. Before giving a reluctant yes, she needed proof that I was ready. I passed her tests—all four more of them, including reading a necklace I was sure had been her mother's or grandmother's—with little difficulty.

I left her office that night feeling lighter than I had in over a month, and then passed a glorious week of relaxation and fun with Amy in Mexico. It wasn't like we took off by ourselves to Cancun or did anything wild—we visited my aunt's family, and she even joined us for a few days—but the beach, the sun, and the freedom from the Academy were wonderful. More than wonderful. They were exactly what I needed.

Boyfriends were strictly forbidden. Amy didn't know the real reason, but she agreed our trip would be girls-only and, to my complete amazement, she stuck to it. I considered Spring Break as my final, well, break. How I felt when I returned would determine whether Carter and I got closer again or continued to move apart. I was testing that old theory about absence making the heart grow fonder.

The time flew by, and though I was sad to see our break end so quickly, I was eager to return home and, more importantly, to return to Carter. I was sure of it. In fact, I probably should have known I'd react that way. I was in love with the boy, after all. But I was also stubborn, and it took a week of warm sunshine to melt away my lingering doubts.

We arrived back at Northbrook early Sunday evening after the long ride from the airport with Amy's parents. I dragged my bag up to our room, said a quick thanks to the Morettis, and then practically sprinted across the street to Carter's apartment.

He opened the door and I threw myself on him, nearly knocking us both to the floor. But he caught me and held tight. I think we both knew how the other felt before either of us said a word.

"Welcome back," he whispered into my ear.

"I missed you so much," I whispered back and, with that, we were inseparable again.

       ಶ   ಶ   ಶ

IF THE BEGINNING of April was the dark days, the end of April was its complete opposite. Spring truly sprung and like the weather, everyone seemed to grow brighter and happier. Classes were so busy there wasn't enough time to be depressed even if I wanted to, and the end of the school year felt blessedly within reach. There were barely a few weeks left before finals, graduation, and, for pretty much all of the students but me, moving out for the summer.

Much to Carter's delight, I'd joined the track team as my spring sport. I was even learning to appreciate it, though I honestly enjoyed swimming and volleyball more, not that I admitted that out loud. I'd been delegated to running hurdles along with long relays and I was average at all of them. The one thing track had in common with volleyball was the constant bruising. I began to believe I'd forever be colored yellow and purple.

In fact, everything was going along so perfectly, almost as well as my first few months on campus, that I probably should have been worried. With my weekly practice sessions ended, and no more secrets or surprises looming over my head, I'd actually found myself able to relax and, for the most part, to forget about being Sententia entirely. It was a little strange, going from living immersed in the world of it to generally just…being normal.

Carter said that generally being normal *was* normal, even for him. It had only seemed like such an enormous deal to me because I was so late to the game. This was a welcome change. Without constant reminders of them—Carter and I talked about his second job only when something interesting happened, which was rare—I even started to let go of my fears of the Perceptum. Life was, in a word, good. Busy as all heck, but good.

The very last week in April, I got a surprise. I returned to my locker after track practice, tired and sweaty and ready to relax, when I found it. As I opened the door, a neatly folded note fell out at my feet. It must have been shoved through the grates at the top. I expected a joke from a teammate, or something from my roommate, but it was neither. It was, of all the unexpected people, from Jill.

Though she and I seemed no closer to speaking terms than we had since the Winter Ball, I hadn't been the only one for whom absence had made an impact. The week following our return from break, during an impromptu stop at the bookstore after class, I stumbled upon Carter and Jill embracing at the register. Apparently he'd finally gotten her to speak to him, or she'd finally decided she couldn't stand avoiding him anymore. Carter really did love her—like a cousin—and they'd been so close for years. Whatever she felt for him, it had to have been as hard for her as it was for him not to be friendly.

After they reconciled, Jill still avoided me completely—I almost thought she had a second Sententia ability that let her know where I was going to be so she could make sure she *wasn't*—and Carter's gentle efforts to encourage her to talk to me, too, had had little impact. Or so I'd thought.

I looked around, but she obviously was not in the locker room anymore. She wasn't on any of the sports teams this season, as far as I knew. A note from her was not only a big surprise, but perhaps a step in the right direction.

Dear Lainey, she wrote, in her expectedly small and neat handwriting,

I'm so sorry and embarrassed about everything that's happened. I should have apologized sooner, but I didn't know what to say and I thought you would probably hate me anyway. Carter said that wasn't true and I guess maybe I believe him.

I shouldn't have done what I did either. I am sorry. I'm not sure what I was thinking. It's not an excuse, but I'd been drinking and just got caught up in the moment. I guess you know what it's like to want to kiss him, but you get

to do it all the time. I'd wanted to do it for so long, even if I shouldn't have. Anyway, I'm sorry.

I'm not very good at being friends with people, but I hoped maybe we could try. If you were willing. I feel like hiding on campus all the time, but I hoped maybe if we became friends it would be easier. And I could have someone else to talk to.

I understand if you don't want to, but Carter keeps telling me you do. Will you meet me, so we can talk and maybe I can apologize in person? I don't want to do it around school. People talk about me so much already I can't stand it. But maybe if I finally get to know you, I'll feel more comfortable, and you can help me learn how to fit in.

I know you know where the woods trails come out at the top of campus. If we meet there on a Saturday afternoon, there'll be no one around to see us and it's easy to sneak away. I go there all the time. Please don't tell anyone I've asked you to do this, even Carter. I feel so stupid and nervous about it. I'll wait for you this Saturday at 4:30. If you don't show up, I'll know you don't want to talk to me, and I'll understand. No one else will have to know.

—Jillian

I sat on the bench in front of my locker and reread the note several times. It wasn't that it said anything groundbreaking, but it was such a brave thing of her to do. Of course I would meet her, and I hoped that we really could become friends.

Chapter Twenty-Six

She'd picked a good time to meet on Saturday, right after my work hours ended, when it was pretty empty around campus. I shouldered my backpack and took a roundabout route to the top of campus. Maybe my subterfuge wasn't necessary—I saw no one on my way there—but I didn't want to be caught sneaking into the woods. I liked to avoid Headmaster Stewart as much as possible, so getting in trouble, even for minor infractions, was never on my list of things to do.

When I finally got up there—the library was almost at the other end of campus from the trailhead—I understood why the grounds were more empty than usual. It was sunny out, but deceptively so. A biting wind had come up while I was at work, making it the coldest day we'd had in weeks. I'd worn only a light spring coat and was shivering by the time I arrived. Jill was already waiting in the shadows of the trees. I hoped she hadn't been there too long, because it was even chillier in the shade, but she was smartly dressed. She had a cute knit hat that covered her ears, a pretty silk scarf, and soft-looking leather gloves. I envied her for being so prepared, not that I should have been surprised.

She was always very put together. In fact, aside from her own shyness, she exhibited none of the classic reasons kids were unpopular. She might not have been the prettiest girl in her grade, but she was nice enough looking, with her petite figure, pretty blond hair, and especially those stunning blue eyes. She always dressed well, was good at sports, and was smart too, a must at Northbrook. Really, she should have been able to make friends easily, but I guessed it wasn't the surface things about you that made it easy.

I thought I had similar surface advantages to Jill's, but I didn't make friends easily either. I might not have been shy—I didn't have trouble *talking* to people—but I didn't have much practice at really making friends. Before my time at the Academy, I wasn't usually around long enough to keep them. Maybe I understood Jill better than I thought I did.

"Hi," I said to break the ice. She was obviously very nervous. "Sorry I'm a little late. I didn't want anyone to see me."

"It…it's okay," she said. "I…I just thought you might not come. But thank you."

I kind of wanted to hug her, she was so jittery, but I didn't think that would be welcome. Instead I said, "Of course I came! Everything Carter said was true. I *do* want to be your friend. I hope we can be."

"Thanks," she replied, looking a little relieved. "Do you mind if we walk? It's a little cold out, and we probably shouldn't get caught hanging out up here anyway."

I *definitely* wanted to walk. My light jacket and backpack weren't doing much to keep me warm. I followed her lead down the path Carter and I had once taken, but after not very long she broke off onto a smaller path I'd never been on. She explained the side trail went off campus completely and would also get us out of the trees. It was getting later, but even the late afternoon sunshine would be welcome.

As we walked, she apologized, haltingly, and I knew it had to be hard for her, but she did it. I told her how impressed I was with her for it; I thought she was a lot stronger and braver than she gave herself credit for. This seemed to encourage her, and she became more open and relaxed the longer we walked.

Carter was a lengthy topic of conversation. More than anything, I think Jill just wanted *someone* to talk to. She couldn't talk to Carter about how she felt, and she didn't really have girlfriends to confide in either. I was a willing and sympathetic ear, and she took it eagerly.

"I've had a crush on Carter for as long as I can remember," she told me. "It's not just a crush though, I don't think so. I've never really thought about any other guys. I mean, some of them are cute but, you know…they're not Carter. I know he's never felt the same way, but I always thought maybe, with time. And then for the last more than a year, he didn't date *anyone.*"

She played with her scarf as she talked. I couldn't help noticing how pretty it was and how the copper tones in the pattern made her eye color pop. "I know I probably shouldn't even think of him that way," she went on, "but I couldn't—can't—help it. I'm sorry again, by the way. I was really jealous of you since you got here. I guess I still am a little, but…I'm getting over it. I don't even know why I'm telling you all of this, but I…you know what it's like to like him, to watch him flirt with another girl and wish…" She trailed off and sighed.

I still didn't hug her, but I smiled and nodded in a way that I hoped seemed sympathetic. "I know what you mean," I said. "And I don't want you to be jealous of me, but understand if you can't help it. You don't really show it, though, and you deal with it a lot better than some other people."

I told her about everything Alexis had done, including the night of the Ball, and the horrible things she'd said to me earlier. And then…we just talked. Like two normal girls getting to know each other. It was nice, and once Jill got going, she was easy to talk to. Breaking the ice seemed to be the hardest part for her. I almost thought we *could* be friends, real friends, not just girls who were friendly when they were around each other.

After a while, the small trail led into open and well-manicured grounds. It reminded me of the Academy, until I realized that the small buildings I could see between the trees and flowers were actually mausoleums, surrounded by neat swaths of gravestones. We'd entered a cemetery.

"Sorry," Jill said quickly. "I hope you don't mind. I walk here a lot; it's pretty and…peaceful. The gates are closed at five, so I know it will always be quiet if I come around now."

Parts of the cemetery were very old, with worn, white stones dating from more than a century ago, leading into areas with newer, larger monuments in all colors of smooth marble and granite. I found I liked reading the gravestones, especially the inscriptions. I wondered if I touched them and tried hard enough, if I could divine anything about the person's death. I doubted it, but thought Jill might know better than I did. I was about to ask her what she thought when she started talking.

"So you don't really have parents either, just like Carter, huh?" she said.

I hesitated. I was pretty sure most everyone knew about my parents' accident, but I was taken aback by a sort of abruptness in her question. "Um, well, I don't remember either of mine, since they both died when I was young," I finally said. "But yeah, I guess Carter and I have that in common."

Jill had wandered off the trail and though I thought she was moving at random, I realized the name PENROSE was carved in the center of the simple, pale gray double headstone where she stopped. This was Carter's parents' grave. I glanced around and got the impression the cemetery was enormous. And empty. We were near the edge of the grounds, with a fence bordered by trees not too far away, and no entrances or other people in sight. I shivered, suddenly feeling cold and very alone.

"I think that's one of the reasons he likes you so much," she went on, almost as if I hadn't spoken, gesturing at the carved stone before us. "He thinks you can understand what he feels. He hates being an orphan, even though, honestly, Melinda and Jeff are better parents than his father ever was. But...I think he feels extra pressure too, because he's the last one in his Sententia line." She paused then added, in what I thought was a slightly harder voice, "I guess you understand that too."

I looked sideways at her, but she was staring at the grave, oddly impassively. There didn't seem to be anger in her face like I swore I'd just heard in her voice. I couldn't believe Carter would have told her that I was a Marwood, and I knew Daniel Astor himself had mandated my heritage remain a secret while I was still at the Academy. "What do you mean?" I asked cautiously.

She smiled, with all the coldness I really *had* heard in her words, and it practically froze me where I stood. Out of surprise, or fear, or maybe unwitting surrender, I did manage to hold up my hands.

Which, of course, made it easy for her to punch me in the stomach. *Hard.*

I doubled over in pain and shock, and couldn't even catch my breath or shout what my brain was thinking—something that sounded distinctly like *what the fuck?!*—before she hit me again. Her gloved fist slammed into the side of my head and knocked me to the ground. She kicked me once in the side, which hurt like *hell,* before I could scramble away and push myself up.

I didn't get very far.

She kicked me in the side again, for good measure, and then in the shoulder, sending me careening into the gravestone behind me. The Penroses' grave. Before I had time to wonder if I might be on my way to joining them, or exactly why she was attacking me in the first place, Jill stomped on my hand with one foot and pushed me onto my back with the other. She dropped to her knees on my chest, pinning my arms to the ground. God, that hurt, and I cried out in pain.

Unfortunately, only the dead were around to hear me.

"Jill?" I croaked, shocked and confused, a question in my voice as if this were somehow a mistake. Which showed how fuzzy my brain was, since she'd practically beat the shit out of me. And it didn't look like she was done. She was staring down at me, the scarily impassive expression back on her face, but I could see the malevolence in her eyes. I realized then, more than a little too late, that her problem with making friends wasn't that she was shy. She was actually psychotic.

"You know exactly what I mean!" she shouted, answering the question I'd completely forgotten I'd asked. "It's bad enough you show up with your mysterious Legacy and, and, your beauty and your money and everyone loves you, including Carter. But then you have to go and be *special*. A Hangman, for God's sake! You're all supposed to be *dead!*"

Half of my pounding head followed her words, amazed at the depth of the hatred in them. The other half desperately hoped she'd keep talking long enough for me to formulate a new plan. What I was doing—lying on the ground trapped underneath her—didn't seem like the best one. As she spoke, I tried kicking her, failing completely and snapping my own knee awkwardly in the process. My legs were effectively immobilized by her shins, locked tightly across my hips and upper thighs.

Thrashing and jerking did no good either, along with trying to roll over, head butt her, even bite her. Spitting at her might have helped if I'd thought of it. Instead, I was hopelessly stuck, though I swore I *should* have been able to shake her off. I was many pounds heavier, several inches taller, and a brown belt, for freaking sake! All I needed was one good punch. I bucked and twisted some more, and all around did whatever I thought might get me free.

To absolutely no avail. I didn't even know how it was possible, but I remained solidly pinned, with a wicked slap in the face and knees ground harder into my chest for my efforts. Air was quickly becoming a very important commodity.

"Stop trying to get up!" she hissed at me, and then slapped me again, even though I'd stopped struggling. I was too dazed even to take advantage of my momentarily free arm.

"I'm sorry!" I rasped. "Jill, I'm sorry. But this is crazy, stop this!"

Apparently the c-word was the wrong thing to say.

"I. Am. Not. Crazy!" she screamed. I wanted to disagree, but didn't. Though she might have been small, and absolutely more than half out of her mind, she was *strong*. And she was really starting to scare me.

"I'm sorry!" I tried again. It came out weak and soft because I couldn't draw a full breath.

I didn't think she even heard me. Or cared what I said. She was almost babbling in her frenzy. "How could you possibly think I'd want to be *friends* with you?! You have *everything* already. You don't need more friends. You don't even need Carter! You could have *any* guy! And *now?* Now you're all my father will talk about either. 'The Marwood girl, the last Hangman…' blah, blah, blah. *You're* all *anyone* talks about and I can't stand it anymore!"

"Your father?" was what I said before realizing, *Daniel Astor!* Apparently, it wasn't true that she didn't have contact with him. And apparently, he *wasn't* keeping my secret, either.

"Yes, my father, you idiot!" she yelled. "But he won't shut up about you…what an important discovery you are, how useful you'll be, and on and on. And the *worst* part, do you know what that is?!"

I shook my head, maybe in answer to her question, maybe in denial of this whole insane conversation, but she just kept talking. "He keeps blaming *me* for not figuring it out sooner. Why didn't I sense it when I touched you? Why can't *my* gift be as strong as yours? All these years, and he doesn't even understand how my gift *works!*"

Her head whipped from side to side as she spoke, her cheeks flushed and blond hair flying around her small face. I had no idea where her hat had gone. And in a further sign that my brain was not working right, what with the lack of oxygen and the crazy girl shaking on top of me, I also noted that there, in all her passion and the glow of the setting sun, I'd never seen Jill look prettier.

When she was killing me.

I came to that realization pretty quickly, that I was not meant to get up off the cemetery ground. Surely no one else knew we were here. Jill had asked me to keep it to myself and, perhaps stupidly, I had. But then, could I logically have suspected *this* would be the afternoon's outcome? I wouldn't have suspected it in a million years and, I was sure, thanks to my careful trip into the woods and the only evidence of my companion—Jill's note—tucked safely in the bag I'd carried with me, neither would anyone else.

Jill took advantage of my distraction, contemplating the grim certainty of my impending death, to let go of my arms only long enough to slam my head on the ground. While the world spun around me, she tugged the scarf from around her neck and wrapped it twice around mine, spreading her knees wider to pin down my upper arms.

This was very bad news. The scarf I'd so admired earlier might have been thin and stylish, but it was long and, most importantly, it was silk. The strongest fabric known to man. I had no hope it would break before I did, and that would not take very long.

She wound her small hands in the ends of the scarf and began to pull.

While she choked me, she actually smiled. It was wide and lovely, all teeth and happiness, and was, perhaps, the first genuine smile I'd ever seen on her usually somber face. It scared me more than anything, more than the scarf around my neck or the lack of air in my lungs. It had already been difficult to breathe, with her weight on my chest and my burning ribs, but it was rapidly becoming impossible.

She started to go blurry, and I wasn't sure if I was crying or finally about to pass out. That would be it for me, if I slipped into the dark oblivion that was very close, so I struggled to remain conscious.

Jill's voice became my only lifeline.

It was low, but I heard her, would have heard her if she'd whispered. Probably even if I'd had to read her lips. There was nothing in my world at that moment except Jill and her rage.

"I would have let it all go," she said, with an equal mix of venom and sincerity. The strangest thing was, I actually believed her, believed that she was just one or two sentences gone over this crazy cliff. If not for a few words, I might have been spared.

Too bad for me.

"I would have," she continued. "You'd be gone in another year anyway, and Carter will tire of you eventually, just like he always does. He always comes back to me. But you *can't* have my father. He's the most important man in the world, and he is *mine*. I wish you'd never come here, Lainey, but now, I won't have to wish anymore."

With that, she leaned back, pulling even harder. Time was almost up.

I didn't have the energy, or the oxygen, to try to fight her, so in my last few moments I said silent goodbyes to all the people I loved and all the things I would never get to do. I also decided to pray, just a little bit. It was something I'd never done much of before but I figured couldn't hurt. If there was ever a time I needed divine intervention, this was it.

Just maybe, it worked.

While Jill smiled down at me from what was beginning to seem like a very long distance, I noticed my last, really *only,* chance. She was pulling tightly, arms down near her sides for leverage—honestly, it had to be difficult work, strangling me—and her coat sleeves had slipped back, exposing a tiny stretch of skin between them and the ends of her gloves. With all the energy I had left, I threw my hand up and caught onto her pale wrist.

And then, out of complete desperation and a very, very strong desire to live, I killed her instead.

Chapter Twenty-Seven

It was surprisingly fast. Not instantaneous, but quick enough to spare me. I had no idea if it would work, or how—had never *wanted* to know either—but between my life and hers, I had to try.

Carter had been right, that I'd be able to feel it. I experienced it inside myself almost the moment I Thought, capital T, about killing her.

The specific words of the Thought didn't seem to matter—in fact, if I had to put into words *what* I'd Thought, it was probably something like, *please God, let this work*—but the intention was the most important part, and apparently I'd meant it. For me, the internal sensation was almost indescribable. The closest I could come up with was a cross between being able to *feel* your blood flowing combined with a light electric shock. Maybe that's what it was, some kind of electrical pulse, from my body into hers. I didn't know.

All I was certain of was that, after a few seconds, the pressure around my neck slackened. Jill gasped at the same time I did, as I sucked in the first blissful, cool breath I'd had in far too long. She looked down at me—eyes wide with shock and, if possible, even more hatred—clutched at her chest, and then fell sideways.

She was dead. And I had done it.

For a second, I lay there, gasping, trying to figure out what the hell I was going to do. Jill was *dead*. I mean, I hadn't taken her pulse or anything, but I knew she was. Carter hadn't said this "gift" of mine knocks people out. No, it stops their hearts…but I *knew* what to do if someone's heart stopped.

I bolted upright, which was a bit of a mistake since I was still light-headed and weak. Luckily, adrenaline, mixed with a little bit of self-loathing for what I'd done, took over. Maybe it was a ridiculous notion, but even though Jill had been trying to kill me, I certainly didn't feel the same about her. I hadn't ever wanted to hurt her at all.

For once, finally, training prevailed. Where my obviously rusty martial arts instincts had failed to protect me, at least my CPR kicked in to save someone else. *Thank you, Coach Anderson, for making us all get certified!* I quickly checked for a heartbeat, which, not surprisingly, wasn't there, then threw open her coat and started compressions. I also remembered there were professionals who could help me save her, if only I could get them here. I paused after a round of breaths and pulled out my cell phone.

Blessedly there was service.

I made a frantic call to 911, doing my best to describe the situation and where I was—I had no idea the name of this cemetery nor how to get to it except through the woods—but they seemed to know where I meant and said they were on the way. The dispatcher wanted me to stay on the phone, but I couldn't do CPR and listen to her at the same time. I tossed my phone to the side and continued trying to revive Jill.

There was almost nothing left to do but compress, breathe, pray, and wait, but something, I couldn't say what, made me quickly search her pockets. I didn't know what I thought I'd find, maybe a note or something professing her guilt, but I was surprised instead to pull out a small bottle of lighter fluid and a pack of matches. *Was she going to* burn *me after I was dead?* I shuddered at the thought, but shook it off. It didn't matter what she'd been planning to do.

I tossed the small can as far as I could—it bounced behind a row of headstones and out of sight—then resumed CPR. When the paramedics and, no doubt, the police finally arrived, they'd have nothing but questions for why she was carrying lighter fluid. They'd have nothing but questions anyway, but that was one thing I didn't want to have to explain.

I could hear the sirens wailing in the distance, getting closer every second. I stopped my efforts only long enough to adjust Jill's scarf around my neck so that it completely obscured the bruises I could already feel blooming. Those were also questions I didn't want to answer.

Other than that, as far as I knew, I had no obvious injuries. My flushed cheeks and mussed hair could be written off to my frantic attempts to save my friend. A plausible amount of screaming when Jill "collapsed," plus the fact that I was crying freely and breathing heavily, would be cover enough for my bruised voice.

As I kept up my desperate attempt to revive Jill—tiring arms and aching throat be damned—I went over my story in my head. It had to be simple, because those were the easiest lies to tell. In fact, I felt like I could get away with telling almost the whole truth, up until the part where Jill attacked me.

The sirens came screaming up behind me, first one, then two more vehicles screeching to a halt. My back was to them as I leaned over Jill, but I heard doors slam, followed by shouts and running feet.

With little more warning than a rapidly spoken, "Miss Young? We'll take over now," I was unceremoniously picked up and plunked down a few feet from where I'd been. My arms were still in the compression position, and I fell backwards onto my butt, landing hard on the ground despite not being very far from it to begin with. I blinked, and a muscular-looking EMT expertly took the place where I'd been seconds before, his partner already having set up a mobile defibrillator.

Two police officers hovered near where the EMTs were bent over Jill's lifeless body, and a fire truck pulled into the lane behind us, lights blazing but sirens off. A second ambulance pulled in moments later. A blanket appeared around my shoulders as I became aware of two more police officers, a man and a woman, on either side of me. The woman had her arm around me and was gently saying my name. They were trying to get me to stand, to usher me over to the other ambulance, but I refused to move.

I couldn't tear my gaze away from Jill.

There was no place for modesty here. They'd completely cut off her shirt and bra, exposing the pale, flawless skin of her chest, marked now with angry red welts as they shocked her, for the how many-ith time, I couldn't remember. The big EMT tirelessly performed compressions as the other one continued testing Jill's vital signs in between giving her regular breaths. With nothing for them to do, the firemen milled about, watching anxiously.

I was beginning to despair, rapidly losing hope that she could be saved and that I would not forever carry the knowledge that I killed her. I heard the woman EMT with the paddles shout, "Clear!" again, and watched as the man instantly held up his hands and leaned out of the way. Jill's body convulsed as she was shocked one more time, arms flopping loosely at her sides.

The man was about to recommence compressions when the woman held up her hand, listening intently with her stethoscope and looking at her machine. "PULSE!" she shouted. "I've got a pulse."

I think I might have shouted too.

Everything moved very quickly from there. In what seemed like mere seconds from when the EMT had shouted that Jill's heart was beating, she was in one ambulance, already speeding out of the cemetery, and I was in the back of the other, doors slamming and sirens blaring to life around me. Both my bag and my phone had somehow made it into the cab with us.

The EMT with me was speaking to me gently but firmly. I was not processing words, but he seemed to be encouraging me to sit up. I did that, and he quickly pulled my jacket off my shoulders. He reached for my scarf too—Jill's scarf—but I pushed his hand away.

"No, no, I'm fine," I told him. "I'm fine. It's just Jill." I slumped back into the bed, exhausted.

"You're in shock, miss," said the jacket-taker, and I couldn't help but agree with that. I was most *definitely* in shock. "I need you to try to relax so I can check your vitals," he went on. "Okay?"

"Okay," I replied, limply holding out my arm. He first placed an oxygen mask over my face, which almost instantly made me feel better. I *had* been significantly deprived of oxygen, I realized. My paramedic efficiently did his checks—blood pressure, pulse, breathing, eyes—as we sped away.

"Jill?" I croaked again, when he finished prodding me.

"We'll do our best, Miss, I promise," was all he said.

DESPITE MY PROTESTS that I was fine, my ambulance followed Jill's to the hospital, where all my vitals were checked again in the Emergency Department. That's also where I was, for the first and hopefully last time in my life, questioned by the police. Even though they were friendly and assured me they only needed my statement for their records, it was a frightening experience. Especially when you really did have something to hide.

Thankfully, I hadn't had to talk to them alone. To my surprise, once the doctor declared me healthy—physically anyway—my advisor from school, Dr. Callahan, preceded the officers into my sectioned-off room. I was worried he'd been sent to deliver the bad news about Jill, but it turned out there was no news about Jill, yet. No, he was simply the Academy's representative. Because he was genuinely concerned about both of us, of course, and because apparently the police were not allowed to question me, even informally, by myself. I'd nodded sagely when he explained that, as if I was questioned by the police every day.

So with Dr. Callahan's comforting presence next to my bed, I told them my story. It was simple and brief and generally true: Two girls went for a walk in the woods, hung out talking in the cemetery—I was willing to bet we weren't the only kids who'd ever snuck in to walk around or do worse things—and then one collapsed. As I'd told them when I called 911, it seemed like she'd had a heart attack.

That was it, my whole story.

They asked me to describe, as exactly as possible, what Jill had done before collapsing, and I did. Mostly. I explained how Jill had stopped suddenly, grabbed at her chest, and then fallen down. I didn't mention that she'd been strangling me just prior or that I had caused her heart to stop. When they inevitably asked if Jill or I had been drinking or taking any illegal substances, I told them I hadn't and, as far as I knew, neither had Jill. No, I was pretty sure she'd brought the crazy all by herself, no drugs necessary. I didn't mention that either.

Inwardly, I applauded my performance. Maybe I should have gone out for drama instead of sports. I was both distraught and concerned—that part was completely real—and entirely convincing. Thanks to my gift, and my inability to get a single good hit on her in my own defense, there would be no evidence that Jill had had anything but natural, if highly unexpected, heart failure. I was entirely certain the police believed everything I said and that there was nothing suspicious about the incident. In the best interests of us all, I pretended this was true.

Since Dr. Callahan had to remain behind for Jill, I was discharged in the care of my friends, the police. An orderly wheeled me out of the hospital and I climbed into the back of the cruiser, like the common criminal I probably was. I had momentarily killed a girl, after all, even if it was in self-defense. At least they didn't use the lights. Once we were on the way, I pulled my phone out of my bag and turned it back on, ignoring the missed calls and messages and dialing from memory.

He answered almost before the phone had rung. "Lainey, Jesus, are you all right? What's going on? Where are you?" Carter practically yelled, a heavy mixture of relief and worry in his voice. It was late, much later than I'd expected to get back from my talk with Jill.

"I'm okay," I whispered, my throat raw and aching. "They're bringing me back now."

"Thank God," he breathed. "Christ, Lainey, I saw the police car pull through the gates and I *knew* it had to do with you. What on earth happened? Where were you?" Apparently the second cruiser had gone straight to the Academy after we left the cemetery.

I basically ignored his questions, which I couldn't answer right then anyway, and said, "It wasn't for me, the police, I mean. It was for Jill."

"Jill?! Why were you out with Jillian? What happened to her?"

"I…I'll be back on campus in a few minutes and explain everything then. Meet me there?"

"All right. I'll be waiting. And Lainey?"

"Yeah?"

I could practically feel his intensity through the phone. "Don't ever disappear on me like that again."

Chapter Twenty-Eight

O f course, it wasn't that easy. Carter might have been waiting for me when we pulled into campus, but so was Dr. Stewart. My police escorts, being the good officials they were, took me straight to the Administration Building. The policewoman opened the door to let me out, commended me for at least the fourth time on my excellent work in saving Jill—I *really* wished she'd stop doing that—exchanged a few words with the dour-looking headmaster, and left me to her care. Having no real choice, I followed her into the building.

As soon as she'd shut the door to her office firmly behind us, she rounded on me, anger and accusation clear in her eyes. The room was dark except for one lamp glowing on her desk. Being Saturday night, the rest of the building was empty.

"Explain what happened this instant, Elaine," she said harshly. "And don't even attempt to lie to me."

I hadn't planned on it. I had one abbreviated story for the police officers and the real story for her. I felt horribly guilty for what I'd done, for using the gift I'd promised never to use, but I also knew my only other option had been to die myself. I didn't think Dr. Stewart would blame me for doing what I did.

Instead of answering her with words, I slowly undid the scarf concealing my neck. I hadn't had the chance to check out the damage myself, but even in the low lighting it must have been pretty bad, because Dr. Stewart's eyes widened measurably. For added support, I hitched out of my jacket, gently, because every movement hurt like hell, and pulled up the side of my sweater. This time I too could see what Dr. Steward did, and it looked every bit as bad as it felt. There were dark marks on my stomach, and a huge, ugly purple blotch on my ribcage. It hurt just to look at it. I imagined if I pulled my shirt all the way over my head—an act I wasn't sure I could accomplish if I had to—there would be knee marks on my chest and a variety of other blossoming bruises.

Dr. Stewart was visibly shaken. "My God," she breathed, and dropped into one of the chairs in front of her desk. Gingerly, I sat across from her. "Tell me," she commanded. It was quite a bit gentler than the last time.

So I did. I told her everything, every single detail. I had nothing to hide and no reason to hide it. I dug out Jill's note and handed it over too. She listened without a word, incredulity growing in her eyes, and glanced over the note without comment. She cleared her throat before speaking again. "How much of this did you tell the police?"

"I was discreet," I assured her, pulling out the Perceptum's favorite word to give meaning to my answer. My voice was scratchy and painful to use. "Only what they needed to know. And I didn't let on to any of this." I gestured at my wounds. It had been all I could do to keep my injuries concealed, not to cringe every time the doctor had asked me to move or draw a deep breath.

"I can't believe it," she said, shaking her head. I knew she wasn't talking about me. As if it had been waiting for me to finish, the phone on her desk rang. It was a pretty gentle sound, but I jumped as if I'd been shot. That didn't feel good at all. Dr. Stewart rose swiftly and answered before the next ring.

"Yes?" she said in her best headmaster voice, all clipped tones and in charge. I couldn't hear the words on the other end, but I could tell it was a man's voice. She plunked down in her desk chair as soon as she heard him. I had a good idea who it was before she confirmed it a second later. "Senator…Yes…No…I'm sorry…Thank God…No, I have her here."

After another pause—I was only getting one side of this conversation—she recounted the details I'd told her and also gave a litany of my injuries. She glanced back and forth at me the entire time. After another break, she said, "Yes, completely truthful…I'm certain…No. I had no idea, wouldn't have considered it possible…Yes, I know…I'll tell her…Yes. Good night."

She hung up and redirected her attention to me. "That was Daniel Astor." I nodded. That much had been obvious. "He expresses his sincere apologies for the extreme actions of his daughter, exonerates you from any blame, and thanks you for saving her life and doing what you had to, to save your own." I nodded again. It seemed odd to thank me for killing, then reviving, his daughter to save my own skin, but there it was.

"Jill?" I asked hopefully and held my breath. I got the impression she was still alive, but there were lots of conditions in which a person could be, technically, alive.

Dr. Stewart responded with the most beautiful sentence I'd ever heard. "They expect she'll make a full recovery."

Thank you, God, I said in silent, fervent prayer and exhaled a painful sigh of relief. Strange how it both burned my throat but also felt like an enormous weight had lifted from my chest.

I didn't have time to bask in the feeling before Dr. Stewart was giving me rapid and incontrovertible instructions. "This is what will happen: from here, I will escort you directly to the infirmary where you will stay for several days, recovering from shock and a severe migraine brought on by the stress of the situation. On Monday morning, I will convene the students and tell them of Jill's tragic collapse and your bravery in saving her. When I release you from the infirmary, you will behave as if you are the hero everyone will believe you to be. You will *never*, under any circumstances, tell any more of the story than you absolutely must, and never more details than you told the police. This"—she held up Jill's note—"will be your very general excuse for why you and Miss Christensen absconded from campus, if you must ever give one."

She pulled open a desk drawer, took out a book of matches, and lit Jill's note on fire before dropping it in the empty waste can next to her desk. Dr. Stewart and I both watched the note burn, and then she watched me for a while. She drew in and exhaled a deep breath before saying, almost absently, "I suppose this confirms your bloodline beyond a doubt. I almost didn't believe it was possible...but here you are, a final Marwood under my care."

She straightened up and her imperious voice returned. "This goes without saying, but I will say it anyway: you will never turn your gift on another person while you are a student here, not unless you find yourself in a similar life or death situation. Which is unlikely. I cannot begin to understand what made Miss Christensen take such drastic measures against you, but neither can I deny the verity of your tale. It is disturbing and unfortunate." She stopped abruptly and rubbed her eyes, as if this whole thing had made her very tired. I knew the feeling.

As the silence deepened, I decided maybe it was my turn to talk. I didn't really have anything I wanted to say—I'd already told the whole story—but I did want something. Tentatively, I started, "I'd like to see..." but I didn't get very far.

"I think they can wait," she snapped, but then softened. Sometimes I thought Dr. Stewart struggled to repress her maternal instincts in favor of her more assertive ones. I wished she wouldn't; it might make her happier if she just let herself be likeable. "I will speak to Cartwright and Miss Moretti personally, to let them know you are fine. I'll also speak with your aunt first, to explain what's happened, but I'm sure she'll demand to speak to you herself and you will reassure her. Please discourage her from coming here. Other than that, I prefer you to be isolated in your recovery. It will be easier to contain rumors, camouflage your injuries, and disseminate our story that way. You'll see them all soon enough."

I didn't like it, but I nodded. I had no choice in the situation anyway, short of running out of the office and hoping I beat her out of the building. The way I felt, I didn't like my chances.

She rose and came around the desk, gathering my bag and my coat before I had the chance—effectively dashing my hopes of sneaking my cell phone in to the infirmary with me—before looking down at me. "Are you ready?" she asked, but gently, and I sensed genuine concern for my well-being. It was surprising, but welcome. I nodded again and stood up slowly.

On her way to the door, Dr. Stewart stopped and looked back at me, opening and closing her mouth as if unsure what to say. Finally, she squared her shoulders and put a light hand on my shoulder. "I'm proud of you, Lainey. You were brave and you were smart and, most of all, you protected everyone involved. Not many girls your age would have been able to do that. Thank you," she finished on a murmur, turning sharply and continuing out the door.

Obviously no response was expected of me, but I smiled at her back anyway.

Chapter Twenty-Nine

T*he good news:* My ribs were not broken.

The bad news: I had a mild concussion and bruising pretty much everywhere, which would only get worse before it got better.

The good news: My injuries were fairly easy to cover, except for my neck.

The bad news: Dr. Stewart had been pleased to inform me when I *did* get out of the infirmary, despite my "heroism," I would still be expected to serve the required detentions for leaving campus without permission.

Score: Lainey 1, Injuries 1, Dr. Stewart 1 (Overall, I decided to consider it a draw.)

THE NEXT FEW days would have been unbearable if not for the doses of painkillers that helped me spend more time asleep than awake. The nurse said it would help me heal faster the more I slept, so that's what I did. I didn't have anything else to keep me busy, except for thinking about Jill and what had happened or missing Carter, neither of which I enjoyed spending time doing.

I assessed my injuries daily for progress. My throat was an ugly ring of purple and red and my right side was indescribably frightful. That one would hurt for a long while, and my visible bruises would require a bit of creative dressing once I got out, but there would be no lasting damage. Physical damage, anyway. Psychologically, I was in for a longer road. You didn't kill someone, even in self-defense, without gaining a few issues to work out. Thankfully, the painkillers helped dull the nightmares too.

For her part, Dr. Stewart came to check on me every day and was a surprisingly good counselor. Maybe the Dr. in Dr. Stewart was actually in psychology. She asked me helpful questions, genuinely listened while I answered, and overall made me feel...better. I'd never have believed I'd look *forward* to seeing the headmaster, but during my time in the infirmary, I anticipated her daily arrival with interest rather than dread. I'm sure it had a tiny bit to do with her being the *only* person I really got to talk to the whole time, but that wasn't all it was.

Our responses to what I'd dubbed in my head the *Jillian Incident* had built what I sensed was a mutual level of respect between us. We both let our guards down, at least a little, and learned more of what the other was made of. I was glad for it; I preferred being on, if not exactly what I'd call friendly, more *understanding* terms with her.

As promised, I spoke to my aunt on my second day of confinement. Because the public story was significantly less traumatic—for me, anyway—than the real one, Aunt Tessa was not as concerned as, well, she *should* have been. Of course, I couldn't tell her that. I couldn't tell her anything. Mostly she was proud of me, plus a little worried about my "migraine" and how I was dealing with the near-death of a "friend."

Like the good mother she was, she also chastised me for breaking the rules about leaving school grounds. If we hadn't left the school like we weren't supposed to, she reasoned, we wouldn't have been so far from help when Jill collapsed.

It felt so great to hear her voice, I chatted with her for as long as I could keep my eyes open. To my relief, she never threatened to come to campus—because, as far as she knew, there was no real need—and I would see her soon enough when she came to install the art piece she'd promised to donate. I looked forward to it immensely.

Though not quite as much as I looked forward to seeing Carter. Not talking to him the entire time of my forced isolation was quite possibly the most difficult part of the whole incident. With almost tangible need, I longed to see his face, hear his voice, feel his arms around me, and, most importantly, know that he understood why I'd done what I did and forgave me.

On Wednesday, I finally got my wish. Dr. Stewart had brought me a selection of comfortable clothes from my dorm room to wear during my infirmary stay, and she brought me a hand-picked outfit, featuring an appropriately high-necked shirt, to wear upon my release. All she said when she let me go was, "Remain discreet, Elaine. And come see me whenever you need to talk." I assured her that I would, and she and I both knew it was the truth.

You'd think the first thing I'd have done was run straight to Carter, since besides the bad stuff, it was about all I'd thought of for four days, but I didn't. I restrained myself admirably. It was late afternoon and he was in the middle of the busiest time at the bookstore. I knew he'd drop everything the moment he saw me, but I wanted privacy and I wanted time. So instead, my first stop was my dorm room. I had no guarantees Amy would be there, but she was. I wondered if Dr. Stewart had told her I'd be coming back today.

Almost as soon as I came through the door, she slammed into me with a giant hug. I wasn't quite prepared for the assault. I squeaked in pain—I couldn't stop myself—but she released me quickly, smacking her own forehead as she did. She tugged me down on my bed and flopped beside me, sweeping up a pillow as she landed.

"Shit, Lane, sorry! Your head is probably still killing you." The irony in her words was hysterical, but this time I managed to keep from laughing. "But seriously," she continued, "it's so good to see you. I can't believe what happened! Are you okay? They say Jill is going to be all right, but she won't be back to school this year. It's so crazy that she just *died* like that! And you saved her! But...what were you doing off campus with her? That's what I don't understand." She worried at the pillow while she spoke.

I let the comfort of my roommate's familiar chatter wash over me like a balm. I felt better in her presence almost immediately. I even leaned in and gave her another, gentler hug before I responded. Not quite as much as Carter, but I'd missed Amy too. I couldn't tell her the real truth, but I knew she would help me cope with the *Jillian Incident* in her own way. Neither could I be completely vague with her, because she was too smart for that, and also because she was my best friend, so I'd carefully crafted an answer that painted Jill in the best possible light and was, mostly, true.

I explained that Jill had finally responded, tentatively, to my attempts to befriend her, how we'd agreed to try hanging out without giving people a chance to gossip, and had stumbled on the path to the cemetery pretty much by accident. I described how scary it had been when she'd collapsed and how hard it was to save her. I even told her about how helpful Dr. Stewart had been about the whole thing.

"Wow," she said drily. "That's the most surprising part...I didn't think the woman had a caring bone in her body." She shook her head and was back to serious. "But yeah, how crazy. You're fantastic, by the way! I think I might have freaked out and fainted or something. And I want to learn CPR too. A doctor's daughter, you think I'd know…Your voice sounds like you've been crying for days. Have you? Are you *really* okay?"

She squeezed my arm affectionately and I almost did start crying. I *hadn't* been doing that, not since Jill's heart had started beating, but Amy's concern, and my inability to share what had really happened, almost had me weeping again.

So, I lied some more. I had to. "Yeah," I said. "I can't help thinking about her. It was…really scary. The nurse gave me some anxiety pills to take for a while, though, and I think they're helping. It's getting easier." My "anxiety pills" were actually Vicodin, but it was a good cover for why I was popping the pain medication several times a day.

Amy was quiet for a while, probably thinking about what it would be like to watch a classmate die, but as always, she rebounded quickly. "God, you're a high maintenance friend," she joked. "When I asked for a roommate, I didn't expect to get one that came with so much *drama*. I'm thinking of getting a single next year, or maybe you'll have to move into the infirmary full time and I can keep my awesome room for myself."

We laughed and I hugged her again. It was true, I did seem to bring the drama, though mostly through no fault of my own. But we both knew that Amy loved it, same as she loved me. Being Sententia was hard, but it was what had brought me here, to this school, and this room, and this girl who I hugged one more time just because I could. I wouldn't trade it for anything, even if I had the chance.

Chapter Thirty

peaking of things that were not always easy to deal with but I wouldn't trade for the world, it was finally time for me to see Carter. I waited until after dinner—where I told my abbreviated story about a million times to my friends and nearly everyone else on campus before Amy shooed them all away—and hurried as much as I was able across the street to the bookstore and up the back stairs. I was sure that Dr. Stewart *hadn't* told Carter I would be released today, so it took a minute or two for anyone to answer the door.

It was Melinda who greeted me. She instantly burst into tears. "Oh God, Lainey," she sobbed, hugging me gently before pulling back to look at me. "Are you okay? Oh, honey. I can't...I don't..." She struggled for words between her tears.

"I'm okay," I interrupted, and hugged her again. I was a little overwhelmed by the strength of her response. I knew she had real affection for me, but Jill, even if she was a little crazy, was still her niece. "I'm so sorry," I told her truthfully, "but I'm okay."

"Sorry?! You don't have to be sorry! What Jillian did…Oh, Lainey, I can't believe it. But we'll have plenty of time to talk about this later." She wiped her eyes and stepped to the side.

Carter had appeared behind her not long after she'd opened the door and shouted. He waited patiently, hovering by the hallway entrance that led to his room, though I could tell he was eager to hug me himself. Relief rolled off him in waves.

Jeff Revell, too, had appeared on the other side of the kitchen. He nodded at me and murmured, "We're just thankful you're all right," before disappearing through the living room door. Melinda followed him after one last squeeze of my arm, leaving Carter and me alone.

For a moment, neither of us moved, staring at each other from the few paces that separated us instead. I was so relieved to see him that I was frozen in my spot. Finally, despite knowing it would hurt, I threw myself at him, and he swept me up into his arms and carried me into his bedroom, shutting the door behind us with his foot. He set me down on the bed, gently, and then ran his fingers through my hair and across my cheek.

"I was so worried about you," he said. It was barely audible, but it didn't matter. I could practically *feel* the words seep under my skin and warm me from the inside. *"Are you okay?"*

"I will be," I told him, and I would. Eventually. "It's going to take a little while. For everything."

"Can I see?" he asked tentatively.

I always thought it would be more romantic, or maybe passionate, the first time I took my shirt off in front of him, but it was neither. It was actually painful. It was also the easiest way to show him the extent of what she'd done. At least Dr. Stewart had brought me a decent-looking bra. Wordlessly, I slipped my shirt over my head.

I think he was more shocked than the day we'd discovered I was a Marwood, or the day he accidentally revealed his incredible abilities.

He gasped sharply, blue eyes enormous as they looked in mine, asking silent permission. I nodded and he gingerly reached out to touch the worst of my injuries, first my neck—there was still a dark purple band, but it was starting to yellow at the edges—and then my side. I couldn't help flinching when his fingers grazed the still-deep bruise there.

His eyes snapped back up to mine and he pulled his hand away. "Jesus," he whispered, raking his fingers through his hair. I pulled my shirt back on. "She did all that to you?"

I nodded again. "It's getting better, though."

"Jesus," he repeated.

"Carter, I'm so…"

He chopped his hand through the air to cut me off. *"Don't* apologize. Please. I can't take it. This was *not* your fault."

"But Jill…she's family. And I…I killed her."

"You *saved yourself.* And her too. That's all that matters." His words were almost angry, they were so vehement. He hopped up and started to pace the length of his room. With anger came his nervous energy. "I don't care if she's family. At this point, I wouldn't care if she'd died. She tried to *murder you.* You think I'll be upset that you didn't let her? God, Lainey. You really don't get it, do you?"

He dropped down in front of me, gripping my face between his hands. "I love you, Lainey Young. I. Love. You. I think I might have killed her myself if anything worse had happened to you!"

It was my turn to be shocked. Not because of what he'd said, even though neither of us had ever said it before. I knew he loved me. I'd known it for weeks, maybe months, and I knew I felt the same way. No, it was the *intensity* with which he'd said it. It both exhilarated and frightened me. I didn't know if I was ready for such serious emotions, but that didn't matter. I felt them too.

"I…I love you too," I stuttered, then gathered strength. "I mean it. I have for longer than I want to admit."

He didn't say anything else, but I could see the elation in his eyes. Somehow, I think he'd doubted that I returned the feelings. Which was stupid, but I guess maybe I'd finally found the one thing about which Carter wasn't wholly confident.

He kissed me then, gently at first, but it grew, slowly and steadily, until we were lying together on his bed, completely entangled in the comfort of each other. If my injuries hurt, I didn't feel it. I felt great, and *right,* and better than I had in months. I loved Carter and he loved me and we'd both finally admitted it out loud. What could possibly be wrong?

But there's always something.

I'm not sure what made me do it, or whether or not it was conscious at all. Maybe it was because I'd never felt happier or safer than I did in that moment. Maybe it was my feeling of utter relief. Maybe it was simple exhaustion. With his arms hard around me and lips soft against mine, it was a miracle I could have any other thoughts at all. Maybe there was nothing I could have done to prevent it even if I'd tried.

I'll never know what caused me to open all of my senses at that moment, but I will never forget what came afterwards. In a brief and vibrant vision, with no real details but utter certainty, I knew that Carter Penrose had been an instrument of death before and that he would be again.

The next face I saw was my own.

Acknowledgments

THANK YOU:

To my agent, April Eberhardt, for the tireless support of me and my words.

To Amazon, Penguin, Createspace, Thom Kephart, and the rest of the team, for the Breakthrough Novel Award contest and for bringing me one step closer to living a dream.

To Tracy, Chris, and the entire Luminis team, for the *next* step and for taking the chance.

To Jill Baguchinsky and Rich Larson, for being competitors *and* friends.

To Geri Barrison, for being my first and best reader.

To Kristy Farrell, for the graphics and, most especially, the enthusiasm.

To my husband, for everything.

To my family, for everything else.

About the Author

Cara Bertrand is a former middle school literacy teacher who now lives in the woods outside Boston with: one awesome husband, two large dogs, one small daughter, and lots of words. LOST IN THOUGHT is her first novel and was one of three finalists for the Amazon/Penguin Breakthrough Novel Award in the Young Adult category.

Visit her online at www.carabertrand.com or on Twitter @carabertrand

BERTR   HEI
Bertrand, Cara,
Lost in thought /

HEIGHTS
12/14